MW01138210

Copyright 2012

Laurence E Dahners

ISBN: 978-1478344056
ASIN: B008RBN7TA

This book is licensed for
your personal enjoyment
only

Rocket!

An Ell Donsaii story #4

———

Laurence E Dahners

Author's Note

This book is the fourth in the series, the "Ell Donsaii stories."

Though this book *can* "stand alone" it'll be *much* easier to understand if read as part of the series including

"Quicker (an Ell Donsaii story)"
"Smarter (an Ell Donsaii story #2)" and
"Lieutenant (an Ell Donsaii story #3)"

I've minimized the repetition of explanations that would be redundant to the earlier books in order to provide a better reading experience for those of you who are reading the series.

Other Books and Series
by Laurence E Dahners

Series

The Hyllis Family series
The Vaz series
The Bonesetter series
The Blindspot series
The Proton Field series

Single books (not in series)

The Transmuter's Daughter
Six Bits
Shy Kids Can Make Friends Too

For the most up to date information go to

Laury.Dahners.com/stories.html

Table of Contents

Author's Note 4
Preprologue...7
Prologue 9
PART ONE 16

Chapter One *16*
Chapter Two..*28*
Chapter Three...*45*
Chapter Four *60*
Chapter Five *78*
Chapter Six *87*
Chapter Seven *107*
Chapter Eight *133*
PART TWO 137

Chapter One *137*
Chapter Two...*158*
Chapter Three...*181*
Chapter Four *197*
Chapter Five *216*
Chapter Six *232*
Epilogue..251
Author's Afterword 257
Acknowledgements 258

Rocket!

Preprologue

Ell's father, Allan Donsaii, was an unusually gifted quarterback. Startlingly strong, and a phenomenally accurate passer, during his college career he finished two full seasons without any interceptions and two games with 100 percent completions. Unfortunately, he wasn't big enough to be drafted by the pros.

Extraordinarily quick, Ell's mother, Kristen Taylor captained her college soccer team and rarely played a game without a steal.

Allan and Kristen dated

more and more seriously through college, marrying at the end of their senior year. Their friends teased them that they'd only married in order to start their own sports dynasty.

Their daughter Ell got Kristen's quickness, magnified by Allan's surprising strength and highly accurate coordination.

She also has a new mutation that affects the myelin sheaths of her nerves. This mutation produces nerve transmission speeds nearly double those of normal neurons. With faster nerve impulse transmission, she has far quicker reflexes. Yet her new type of myelin sheath is also thinner, allowing more axons, and therefore more neurons, to be packed into the same sized skull. These two factors result in a brain with more neurons, though it isn't larger, and a faster processing speed, akin to a computer with a smaller, faster CPU architecture.

Most importantly, under the influence of adrenalin in a fight or flight situation, her nerves transmit even more rapidly than their normally remarkable speed.

Much more rapidly...

Prologue

Boston, Massachusetts— PGR Comm, a privately held company in Boston MA, announced today the initial public sale of a new communications chip. These chips have apparently already been in use by US military services. The chips come in pairs, said to be "quantum entangled" and are purported to allow instantaneous communication between one chip and its mate over very large distances at extremely low cost. It's further claimed that such communication is uninterruptible, uninterceptable, undetectable, and requires no infrastructure. The company claims these chips will revolutionize communications.

If such claims are substantiated the chips will certainly alter...

The Friday night before Thanksgiving Phil Zabrisk walked into the Gold Rush, looking around for Jason Daventa. He and Jason had been buddies since basic training at the Air Force Academy. They were meeting there for a night out on the town in the big city of Denver. It'd been a while since they'd last gone out together since Phil, to his own surprise, hadn't really been in the mood to chase the ladies.

He hadn't felt like it since that Thanksgiving weekend nearly a year ago when he'd helped foil Ell Donsaii's attempted kidnapping. After the kidnapping he'd tried to tell her how important she was to him and she'd seemed to respond. He could close his eyes and remember the thank you kiss she'd given him. But he'd rarely seen her since then. She'd driven up to Seymore Johnson AFB to see him for a day over his Christmas break when he'd been home visiting his parents. Then he'd driven down to visit her at her mother's home in Morehead City a day later.

In January she'd gone to Officer Training and been assigned to Nellis AFB. He'd hoped to visit her in Las Vegas over his summer break, but that hadn't worked out. He'd kinda hoped that she'd hop over to Colorado Springs to see him, but that hadn't happened either. Now it'd been nearly a year and he'd only seen her those two times during Christmas break. Gradually he'd developed the feeling that he'd better get on with his life. She'd been a lieutenant for almost a year now, while Phil still had more than half a year to go at the Academy before he'd get his own bars. It seemed silly to wait around for her. It'd be even crazier to think *she'd* wait around for him.

So when Jason called and suggested they go out on the town, he'd decided that it was time to get back in the swing of things. He looked around The Gold Rush and saw Jason sitting in a booth. *Not a good tactical base for chasing women, Jason,* he thought as he started that way. *A booth impairs your mobility.* As he approached Jason and could see deeper into the booth he saw Joy Denson sitting next to him. Joy and Jason had been an item back in their Doolie year, but hadn't been together for quite a while now. *Damn! If they're getting back together tonight, and they're dragging me along on a date, I'm gonna be pissed!* Phil rolled his eyes and stepped up next to the booth. Belatedly, he noticed that someone was sitting on the bench seat across from Jason and Joy.

Rocket!

Ell!

Stunned, Phil found himself grinning vacuously at Ell's trademark crooked smile. Then he realized that Joy and Jason were laughing at the silly look on his face and turned to glare at them. "You guys kept this a secret?!"

Ell grinned up at his Norse God good looks and giggled, "Are you gonna sit down and give me hug? Or am I gonna have to climb way up *there* to get one?"

Phil dropped to the bench beside Ell and threw his arms around her, *Hmmpf, she feels good!* He drew back, leaving one arm around her shoulders, "Man! It's *great* to see you! I'd just been thinking how it'd been a long time! How is life up there in exalted lieutenant land?"

Joy laughed, "Lieutenant!? Boy are you behind the times! She's been a captain for whole days now!"

Ell looked sharply at Joy, "How'd you know about that?"

Smugly Joy said, "I have my ways."

Phil and Jason goggled, "Captain?" Phil asked.

Eyes sparkling, Joy grinned, "It seems that President Teller has been up to some of his old tricks. Let's see," she looked musingly up at the ceiling. "I believe a certain someone may have been awarded the Presidential Medal of Freedom as well as being promoted two ranks, the maximum possible in peacetime?" She waggled her eyebrows at the two men. "If you guys knew how to keep your ear to the ground, *you too* could be aware of such things."

Phil turned to stare at Ell, "Really?!"

She shrugged, looking uncomfortable, "Yeah, but they're letting me out of the rest of my military commitment so the promotion doesn't really matter."

A stunned pause followed, then Phil said, "What'd

you do?!"

Ell looked uncomfortable and shrugged minutely again. "I let them use some of my chips…" she trailed off.

Joy grinned, "What the indomitable *Captain* Donsaii means to say, is that she single-handedly staved off a war in the Western Pacific."

Jason turned to stare at Joy, "You mean that Fleet Exercise of the PRC's really was an invasion that got turned back? I've heard people claiming that, but…"

"Yep! A certain someone got in their way." Joy chortled.

"Joy!" Ell said blushing brightly, "*I* didn't stop them! All I did was help with the comm problems we were having after the Chinese shot down our satellites!"

Joy snorted, "Yep, that's *all* my old roomie did…" Joy raised her eyes to the ceiling. "Holy crap! Isn't that enough?"

Phil lifted his arm off Ell's shoulders, "Holy crap is right! My arm's on fire just touching such a hot commodity."

Ell grinned up at him and grabbed his hand, pulling his arm back down onto her shoulders, "Hey, a girl needs her hugs, the least you can do is keep your arm around me until you have a few blisters." She tilted her head and frowned seriously. "But really, it wasn't that big a deal. It just happened that the comm chips I came up with last fall could substitute for the lost satellite links. Joy's making it sound like I went over there and stopped the PRC myself."

Phil rolled his eyes, "So, tell us, what did happen then?"

Ell was saved by the waiter. He stepped up to the table, asking, "Can I get you some drinks while you look

Rocket!

over the menus?"

However, once their orders had been placed, they dragged the story of what had happened out of her, including the story of her PGR chips, their quantum entanglement and instantaneous communication capabilities. At every turn, a flabbergasted Phil heard her describe her accomplishments as if anyone else could have done the same, if only they'd been as lucky as she had. She played down her role and asked them not to make a big deal out of it, especially in view of the fact that the President wanted public acceptance of the fiction that the PRC had only been undertaking a training exercise.

Eventually Ell managed to deflect attention from herself by using the tactic of asking them what their own plans were. Jason had applied to med school. Ell gave him a high five. "Hey, I didn't know you were that kind of student!"

He lifted his chin, "I have been forced to hide my light under a bushel so you bourgeois individuals would accept me into your circle." He raised an eyebrow aristocratically and held up his beer mug.

Phil said, "Put your pinky out when you lift that beer, Mr. Academics!"

Joy chortled, "You were worried that you were too smart to hang out with Donsaii!? That's a good one!"

Ell turned to her, "What about you, Joy?"

Joy shrugged, "I applied to flight school. I think I've got a pretty good shot at being accepted 'cause my vision's 20/20, hearing's good and my reaction time's better than average. Like everyone else I'm dreaming of being selected for fighter aviation, but there aren't all that many slots, now that UAVs are doing so much. I'm trying not to set my hopes too high."

"When do you find out?"

"After Christmas."

Ell turned back to Jason, "When do you find out about med school?"

"Sometime Spring semester."

Ell looked up at Phil, "What're your plans big guy?"

Phil shrugged, "I've been applying for astronaut training. I may be screwed though. They recently reduced the height limit to 6' 3" when they took the R20 capsules out of service. I'm 6' 3" plus a half-inch. They have so many good applicants they probably won't overlook that extra half inch. If so, I'll try for aviation I guess."

Phil sounded pretty depressed about it to Ell. "Aren't they talking about a bigger launch vehicle?"

Phil shrugged, "Yeah, but if I were running things, I probably wouldn't take on an oversized astronaut trainee in the *hope* that we'd have a bigger vehicle by the time he was trained."

Joy said, "Have you tried slouching for the measurements?"

Phil frowned, "My height's all over the Academy documentation!"

Joy shrugged, "Just say they inflated your height to make you look bigger on the wrestling programs, then slouch when they measure you. I can change my height a couple inches by slouching or standing up straight."

Phil gazed at her musingly a moment, "That's what I like about you Joy. Your mind's *soooo* devious." His eyes sparkled.

"Think nothing of it," She grinned, "Actually, I'm just trying to reduce the competition for my aviation slot."

~~~

Rocket!

After finishing their meal, they went out bar hopping. Ell ordered a Coke and for a moment Phil started to chide her, then he remembered she was only nineteen. She leaned up against a rail next to him as they looked out over the crowd in the Roost. "Astronaut huh?"

Phil shrugged, "Yeah," he said, looking mildly embarrassed. "Always been a dream."

She smiled up at him, "What do you want to do up there?"

He smiled, "Be weightless, fly a spaceship, go to the moon—if we ever go back. Maybe cowboy up an asteroid or two and bring them back to earth orbit for space resources." Come back down to earth and brag about it." He waggled his eyebrows and grinned, "Have pretty girls like you go all googly eyed over me. You name it; I've dreamed about it."

Ell raised an eyebrow, "But I'm already all googly eyed over you." She frowned at him, "How many googly-eyed girls you shootin' for anyway?"

Phil stared at her a few moments, eyes darting from place to place about her delicate features, then he said huskily, "If she were you... one would be far more than enough."

Ell stared at him for a moment, then said huskily, "You *do* say the nicest things lately Mr. Zabrisk."

Their moment was broken when a soprano voice rang out, "Phil! I haven't seen you in ages!" A blond girl threw her arms around him for a big hug.

Phil's eyes widened in alarm at Ell, but he said, "Um, hi Cathy. Good to see you." After a moment he disentangled himself, but after Cathy'd moved on, he and Ell never regained the closeness of the moment they'd had.

PART ONE

Chapter One

Boston, Massachusetts— PGR Comm confirmed today that their new communications chip technology is based on the physics paper published last year by Ell Donsaii, the young gymnast who stunned the sports world two years ago, receiving three "10's" and four gold medals in the Olympic gymnastic competition...

Chancellor Joseph Kellet surveyed the room. To his relief their "anonymous" donor had apparently not arrived as yet. He saw that the Chair of the UNC Department of Physics as well as her Vice Chair were both present as the donor had requested. His own assistant and a couple of the other Vice Chancellors were also there. He walked over to check on the refreshments and noticed that a good deal of the ice had melted. He turned to the pretty brunette student who'd been examining the refreshments and said, "Would you mind refilling the ice? There's an ice machine behind that door." He pointed her in the right direction.

She grinned at him, saying "Yes sir," and picking up the large glass bowl.

He turned to his Executive Vice Chancellor and said, "Hi Mary, any word on when the donor's going to arrive?" She was looking after the girl with the ice with a horrified expression

Mary said, "I think you may have just sent her for ice…"

"What!!!"

"Mary darted a glance at the door, just closing behind the young, brunette woman, "I'm not sure, but I'd been wondering when the donor might arrive myself. Then I found myself looking at that girl. She came in the main door and didn't seem to know her way around. She doesn't work in our offices. She *can't* be the actual donor, but she may be a representative."

"*Oh my God!*" Kellet turned and stared, "She looks like a freshman! Are you sure?"

Mary said, "Of *course* I'm not sure! But we don't know *anything* about the donor and I *do* know everyone else here!"

Kellet started for the door he'd sent the young woman through. As he opened it he found the young woman standing on the other side holding the newly filled bowl of ice. She grinned at him and breezed through the door he was holding open. He reached for the bowl of ice.

She smiled sunnily and sailed by him to the refreshment table.

Kellet followed, nervously attempting to reach out and assist with the bowl. Embarrassed, he realized that everyone in the room was staring at him.

She set the bowl down, scooped up some ice and put it in a glass which she handed to the Chancellor. She filled a second glass for herself. "Coke?" she asked smiling at him sunnily.

"Uhhh… ginger ale."

She poured ginger ale for him and a Coke for herself,

then raised her glass to him. When he touched his to hers she winked, "Yes, Chancellor Kellet, as you're probably realizing, I *am* your donor's representative."

Mortified, Kellet said, "I am *so*, so sorry! I thought you were one of the student interns we have in our offices from time to time."

Still grinning she whispered, "I could tell."

A few nervous titters broke out among the people in the room near enough to have been watching the interaction. They were watching with the fascination reserved for a slow motion train wreck.

Ell turned to the room with a broad smile. "Hello folks, I'm Raquel Blandon and I represent your anonymous donor. Please call me 'Raquel.' I've met Chancellor Kellet here, but I'd like to meet the rest of you before we talk about the donation I've been sent here to make today?"

She circulated amongst them, shaking everyone's hands and exchanging a few brief words. It was obvious from her comments that she'd researched everyone in the room and already knew their backgrounds. When they were all seated, she smiled sunnily at them again and said, "So far you're aware that I'm representing the donor of a substantial sum of money to the University. To clarify, it's expected to be approximately 115 million dollars a year for ten to twenty years."

A stunned silence greeted this announcement. Chancellor Kellet said, "My goodness, that's wonderful. May we know the name of the donor?"

She shook her head. "I'm *meeting* with you because there are a few strings attached." She grinned at the Chair of the Physics Department as she said, "Fifty percent of this money's to be spent on Physics, from buildings, to research, to hiring faculty, to special physics scholarships. Essentially, in-state students admitted to the Physics program are *all* to be able to attend UNC tuition free. Out of state Physics students are to have very low tuition.

"This funding for faculty and research should enable you to make this one of the best, if not *the* very best Physics program in the country. One page summaries of physics research requests for funding must be submitted to the donor for approval. Some recipients of Physics scholarship slots *might* be specified by the donor. Finally, the donor wishes to remain anonymous. This last is very important—so important that attempts to determine who the donor is will result in the loss of this funding."

They all stared at her in consternation. Finally, the Chancellor said, "Um, we'll just have the University's attorneys write up an agreement..."

He paused at a minute shake of Ell's head. She said, "You can readily access your AI's (Artificial Intelligence's) audio record of what I just specified. You'll find the first 115 million has been deposited anonymously into your public account in the past few minutes. I've ported you the website where Physics research proposals can be posted for approval." She looked at the Physics Chair, "You might warn your faculty that they *won't* be funded if they aren't enthusiastically teaching their undergrad and grad students.

"Otherwise, there need not be any interaction between the University and the donor. The money will continue to arrive as long as the donor is satisfied that you're fulfilling the *spirit*, not just the letter of what I've laid out for you. No need for an agreement. Thank you for your attention."

Before anyone in the stunned room got enough of a grip to say anything else she'd slipped out the door.

***

Washington D.C.— Today the White House announced negotiations intended to reduce the anticipated disruption of the communication industry by the quantum entangled chips introduced by PGR Comm. The stock markets have reacted violently as the capabilities of the new chips have become evident. This unrest...

Dave Slager looked around as a loud "bang" sounded behind him. A tremor ran through the Space Station. Slager closed his eyes. It was a micrometeorite strike. Sounded like a pretty big one. The station was armored with Kevlar padding to protect against strikes, but the sound of this one had been different. He wondered if it'd hit something that wasn't armored?

Jim Sasson yelled, "I think it hit the CRV!"

Slager grimaced. Sasson was more excitable than the typical astronaut, but everyone cut him some slack because he was so brilliant. However, yelling that the meteorite had hit the Crew Return Vehicle that was intended to evacuate the space station scientists in case of an emergency? To Slager that seemed somewhat akin to yelling "fire" in a crowded theater.

However, the CRV *was* one part of the Station that wasn't covered in Kevlar, so Sasson might well be right.

About thirty minutes later Emil Taussan pulled himself into Slager's area.

Slager looked at him with a raised eyebrow.

Rocket!

Taussan shook his head, "I've inspected the interior of the CRV. It seems fine. No atmosphere leak. But I think Sasson's right about it hitting the CRV somewhere. I'll suit up for an EVA (Extra Vehicular Activity or spacewalk) and inspect the exterior."

Slager shrugged his shoulders, "OK, better safe than sorry." He turned back to his own work.

***

Washington D.C.— Today NASA announced that a meteorite strike had damaged the rocket nozzle of the Crew Return Vehicle which serves as an "escape pod" for the International Space Station in case of emergency. NASA said they expected to be able to send up a replacement nozzle on the next supply ship. Apparently they believe the nozzle can be replaced with an EVA.

Mary and Ell strolled together across the campus of NCSU in Raleigh. Steve prowled about a hundred feet in front of them. As head of Ell's security detail, Steve had agreed that having her walk with Mary made her look more like the other students and so was good coloration. Steve himself was pretending to be a grad student crossing campus on a similar course.

Ell nudged Mary, "Steve doesn't do 'oblivious grad student' very well does he? He looks more like a panther searching for its next meal."

Mary stifled a laugh, "It *is* difficult to make six foot two inches of solid muscle look like it spends its time studying."

Ell snickered, "I swear I can see the ghost of his M-25

Laurence E Dahners

in his hands!" She paused, "Well, this is the Physics building. You guys could have some coffee in the little shop over there while I'm upstairs."

~~~

Roger Emmerit fidgeted and slid a finger under the collar of his shirt. He seldom wore a tie and so this one was driving him crazy. Of course, his nerves might also be on edge over the fact that he was about to defend his thesis for his PhD.

Dr. Johnson and the other two professors on his committee had arrived and seated themselves in the front row of the small conference room. Dr. Johnson had insisted that he redo his experiments repeatedly when they failed to support classical theories in Physics.

Then Roger'd had to repeat and modify his experiments many more times, once he'd demonstrated that the results he was getting *were* compatible with the new math conventions and theories that Donsaii'd published in Nature. For a while Roger had wondered whether Dr. Johnson would *ever* allow him to defend his thesis, but as experiment after experiment agreed with Donsaii *and* failed to follow the predictions of classical theory, Johnson'd finally relented.

Several other people had gradually filtered in and seated themselves in the audience. More than he'd expected. They registered mostly as blurs to Roger, though he assumed that some of his grad student friends were there. Johnson said, "Let's get this show on the road."

Roger turned to the big screen at the front of the room. He began to speak as his first images appeared on the screen. Forty minutes later by the clock, and

Rocket!

forever by his internal time sense, he finished his presentation and asked for questions. An initial barrage of questions flowed over him.

Some other faculty had shown up, having heard of Roger's surprising results. Their questions reflected their dubious feelings regarding his results, or at least about his interpretation. Here Professor Johnson's earlier attacks served him well, because he'd already heard *all* of their objections from Johnson. And therefore, he'd done the experiments to show their contentions incorrect. The questions slowed and eventually trickled to a stop. Finally, his committee asked that the room be cleared for their deliberations. Roger stepped outside with everyone else and his friends clustered around to shake his hand and wish him well.

Al and James promised to buy him a beer at West 87 no matter the results. Emma gave him a hug and fiercely whispered, "They'd *better* give you a pass."

Jerry gave him a "bro" hug with a slap on the back and said, "Good luck. We Alpha Centaurians are on your side." Everyone chuckled at Jerry's old joke.

Roger looked around. A couple of his more distant friends spoke amongst themselves. Suddenly he recognized the familiar posture of the slender girl leaning up against the wall with her hoodie up so it partially hid her face. "Ell?"

She turned to face him full on, grinning. Everyone else standing in the hall turned to stare. She pulled her hoodie back exposing her short reddish blond hair and crossed the distance to him in three strides, throwing her arms around him and giving him an intense hug.

Hugging her back Roger said, "Damn, girl! Why didn't you say something?"

She drew back and raised an eyebrow, "Didn't want to throw you off—or make the professors think I was trying to influence your findings as they regarded my theory."

The door opened behind Roger. Professor Johnson leaned out, "Roger?" He motioned him back in. Suddenly Johnson's eyes lit on Ell. He turned back to the room behind him and said, "I'll be just a moment." Then he stepped out into the hall and said, "Ms. Donsaii, a word please?"

Ell, dreading the possibility that Johnson would be confrontational again, stepped down the hall with him.

He said, "I'd like to thank you very much, not just for funding my research application. Though, I'll admit that your prompt authorization of the funding for my project surprised me no end. But, what I really want to thank you for is the audio-video record you forwarded of our interactions. I'm embarrassed to say that I had no idea just *how* obnoxious I can be until I watched your video of myself being an ass *from the perspective* of the person I was treating so badly." He took a deep breath, "Old habits are very hard to break, but I *am* making a sincere effort."

Ell's eyebrows rose, "I'm *so* happy to hear that!"

He said, "I have to get back in there with Roger's doctoral committee, but I hope you'll have a drink with us at the traditional West 87 celebration?"

"Wouldn't miss it for the world."

~~~

West 87 was crowded with well wishers. James held up his glass, "To *Doctor* Emmerit!"

A chorus of "Hear, hear," resounded.

Johnson said, "I'll buy one more round for you

hooligans, then *Dr.* Emmerit and I are going to take on all comers at the pool table."

James chortled, "Oh, you're going *down* tonight Professor. Ell, will you be my partner again?"

Laughing, Ell shook her head.

Once some more drinks had been delivered, James again turned to Ell. "Come on. You know the Professor just thinks it was luck that we beat them last time. We've got to take them on again and show them the error of their ways!"

Ell raised her eyebrows, "It *was* luck!"

"No way!" James grabbed her elbow and tugged her toward the tables where Roger and Dr. Johnson were racking the balls.

Ell dragged her feet, protesting feebly, but then Emma said, "Come on Ell. Show us what you can do at pool, the way you did at foosball."

This urging reminded Ell how she'd regretted playing "full on" at foosball the year before. Her athletic abilities had stunned the group, but left her feeling embarrassed to be known as someone with such bizarre abilities. She turned to Emma and whispered, "No! There're too many people watching! I don't want strangers thinking I'm some kind of freak! Help me get out of this?"

Emma looked into Ell's eyes a moment, saw the anxiety there and said, "Sorry James, Ell and I need to have a little girl talk. Jerry, you play as James' partner." She assertively led Ell back to the booth despite some lingering protests.

Once they were seated Emma said, "So, if I'm going to protect you here, you're going to have to spill the beans. What's going on between you and Roger?"

Ell shrugged, "We're just good friends."

Emma's eyes widened, "Hah. 'Just good friends' don't submit a paper to the APS in the hope they can visit their 'friend' in Las Vegas."

Ell tilted her head, "Really good friends?"

Emma snorted, "I should say. You gonna make an honest man out of him?"

Ell rolled her eyes, "He'd need to participate in that you know. Besides, remember I'm only nineteen? You might find it hard to believe but Roger's the first boy I ever kissed. I should probably see a little more of the world before I settle down, don't you think?"

In shock Emma said, "Your first kiss! At age eighteen! You've *got* to be kidding!"

Ell stared at her hands, "I'm a late bloomer?"

Emma grinned at her. "So you're gonna play the field first?!"

Ell shrugged and looked embarrassed, "Maybe? I don't know. I like Roger a *lot*."

~~~

When almost all his well wishers had left West 87, Roger turned to Ell, James and Jerry, saying, "I'm done in and heading to the barn. See you guys next week."

Ell said, "I'll walk you home. You'll be needing some protection from the Rigellians." She winked at Jerry.

Jerry put a hand over his heart, "But then who'll protect *me*?"

Ell raised her eyebrows, "Surely you jest! Everyone knows the Rigellian digestive tract can't handle Alpha Centaurian protein! You're the only one who's completely safe."

~~~

As they walked Ell was happy to find her hand in

Rocket!

Roger's again. "So, what *are* you gonna do with that shiny new doctorate?"

Roger shrugged, "I really don't know. I *want* to do research. Sometimes I think I'd like to work for industry, but I'm afraid of being told to work on some problem I'm not interested in. I've been thinking I'll have to stay in academics, do a post-doc or something, then join the ranks of the professors. Right now I'm planning to spend some time looking around at what's available since I've got the PhD pretty much wrapped up. Maybe the perfect job'll find me?"

"What do you want to study in your research?"

"Hmmm, I'm kinda interested in a crazy new theory by this chick named Donsaii. Maybe you've heard of her?"

Ell grinned up at him and punched him lightly on the shoulder.

Roger said, "This is my place. I'd love to have you come in as long as you promise to behave yourself? No taking advantage of my drink addled state?"

Ell stopped, and when he stopped too she put her arms around him for a hug. "Maybe you shouldn't invite me in then. Who knows what I'll be tempted to do with you in such a pliable condition? I probably wouldn't be able to leave without some kisses..." She leaned her head back and smiled up at him again.

He shrugged, "Well... I guess I could part with a few of those." He grinned back and turned to open the door...

Chapter Two

Cape Canaveral— Today's launch of ILX Corporation's Vulcan 5 rocket ended in failure when the rocket failed to stay on course and had to be destroyed. This is the second failure of the new Vulcan 5 launch vehicle that was expected to take over supply of the aging International Space Station. More concerning is the fact that this launch was carrying the replacement rocket nozzle for the Space Station's Crew Recovery Vehicle. The CRV's nozzle had recently been damaged by a micro meteorite, leaving the astronauts without an escape vehicle in case of an emergency. NASA director James Epaulding described this as one of a "perfect storm" of problems for the Station, but said they fully expected to solve these problems...

Ann Tandy parked her car so that the Century 21 Commercial Real Estate decal on its door would be obvious to anyone entering the empty parking lot. She walked over to the door of the closed QemZ research facility and checked to be sure that the digital key her AI'd downloaded would in fact open the door. She stepped inside, *Good, the heat's on.* She'd sent Jake out to warm up the building and check for any other problems that morning. Jake rarely failed to perform— but she always worried. She flipped on the lights and looked around. *Good, looks clean.* She walked down a hallway looking into the various offices and cubicles.

Ann briefly checked the research and production area which consisted mostly of a huge empty space with a number of big chemical tanks and some industrial sized stainless steel tables. Satisfied, she walked back outside to wait for the prospective buyer. She'd been communicating with this Raquel Blandon for several days now.

Blandon had been very reserved about who or what company she represented. This made Ann nervous. Blandon sounded kind of young and Ann'd had the unsettling thought that she might be getting pranked. Blandon had specified a facility in the Research Triangle Park near Chapel Hill with some large "industrial" rooms and a total of 20-40,000 square feet. Even with those broad specifications this QemZ facility was the only available place that really came close. Ann hoped it would meet their needs; she could really use a commission about now.

A car pulled into the lot and parked near Ann's. A young brunette woman got out and began walking towards her. Ann's heart sank. She was just a girl! Then to Ann's immense relief another car pulled in and parked a few spaces away from the first car. Hopefully these would be the actual buyers?

"Ms. Tandy?" The young woman said, putting out her hand to shake, "I'm Raquel Blandon." Because Ann had her attention focused on the other car Blandon looked back over her shoulder at it. Three men had gotten out of the vehicle, but they just started walking off around the far corner of the building. "Uh, the guys are just gonna walk around the outside." Blandon said.

Ann's shoulders sagged minutely. "*You're* the one interested in this building?" she said dubiously.

Laurence E Dahners

Blandon grinned at her and said, "Yep. I'm guessing you're worried that I'm too young?"

Ann raised her eyebrows and said, "This facility *is* listing for 5.7 million dollars."

Blandon nodded enigmatically and said, "I know. Shall we look around?"

Trying to avoid gnashing her teeth, Ann dispiritedly said, "Sure," and opened the door.

To Ann's surprise, the girl only spent a few minutes in the office space, giving it at best a cursory examination. But, she went over the industrial space with a fine-toothed comb. She examined each of the vats, looking at their outsides and then peering at their insides with a brilliant flashlight she'd brought in her purse. She went outside and scrutinized each of the huge insulated liquid and gas storage tanks in the fenced enclosure out back. Back inside she carefully tugged and pulled on all of the industrial stainless steel tables and cabinets. She spent forty minutes in the machine shop, exclaiming over and turning on and off every one of the large machines, including some that apparently communicated with the young lady's AI once they'd been powered up.

As she left the machine shop Blandon said, "We'll offer 4.4 million. Please let me know if the sellers are agreeable?"

"What! Wait! Who do you represent? You haven't even talked to them!"

"I have," the young woman said, "because *I'm* the buyer."

And blinked, then said, "I'll have to assure the buyers that you can actually finance the purchase."

"Say that I represent..." the girl looked to one side as if thinking, "'D5,' a... new company. Check your account.

Rocket!

I've just deposited 3.4 million for earnest money. Of course I'll expect to get that back if the sale doesn't go through."

In astonishment Ann looked up at her HUD (Heads Up Display) and saw her AI's confirmation of the deposit.

"D5?"

"Yes Ma'am." She grinned, "for 'Dimension Five.' Let me know what the sellers say." she said, and turned to walk to her car.

***

Boston—Today, President Teller announced he'd brokered a deal with PGR Comm to license their "quantum entangled chip" technology to existing communications companies. This agreement has been trumpeted as a means to prevent the collapse of current cell phone, cable and other telecommunication companies due to their inability to compete with PGR Comm's new chips. Such a meltdown of the communication industry had been forecast to result in the loss of hundreds of thousands of jobs. Those predictions had already resulted in huge losses in the stock market.

President Teller proclaimed the agreement as a means to "provide an orderly transition to a new technology in this important industry…"

~~~

Aaron Miller's receptionist Sally looked up when the door to their waiting room opened. A slender young woman stepped in and walked over to Sally's desk. The young lady had reddish blond hair and a pixie face. As she got closer Sally realized she was quite young. She had even features, brilliant green eyes and a flawless complexion. The young woman looked like a model. Sally frowned, *Is she lost? What would a model be doing in a patent attorney's office?*

The young lady said, "Hello, I'm Ell Donsaii. I have a spot on Mr. Miller's schedule under the pseudonym 'Blandon'?"

Startled, Sally recognized the young lady now. "Um, yes Ma'am! I'm sorry I didn't recognize you. I'm sure Mr. Miller will see you now. He's told me he'd see you anytime." She tilted her head, "Why'd you use a pseudonym?" With some embarrassment Sally felt like she was burbling.

"Sorry, I don't like having my real name on anyone's calendars. There are some people out there who've caused me a lot of trouble."

Sally's AI confirmed that Mr. Miller wanted her to bring Ell back to his office. Sally said, "Right this way." She indicated a door decorated with a Christmas wreath.

Miller enthusiastically met Ell at the door to his office, "Hello, hello, what can I do for you Ms. Donsaii?"

Ell shook his hand, "I'd like to submit another patent application please."

Miller looked over her shoulder, "Is Dr. Smythe here?"

"Uh, no, this patent's separate from the previous one he helped me with. And..." she grinned at him, "thanks to you guys I have plenty of money to take *this* patent out without his help."

Miller shook his head briefly, reminding himself that the previous patent had actually been for Ell Donsaii's intellectual property, not Dr. Smythe's. It was difficult to keep a grip on the fact that this teenager was a genius of the first water. Because Smythe had brought her in the first time, Miller's subconscious somehow always managed to attribute her brilliant ideas to Smythe. He kept feeling like Donsaii was Smythe's protégé despite, intellectually, knowing better. "Excuse me, Ms. Donsaii. Step into our conference room and tell me about this new invention."

Miller sat listening with more and more incredulity as the young woman described a method she'd worked out to connect one location to another through "ports" defined by pairs of entangled molecules. The PGR chips she'd invented sent data instantaneously from one location to another using a single pair of entangled molecules. Her new invention apparently worked on an extension of the same principles by using entangled molecules to form a connection from one location to another through her fifth dimension. Instead of *one* pair of entangled molecules, this new invention used many entangled molecules arranged in a circle to make a physical connection from one location to another. The entire concept was quite similar to the "wormholes" proposed by a number of science fiction writers and some serious scientists. The big difference was that this apparently wasn't a hypothesis. The girl claimed that she'd actually created microscopic versions of these ports. Making a large opening would be extremely difficult and expensive because of the need to construct the opening one entangled molecule pair at a time.

Before she hired people to work out techniques for making such ports more efficiently and to investigate possible methods to make the ports without such labor-intensive manipulations, she wanted the concept to be patent protected.

Resisting the urge to call Dr. Smythe to confirm this wasn't all just a pipe dream, Miller took extensive notes and began planning out a patent application.

***

Los Angles— ILX Corporation admitted to finding a design flaw in their Vulcan 5 launch vehicles that have failed recently. Apparently the modified rocket nozzles that allowed ILX to engineer a greater thrust to weight ratio and undercut their competitors are at fault. It's unclear whether ILX will be able to honor its commitments to provide cheaper service to space. NASA director James Epaulding was heard to say "This is a disaster of unbelievable proportions…"

Amy and Steve entered Ell's room at the Red Roof Inn in Chapel Hill. Amy choked back a giggle at the incongruity. Here was a woman who'd soon be receiving her second minimum royalty of 2.1 billion dollars, sitting cross legged on the bed in a cheap hotel instead of in a suite in the most prestigious lodgings available. However, as head of Ell's security team, Steve liked the anonymity provided by such a modest and unlikely location.

Plus, Ell didn't have any desire to stay in an elegant hotel.

She turned to them, "OK, tomorrow I'm going to be starting to interview people out at the old QemZ facility. Steve, how are you coming with regards to providing security out there?"

"The company you hired to do remodeling and

renovation of the building has subcontracted installation of some of the security features I wanted. They've already brought out a portable guard shack and placed it at the entrance until a permanent one can be built. For now, I've hired a local security firm to provide a guard presence at all times. They aren't of the same quality of your personal security team, but with the budget you've provided we should have enough of them to do what we need around the clock."

"Amy, what about a more permanent place for us to live?"

Amy looked up, "First I want to mention that the equipment from your lab in Las Vegas was delivered to the QemZ facility yesterday." She frowned, "I really think we should refer to it by our new name D5, but I'd like to suggest 'D5Research' so it doesn't just sound like a quadrant on a map?"

"Great idea, we'll incorporate using that name. Can you get the lawyers on that?"

Amy said, "OK." She had her AI make a note, "Regarding your first question, I've found three houses for you to look at. And, Ell, I wanted to say that I truly appreciate your willingness to live in the Chapel Hill area where the public schools are good. That'll set my mind at ease about Mike and Janey."

Ell shrugged, "No problem, I'm looking forward to living there myself. Besides, it'll make my commute to class shorter."

"You're really going to go back to school?"

Ell shrugged again, "Yeah, there are a couple of classes I want to take. I could learn this stuff by reading on line, but I really like being in a class and having somebody explain some things to me. Besides, it gives me a chance to hang out with other kids my age."

Laurence E Dahners

Steve chuckled, "Well, you aren't going to have complaints from the security detail about having to follow you around a college campus. I'll have to work out something to keep them on task instead of girl-watching."

Ell grinned, "I don't mind if they enjoy the scenery, as long as they're ready to go if I need 'em."

She turned to Amy, "I don't have my first interview until 11. Can we look at houses first thing in the morning?"

"I'll call the agent, but I'm sure she'd be willing."

The next morning, they drove out to look at the houses Amy'd picked out. Ell really liked the first one, but Steve was *not* happy, saying "There's no place for your security team to stay in this place."

Ell said, "It's pretty big, couldn't they stay in one of the rooms?"

"Either they'd have to really stay in that one room, which would be uncomfortable for them, or they'll be out wandering around your house which won't give you any privacy. What you need is a house with a 'mother in law's' apartment out back. Or one with another small house next door that you could buy as well." He turned, "Amy, you should live nearby as well."

Amy grimaced, "I hadn't thought about those issues. I don't think the other two houses I picked out are going to be any good either. Maybe we should give it up for today and I'll ask the agent to look around some more with me over the next few days?"

They spoke a few minutes more and agreed to Amy's suggested plan. Ell and Steve started driving out to the "D5Research" facility. As their cars left the neighborhood they'd been in, they drove past a small farm. Steve asked his AI to call Ell. "We need a place like this farm we're passing. It looks like it has several small buildings the team could stay in and work out in. Lots of space to run and circulate guard details. You could even have your own separate small lab in that barn."

"Is it for sale?"

"Well, no. I meant we need to find a place *like* that."

"Hmmm, let's go talk to them." Her car slowed and started to turn.

"What?!" Steve sounded scandalized. "It *isn't* for sale."

"Come on Steve. *Everything's* for sale."

A few minutes later Steve found himself standing behind Ell as she knocked on the door of the farmhouse.

A stout, pinched looking matron came to the door wiping her hands. She grimaced and said, "Sorry, we're Baptists. Not interested."

Ell grinned at her. "We're not here to convert you or sell anything. Actually, we'd like to buy your farm. How much would you take for it?"

"It *ain't* for sale." The lady made to close the door.

Ell called out, "Five million dollars."

The door, mostly closed, stopped and opened a little again. The woman stared at Ell wide eyed.

Ell said, "Your family bought these 21.4 acres with the house, two outbuildings and the horse barn for 2.4 million dollars 19 years ago. Current appraisal value would be approximately 3.3 million dollars. I'm offering quite a bit more than that, but I'd want to take possession of it very soon.

The woman turned her head and hollered, "Harald…"

~~~

"You've what!" Amy said incredulously.

"Bought the farm." Ell said with a little giggle. "Actually, we only 'agreed in principle' to buy a small horse farm. Allan (Ell's AI) just sent you the address. I've offered a lot more than the appraised value and they've agreed to move out within the week, but they'll continue to maintain the property for at least six months. Steve likes it. It's in the right school district. It's an easy drive to work and to the University for me. And... I think it's pretty."

"But there isn't anything like that for sale out there!"

"Sure there is. If you offer enough money... I'm heading over to D5R. Please get that real estate agent to help you work out the details of the sale."

~~~

As his car cruised along I-40, Roger Emmerit wondered what this "D5Research" was. He'd never heard of it, but it'd popped up in his job search engine several days ago. He'd been running a job search for "PhD, physics, research, no experience required, North Carolina..." for a couple of months now with only weak matches until this one popped up. It matched nearly every characteristic he'd given. He was excited to see it was located in the nearby Research Triangle Park. However, he felt concerned about whether a new tech company would have much staying power. *Oh well,* he thought, *even if it folds, it'll at least mean I have some experience to put on my next job application.*

His car turned in at a small facility and stopped at a guard shack where the guard leaned down to get a good image of him. The shack looked very temporary. After a moment the guard looked up at his HUD and said, "Dr. Emmerit?"

Roger looked blandly back at him, "Yep."

"You're expected and can go on in. The main entrance is at the right front of the building."

Roger frowned as he looked around, "How long has this "D5Research" company been here?"

"I think just since last week sir. My security company was contracted to start providing protection on Monday. Lots of construction vehicles going in and out. I assume they've just bought the building and are remodeling."

Roger's heart sank, "Thanks," he said to the guard as he had the car drive on into the facility. Maybe it was just a new facility for an established company? His AI hadn't turned anything up on "D5Research" but it wasn't unheard of for the research wing to have a name distinct from that of a main corporation. The parking lot was about half full, but at least two thirds of the vehicles appeared to be contractor's trucks. Roger's car pulled up to the right end of the front of the building and he got out.

Four men were putting up a "D5Research" sign by the door as he approached and Roger had to wait for one to scooch aside so he could enter. Inside a couple of men were tearing up the carpet. Roger had to step around them and a small Christmas tree to approach a receptionist's window.

The young man behind the window looked up, then down at a monitor. "Dr. Emmerit?"

"That's me."

"If you'll step through the door over there Sir, I'll meet you in the hallway behind it."

Roger opened the door and the young man met him on the other side in a long hallway. Roger said, "What's this company do? I can't find anything about it on the net."

"Research, Sir. I'm afraid I don't know all that much about what the research involves. I was only hired last Friday. So far everything's been focused on hiring admin personnel and researchers like yourself. Well, that and the remodeling of course."

The receptionist took Roger down the hall to meet a lady in an office labeled by a sheet of paper taped to the door. It said, "Human Resources."

"Hey Nancy," the young man said to the dark haired woman in her thirties behind the desk. "This is Dr. Roger Emmerit, one of the physicist applicants."

He turned back to Roger, waving a hand at the woman, "Nancy Moore."

"Nancy" looked away from her screen and smiled at Roger, "Thank you for coming out Doctor Emmerit."

Still finding it odd to be addressed as "Doctor," Roger said, "It's no trouble, Ma'am. Please call me Roger. I'm very interested in learning more about your company, is it new?"

"Well then, call me Nancy. Before I can tell you much about the company, I'll need to get you to sign a non-disclosure agreement or NDA. I've ported it to your AI. Can you look it over and let me know if you'd feel comfortable signing?"

Roger's eyebrows rose. He assumed this was a pretty unusual request for a job interview since he'd never heard of signing an NDA before even interviewing for a job. Nonetheless he looked at up at his HUD and started reading. The NDA specified that, whether or not he took a job here, he wouldn't speak of D5Research, or its field of study, or its founders for a period of two years.

Rocket!

He looked back at Nancy. She was focused on her screens again. "And I can't learn any more about the proposed job unless I sign?"

Nancy looked back at him, "I'm afraid not. The company's studying phenomena for which it has applied for patent protection, but even so, it doesn't want word getting out."

Roger agonized for a moment. This didn't feel right. However, he found the secrecy made him even more curious. "OK, I'll sign."

Nancy said, "OK, your reading of the document and verbal agreement has been recorded as an 'electronic signature,' you *do* agree?"

"Yes Ma'am."

Nancy leaned back in her chair, "D5Research, or 'D5R' as we call it here, is a new company founded to study phenomena predicted by a paper published in Nature a year and half ago. You've probably heard of the paper. It's the one that led to the new PGR chips that are causing the upheaval in the communication industry. D5R has been founded to investigate a different, though related, phenomenon..." She halted as Roger put his hand up in a halting motion.

"Um, you should know that Ell Donsaii's a personal friend of mine."

Nancy tilted her head quizzically. "Okaaay?" she said, drawing it out.

"She's the one that wrote that paper in Nature you're speaking of."

"That's correct."

"I feel like I'd have to tell her that you're working on her theory so you might not want to tell me any more. I could have real conflicts with that NDA."

Nancy cocked an eyebrow, "I'd point out that you've

already *signed* that agreement. But it doesn't matter," she grinned, "Ms. Donsaii's aware of D5R."

Taken aback, Roger said, "Okaaay?" himself.

"In case you decide to join our team you need to be aware that D5R plans to offer *very* competitive salaries and benefits. For instance, we'd expect you to *start* at a hundred fifty thousand a year. I've ported you a listing of the benefits to review at your convenience. If you're still interested, I'll need to take you to talk to our chief science officer?"

Roger, doing his best to appear blasé about the surprisingly large salary figure, looked briefly at the benefits, then shrugged. "Sure, I'd like to hear more."

Nancy stood, "OK, let's go find her." She grinned and slanted her eyes at Roger as if she had some mysterious secret. Roger followed her down the hall. She stopped at another office. The door had another paper sign, this one saying "CEO-CFO-CSO-etcetera." Nancy grinned back at Roger, "Not here." Nancy winked, "She's hardly ever in her office."

She turned and led Roger back the other way and out into an industrial space with a scattering of people around it. Roger's head swiveled every which way, trying to take it all in. Large crates labeled with the names of scientific instrumentation companies lined one wall. Men in coveralls were mounting one of the large stainless steel tables onto vibration isolation supports. A group heaved one of the large boxes up onto one of the tables that already had isolation supports, evidently preparing to open it. Nancy, just in front of Roger said, "Ms. Donsaii? I have Dr. Emmerit here."

Tingles ran up the back of Roger's neck and prickled in his scalp as his head swiveled around to see Ell standing there with a small group. Grinning at him unrepentantly! "Ell?!"

"Hey Roger! How do you like our little setup here?"

"Ell!" He turned his head to see Nancy grinning at him too. The rest of the little group looked puzzled.

Ell held up a finger. "Hold on a sec' Roger. Let me finish up here so I can talk to you without being pressed to come back to this issue." She turned back to the group she'd been with when Roger came up.

Nancy said, "Can I get you a coffee Roger?" She looked at him with an innocent twinkle in her eyes.

Roger snorted, "You had this all set up didn't you?"

"Well, Ms. Donsaii *had* mentioned that she knew you and hoped you'd apply for the position. The coffee machine's over here."

Ell came up as Nancy handed Roger a cup of coffee. "Hey Rog'" she was still grinning ear to ear.

"Hey yourself! What *is* all this?"

"You're not gonna believe this! You know how my theory predicts that quantum entanglement works because the entangled molecules are connected through a very tiny 5th dimension?"

Roger nodded.

"So that when something happens to one of the molecules, effects are seen at the other member of the entangled pair, instantaneously, at least as near as we can tell?"

Roger nodded again.

"Well, it turns out that you can arrange entangled molecules in tiny circles and energize the area surrounded by them. When the energization field's correct, a physical opening appears through the 5th dimension like a little wormhole connecting the two rings!"

"What?!" Roger felt a sensation like an electric shock in his scalp and his head swam a little as if he'd been physically stunned.

"Yeah. The holes I've made so far are microscopic. Some rich investors set D5R up to see if we can make 'em bigger." Ell put a hand to the side of her mouth and lifted an eyebrow as she stage whispered, "The investors are out of their minds! They kinda put me in charge!"

Roger swayed slightly, "A, a, a... wormhole... that stuff can pass through?"

"Well, just gas and water molecules so far, but, yeah. You wanna help us work on it?"

Chapter Three

Washington D.C.— NASA has come under heat for relying exclusively on ILX Corporation's Vulcan 5 rocket launch vehicle. Critics say the excitement over the Vulcan 5's potential to launch larger payloads at significantly lower cost was unwisely allowed to disrupt the commercial space flight industry. When ILX's competitive advantage allowed it to begin getting all of the space launch contracts, several of the companies that had been providing satellite launch and service to the Space Station were shuttered.

Now, however, due to the repeated failures of the Vulcan 5 during actual launches NASA has been placed in the unenviable position of trying to resuscitate some of the companies it let wither…"

"Holy crap! What a mess!" Dave Slager turned himself in place to face Emil Taussan who was running on the Space Station's simulated weight bearing treadmill. "We all should've known the figures for the Vulcan 5 were too good to be true!"

Emil shrugged. "But we all *wanted* them to be true."

Slager grimaced, "You know we're going to be on short rations up here pretty soon. None of the previous launch companies nor the, Russians, Europeans, or Japanese have anything in the pipeline. ILX was supposed to keep one of their old launch vehicles ready until they were sure the Vulcan 5 was reliable, but I'll bet they don't have one they'll be able to send up in a hurry."

Emil shrugged, "If it gets too bad, surely the Chinese would be willing to supply us."

"Hah! Do you know their capsules won't even connect to our airlock? They'd have to work up an adapter and you know nobody will even start designing it until it's almost too late."

"What about India?"

"What about? They could get something up here I suppose, but their capsules are small and I'll bet they don't have the correct mechanisms to lock to our door either."

"Maybe we should do another EVA to re-evaluate the CRV's rocket nozzle? Do you think there's any chance we could repair it up here?"

"No chance at all, none, zippo. Even if we had equipment to weld it, the kind of weld we could make wouldn't hold up to the heat the nozzle generates."

***

Ed Candela looked up at a knock on his door. Mike Voight stood there looking grim. "How bad is it?"

Voight's shoulders slumped. "Bad! ILX *says* they have a Vulcan 4 that they can launch in case of trouble, but it turns out they don't have any motors for it! They'd been planning to fit it with the new motors that they've been building for the Vulcan 5! They didn't want to waste any money' making more of those inefficient Vulcan 4 motors! He"

Candela slammed a fist down on his desk, "Dammit!" He raised his eyes to the ceiling and slumped back in his chair. "How long to make more

Vulcan 4 motors?"

Voight's eyes rolled. "Six months! They repurposed the fabrication equipment to make the Vulcan 5 engines!"

Candela sighed and closed his eyes. "Please talk to the Chinese about whether they'd be willing to send a mission to the ISS. We'll need to start *now* on building an adaptor to fit their capsule to the station. Then tell ILX we want them to try to send up another supply rocket using their existing Vulcan 5, after they've done everything they can to stabilize the problem with their rocket motors. We've got to at least *supply* those guys up on the station if we want them to last until we can get a mission up to retrieve them."

***

Roger pulled his pecan pie out of the oven. Living in a family that owned a restaurant made Christmas dinner kind of weird. The Emmerit family tradition was that everyone made one dish. Some of the family made something exotic and new each holiday dinner. Some made something awful, for instance Aunt Gert's fruitcake. Roger made pecan pie. He'd learned to make a pretty good one years ago and wasn't interested enough in cooking to try to make something different each time. The doorbell rang as he carried it out to the big buffet the family was setting up. He went to pull the door open. "Well, hello Ms. Donsaii." His smile threatened to crack his face, "How are you this evening?"

Ell grinned at him, "Well, I'm just fine Dr. Emmerit, thank you for asking."

Roger grinned back, "Please allow me take that." he took the covered dish she had in her hands. "And your coat?"

She handed him her coat too, then smirked at him. With both hands full, he wasn't sure what to do next. Her eyes crinkled, "Perhaps I should take the dish back while you hang up my coat sir?"

Resignedly he said, "Perhaps so." He made a little bow, "Pray tell, what's in the dish?"

"Mac and cheese. Probably not up to the standards of your family's holiday meals, but it's one of the few things I actually know how to make."

"Oooohh," Roger leaned close as he took it from her to put it on the buffet, "I love a good mac and cheese," he said sotto voce. "People in my family feel they have to prove something by making things that're too fancy, if you know what I mean."

Ell's eyes sparkled and she raised her eyebrows, "I'm looking forward to fancy."

From behind her Ell heard Roger's Dad, "Is this the young lady you've invited Roger?"

Ell turned, "Hi Mr. Emmerit."

His eyebrows rose, "Ms. Donsaii?"

"Yes sir."

He darted an accusatory look at Roger, "Roger didn't tell us he'd invited you to dinner, just kept referring to his 'mysterious guest!'" Brows lowered, he said "I'll have to have a word with him about keeping someone like *you* a secret."

Ell grinned at Roger, "Well, Mr. Emmerit, I'm probably mostly to blame. Ever since I was kidnapped last year I try to keep my intended whereabouts unknown if possible. Hopefully he was just respecting my wishes." She winked, "I do think he could have told

Rocket!

his own family though."

"Well, my son's much too rude to offer you a drink, but if you'll come with me I'll see to getting you a glass." He winked at Roger as he steered Ell toward the next room. "I know you and Roger were in grad school together a year ago, but then didn't you go back in the military?"

"Yes sir, but I'm back out of the military again now. I've moved back to North Carolina..."

~~~

Distractedly, Ell looked around at the swirling menagerie of people pouring in to the Emmerit Christmas dinner. Aunts, uncles, cousins, grandparents, grandkids and a boyfriend for one of the cousins. Ell'd invited Roger to a quiet Christmas Eve dinner with her, her mom and her Gram the night before. So, he'd countered with an invitation to this veritable feast and celebration. The two dinners could hardly have been more different.

Roger's sister Shelly's ebullient acorn had fallen closer to the Emmerit tree than the introverted Roger's. To Ell's amazement they'd drawn lots to determine who sat where at a huge table which consisted of sheets of plywood on sawhorses. The table'd been dressed up with large tablecloths so its lowly nature wasn't evident. Ell had greatly enjoyed their small, quiet dinner the night before, but being with this huge, raucous, loving family felt very special too.

At the dinner Ell found herself seated across the table and several seats down from Roger. Roger had been horrified to find that the lottery had placed Ell next to Roger's Grandmother Emmerit, a notorious snoop. The indomitable lady turned to Ell and said,

"And you're *Roger's* guest?"

"Yes Mrs. Emmerit, I'm Ell."

She looked Ell over, frowning. "Aren't you awfully young for him? How old are you?"

Ell grinned at her, then over at Roger who, appalled by his Grandmother's directness, rolled his eyes. "Yes, Ma'am. I'm only nineteen. I *do* like older men though." She winked at Roger.

"Roger," his Grandmother said turning to him, "How old are you now?"

"Twenty-nine Gramma."

"My goodness, ten years. He *is* robbing the cradle isn't he? So tell me, what are you doing young lady? Are you in school? I do hope Roger isn't dating one of his students."

Finding it refreshing to talk to someone who had no idea who she was, Ell said, "No Ma'am, I've finished school. I did *meet* Roger in school, but I wasn't his student." Ell glanced back over at Roger and, as she did, realized that many of the people in their portion of the table were hanging on every word of the conversation. Some appeared appalled by the way Ell was being interrogated. Others were restraining their mirth at their Grandmother's ruthlessly oblivious questioning of someone who was relatively famous.

~~~

While the rest of the family were pondering asking for an autograph, Roger's grandmother, having no idea who Ell was, was disappointed to learn she'd apparently dropped out after high school.

"So you're working then?"

"Yes Ma'am.

"What kind of work do you do?"

Rocket!

"I do research at D5R."

"Really?" To herself Grandmother Emmerit thought it was pretty uppity for a nineteen-year-old high school graduate to be claiming to be "doing research" herself. *But the girl's certainly good looking, no need to wonder what Roger sees in her. Surprising really, that a quiet boy like Roger would be with such a stunning young lady.* "What kind of research does D5R do?"

Wide eyed, Roger said, "Gramma…" but paused when Ell held up a hand his direction.

"They're trying to find useful applications for the fifth dimension that's recently been discovered."

"Fifth dimension?!" she said, sounding highly dubious.

"Yes Ma'am, another company called PGR Comm is already making chips that use that fifth dimension to make communication devices."

"Humpf. What do you do there?"

Eyes twinkling Ell said, "A little of this, a little of that. I really like working on the research, but the company's *very* new so I spend a lot more time setting stuff up than I do on actual research right now."

~~~

"Gramma!" Ell heard the boy on the other side of Grandmother Emmerit whisper urgently to her. Mrs. Emmerit turned to him, but Ell could still faintly hear his whisper, "That's Ell Donsaii! The girl that won all the Olympic gold medals in gymnastics!"

Mrs. Emmerit turned back to eye Ell speculatively. "So you're a gymnast, eh?"

"I was Ma'am. I don't do gymnastics anymore." Her eyes crinkled, I'm *much* too old for that now."

The conversation moved on to other topics, but it

was apparent that Roger's grandmother remained highly dubious of the suitability of a nineteen-year-old high school graduate for her grandson, the newly minted physics PhD.

~~~

When the main meal had been cleared and people had chosen their desserts Roger's father dinged a spoon on a glass and the huge table fell quiet. He said, "OK time for announcements." He turned to his immediate left. "April, I think you have an announcement?"

Roger's young, blond, blue eyed cousin proudly said "I just got accepted to NC State."

Everyone at the table clapped and then held their glasses up for a toast. "What are you going to major in?" one of the aunts asked.

One of the younger girls stage whispered, "Boys."

Red faced April paused to glare at the whisperer, then said, "I don't know. I'm starting in 'general studies' until I decide."

The same whisperer, "I told you, *boys.*"

They went around the table, some of the older people passing with a professed, "Nothing to report." However, all the young people said something. Some had graduated. Some had new jobs, one had purchased a new boat for his fishing business. Two were engaged to marry.

When it came Roger's turn he blushed and said, "I've completed my degree and got a job."

Someone sang out, "And what degree did you get?"

Still blushing, "A PhD in Physics."

"Woohoo! A toast to *Dr.* Emmerit." After everyone'd raised their glasses, "Where's your new job?"

"I just started work at D5Research in Research

Triangle Park."

At this Grandmother Emmerit turned to look suspiciously at Ell. Ell could tell she wanted to ask more questions, but the announcements went on around the table. When it came her turn Grandmother Emmerit passed and they all looked at Ell. She widened her eyes and said, "Pass."

"Oh, no, all the young people *have* to announce something!"

Ell looked up at the ceiling a moment, then raised her glass and said, "I really like Roger Emmerit?"

Cheers and applause followed this announcement and the spotlight fell on the next person.

Once the announcements were done Grandmother Emmerit turned to Ell and narrowed her eyes. "You and Roger work at the same company?" she asked suspiciously.

"Yes Ma'am."

"Don't they have rules against dating your boss?"

Ell glanced at Roger, seeing he was once again appalled. She winked at him. "Why no. They don't have such a rule, but it's a very new company." She frowned as if concerned, "Perhaps they should?"

Mrs. Emmerit said, "Well I for one think it's bad karma to mix romance and work. But if you and Roger continue to hit it off, perhaps you could find another job?"

Roger finally couldn't take it anymore, "Gramma!" He rolled his eyes in exasperation. "Ell *runs* the company. She doesn't work for *me*; I work for her. If someone had to get another job it'd be me, not her!"

Mrs. Emmerit turned to stare at Roger in disbelief, then turned to look at all the people around her who were smothering their mirth. After a moment she threw her head back and laughed out loud. She turned back to Ell and took on a hick accent, "Well! I guess I done stuck my foot in my mouth! I apologize. I guess you can tell from the way my own family's laughing at me that this ain't the first time I done it?"

Eyes twinkling, Ell said, "Oh no Ma'am! I am absolutely astonished that anyone might think that!"

To her amazement Grandmother Emmerit grinned, turned and stuck her tongue out at her nearby family members.

After the dinner was over a couple of the younger family members did ask Ell if she'd sign autographs for them. By the time she'd signed the entire family was bundling up to go out and sing carols for the neighbors. Ell went along and at first just mouthed the words, afraid of singing badly and spoil the harmony. A few minutes into the first carol she realized that several of the Emmerits sang horribly, but nonetheless joyfully, so she joined in. Caroling turned out to be a funny, sweet, inspiring and joyful endeavor from which she returned home quite late.

***

Cape Canaveral— NASA and ILX today announced that they will attempt to launch another Vulcan 5 rocket with supplies for the International Space Station within the next two weeks. ILX hopes that some recent modifications they've made to the Vulcan 5 rocket motors will be successful in preventing another calamity. Although the supply situation at the Station is not desperate as yet, there is no doubt that a successful mission to the station is becoming a high priority...

Rocket!

The D5R researchers had gathered around one of the big stainless steel tables in the middle of the big industrial room at the research facility for their morning meeting. Ell looked around the group, "Happy New Year to all of you. Since we're all so new, some even newer than others, I'd like to introduce and reintroduce the members of our little research group to each other. I'm Ell Donsaii. Since I wrote the original paper that our research is based on, our investors have put me in charge of directing D5R's research program." Ell waved to her right, "Roger Emmerit here has just completed his PhD in Physics at NCSU and is interested in all aspects of our investigations, but doesn't have a particular specialization as yet. Next is Ben Stavos," Ell indicated a slender thirty-year-old man with a shock of wild blond hair." Ben comes to us from Hewlett Packard where he was a maven of microconstruction. He's going to lead the team attempting to construct port rings by moving entangled molecules into place with high-speed micro assemblers. Fred Marsden," Ell indicated a tall redheaded man, "comes to us from SUNY where he just completed a post doc with Edgar Venter working to quantum entangle macro molecules with some of the new techniques they've developed. He'll lead our team that will see if they can successfully entangle carbon nanotube tori so that we don't *have* to assemble ports two molecules at a time. Next is Brian Short," Ell nodded at a grizzled man, "Brian's a lifelong machinist who can actually run all the equipment in our machine shop and claims he can make *anything* we need."

With an alarmed look, Brian waved his hands in protest, "*Almost* anything."

Ell grinned at him, "I'm counting on 'anything' we

need." She pointed, "Vivian Varka there," she indicated a heavyset woman, "is an electrical engineer who's going to help me build circuits to generate the specialized fields we need. Hopefully, between the two of us we'll be able to energize any ports the assembly teams are able to build." Ell continued on around the table, introducing assistants and minor players in each of the groups that she'd already introduced the heads of.

Ell looked around, "I know that none of you know each other very well yet, but I hope we gel into a real team. Although D5R has backstopped each of you with a relatively generous minimum salary, remember that, if we're successful in making the ports work on a larger scale, there's a profit sharing system in place."

~~~

As the meeting broke up, Ben Stavos rubbed his chin and wondered what he'd gotten himself into. He'd interviewed and taken this job over the net from Texas. Yes, his minimum guaranteed salary was significantly better than HP'd been paying him. But when interviewing over the net he'd thought Donsaii just "looked" young. He also hadn't realized she was *running* the place; he'd thought she was just doing the hiring. When he'd arrived and found out that this girl-child was in charge he'd been completely flummoxed. Then he'd done the research he should have done before giving up his job at HP. She was *just* as young as she looked. Not even twenty yet! Yes, she'd had a moment of brilliance when she'd worked out the math for the 5th dimension and explained entanglement. However, even though Ben didn't understand that math himself, he had the distinct impression that, like she said, it really *was* just a bit of luck that'd let her stumble across it. If this harebrained entangled port idea didn't work quickly, he suspected that whoever was financing D5R would drop it like a hot potato—then what?

Oh well, maybe he'd just stick with this job until the investors gave up on it, then move on. Enjoy the moment. He turned back to the micro assembler setup, "OK, John," he said to his assistant, "let's see if we can persuade this monster to line molecules up in circles."

***

Steve and Mary got out of their car slinging their backpacks. He watched a moment to be sure the car'd begun to drive itself away to the parking lot. Then he turned and looked for Ell who'd been dropped off by her car a few minutes earlier. She was about a hundred yards away, walking one of the brick paths across the campus to her Astronomy class. The platinum blond wig she'd chosen to disguise herself with for her stint as UNC student Belle Donovan made her easy to pick out, even from this far away. He and Mary began walking along the same path, Steve's eyes darting around as he checked for threats. Once they reached the building, Mary stayed in the lobby on a bench. Steve entered the classroom and sat up near the back. He looked over the class. "Belle" was sitting down near the front and she'd started talking to the young man next to her.

~~~

Gordon looked up as someone sat in the seat next to his. Hmm, a pretty blond. Too much makeup for his taste. It looked like she was trying to hide a bad complexion. However, she was cute in a pale sort of way. He turned to her, "Hi, haven't seen you around. You new?"

Ell grinned at him. He had freckles and curly reddish hair. "Yup. Just taking this one class 'cause I'm interested in ET's." She raised her eyebrows at him.

Gordon gave her a look that combined a grimace and a query, "This is a pretty tough class to be taking just because you're curious! You can read about ET's on the net."

She tilted her head. "Maybe so, but I'd like to get a deeper understanding than that."

"Why not just audit the class over the net then?"

"'cause then I wouldn't get to have scintillating conversations with fascinating people like you. My name's Belle. What's yours?"

He put out his hand, "I'm Gordon. A real Southern Belle 'eh? I never thought I'd actually meet one."

"Ha, ha. Didn't yo momma nevah tell you not to make jokes about a person's name? I'm sure I've already heard every 'Belle' joke you can think of."

"Oh ho! Did you just ring the starting 'bell' on a challenge?"

Ell rolled her eyes, but was saved from having to respond by the arrival of Professor Norris. The Professor introduced himself and outlined the class on planetary systems before starting his first lecture. His speaking style kind of droned on, but Ell found the topic fascinating. He was assigning some reading to be done for the next class as the bell rang.

Gordon looked wide eyed at Ell, "There's the 'bell!'"

She grinned and lightly poked his shoulder, saying, "I can see I'll have to be more careful who I sit next to from now on."

Rocket!

As she left the building she had her AI contact her car and send it to pick her up. She saw Mary getting up from a bench in the lobby and leaving when she did.

Chapter Four

Cape Canaveral—NASA and ILX Corporation today announced that the latest Vulcan 5 rocket, carrying supplies for the International Space Station, has also failed to launch successfully. Once again, one of the new, super-efficient motors trumpeted by ILX exploded, driving the rocket off course and requiring it be destroyed by internal charges. More and more concern is being expressed about the supply situation at the Station…

Roger and Ell walked into West 87 together and started toward the booth where the physics grads customarily hung out. Emma looked up. "Hey you two!" She bounced up out of the booth to give Ell a hug. "Am I ever gonna see one of you without the other again?" She was amused to see they both looked a little embarrassed.

Ell said, "Well, you know, we work together now, so if we're gonna go slumming at West 87 with our degenerate friends, it only makes sense to ride together."

"Besides," Roger said, "I'm buying her dinner in a transparent attempt to influence my new boss and the only restaurants I know anything about are here in Raleigh." He shrugged, "If we're gonna be in Raleigh on a Friday night, of course we've gotta drop by West 87 and visit you guys."

They sat down and caught up with their old friends

from NCSU. They were introduced to a couple of new grad students.

Cody, one of the new students wound up sitting next to Ell. He felt like there was something familiar about her, but in the flurry of introductions he hadn't really caught her name. She was hot! He wondered if she and this Roger guy were in a committed relationship. He asked her, "When did Roger graduate?"

"Last December."

"And you two work for the same company?"

Ell grinned at him. The grin lit up her face and he found her even more attractive, "Yep."

"Is he your boyfriend?"

"Well," she considered, "we're very good friends." She tilted her head, "and I'm pretty sure he's a boy…"

Cody, happy to hear that she didn't sound completely committed to Roger, glanced around the table. The others were all lost in their own little conversations. He turned back to Ell, "You seem familiar to me. Do we know each other from somewhere?"

She smiled enigmatically, "I don't believe we've met."

He tilted his head, considering. She looked about eighteen to twenty, younger than he was by a couple of years. "Are you sure? Where did you go to high school?"

"Morehead City."

He grinned, "My parents have a vacation home on Emerald Isle and my dad loves going fishing on Jim Slip's charter boat out of Morehead. I'll bet we've run into each other somewhere down there one summer."

Ell tilted her head, considering. "Maybe we did."

"Did you go to college?"

She grinned again, "A couple of years."

Cody was a little disappointed, thinking she'd gone to a community college somewhere. *But, if she looks* this *good, who cares how far she went in school?* He glanced at Roger. Roger was deep in a conversation with Jerry. "Do you mind if our AIs exchange contact info? I'd love to see you again sometime."

Ell shrugged, "No problem."

Emma, sitting on Cody's left, dug an elbow into his side.

He turned to her and saw her grinning at him. He raised a questioning eyebrow.

"Hey Casanova, have you figured out who you're putting the moves on?"

Cody glanced up at his HUD. It said, "Contact—Ell Donsaii." He closed his eyes and felt his cheeks flush. *She's so famous, how could I not recognize her?* He opened his eyes to see Ell grinning at him. "I guess now I know why you seem familiar?"

She quirked her lip, "Maybe?" She tilted her head in consideration, then frowned a little, "But maybe we met in Morehead too."

A little later Roger and Ell got up to leave for their dinner at the Mellow Mushroom. James said, "You're not taking her someplace fancy now that you've got a job? My God man, you're not gonna impress the girl that way!"

Ell patted James lightly on the shoulder. "Turns out 'the girl' likes pizza better than she does fancy restaurants."

***

Ell stared up at her HUD, watching the results of a

computation she had Allan, her AI, running to calculate the orbits of the planets of Epsilon Eridani. It held interest for her because E. Eridani was only 10.5 light years away and had a planet in the habitable zone. However, it also had a large planet with a highly elliptical orbit. It probably made the orbit of the planet in the habitable zone unstable. Ell was trying to calculate from the known orbits and masses of the various E. Eridani planets just how long the planet had likely been in the habitable zone.

Someone thumped down in the seat next to her. "Whew, got here before the 'bell.'"

Ell looked over, "Hey Gordon. You know, the way you keep arriving to class barely before it rings, you make it *very* difficult to avoid sitting next to you and hearing your awful name puns?"

He grinned at her, "My plan exactly."

Ell rolled her eyes and checked her HUD.

"Hey my roomies and I are having a pre finals party Saturday night, you wanna come? You could be the 'belle of the ball.'"

Ell glared balefully at him for a moment, but then broke into a grin. "OK. Where and when?"

***

Ell arrived back at D5R after her class and headed immediately into the research area for the team's Wednesday morning update meeting. No one looked happy. In fact, their dejected expressions matched her own feelings. They'd been at this for weeks now and there'd been little progress. For a moment she wondered if they'd taken on an impossible task. Or had she assembled the wrong team? Maybe she was the wrong person to lead them? She turned to Stavos, "Ben, let's start with you. Can you tell us something positive?"

Stavos twisted his lips a moment, then shook his head. "The good news is that we've got the micro assembler set up so that it *can* build a pair of rings made from entangled buckyballs."

Ell's eyebrows shot up in excitement. "That sounds great!" She frowned, "Why are you looking so down?"

"You know the entanglement isn't terribly stable until we get them placed in your stabilization field. We actually have the entangled buckyballs moving into the assembler stabilized by such a field. But when we take them from the stabilization field that they're in and move them into the field for the port's ring, they're out of the stabilization field and the action of moving them un-entangles them if we move them very fast. When we try to up the speed of the buckyball placement into the ring, they start losing their entanglement in transit."

"Ouch, that *is* a problem. How fast *can* you place them reliably without breaking their entanglement?"

"About two per second. Since the buckyballs have a diameter of about one nanometer, that means about 5.5 days per millimeter of ring. To make the pair of one centimeter diameter rings you want will take somewhere around half a year!" He paused and shrugged, "We're still working on it though."

Everyone at the table could see that Stavos didn't have any ideas for a solution at present.

"Dang! I'll come look at your set up after the meeting. Maybe I'll have some ideas on how to stabilize the entanglement sooner." She looked up at the ceiling, "Or maybe during the placement?" After a moment she turned to Fred Marsden, "Is your team having any luck entangling tori?"

Marsden rolled his eyes, "Oh yeah, we can entangle them alright. But we have a problem similar to Ben's. Once we've entangled them, we can't *separate* them to put the tori into your stabilization field without breaking the entanglement. Molecules that big only stay entangled for microseconds unless they're stabilized with your field."

"Any ideas on how to solve it?"

He shrugged, "We're going to try to position each torus on a stabilization field plate, then bring the two tori into contact while they're *on* the plates and see if we can get them to entangle with the field all ready to turn on." With a sigh he said, "The entanglement field and the stabilization field are pretty different though."

"Vivian?" Ell turned to Vivian Varka the electrical engineer. "Let's look at their setup together and see whether we can help them work on the transition from one field to the other, maybe a gradual transition." She looked up at the ceiling again, "Or would an abrupt transition be better?" She brought her eyes back down and shrugged, "I guess we can try both."

Ell looked around the table, "Any other news or ideas?"

They all looked morosely back at her, as if hopeless or depressed or something. Ell despondently wondered what she could do to buck them up.

She wondered if she should just give up and disband D5R.

Roger felt nervous speaking up in this group because he was the most junior. Well except for Ell! Nonetheless, he cleared his throat, "Uh."

Everyone turned to look at him. "I'm wondering if an

intermediate approach might work?"

The group looked at him with puzzled expressions. "For instance if we entangled nanotubes say a hundred microns long instead of the much larger nanotori. Then used Ben's micromanipulators to move them into a ring shape at a relatively slow pace…"

Ell's eyebrows went up and she looked around at the group. They all looked somewhat dubious but no one was saying it couldn't be done. "It's an idea. Roger why don't you do some tests and calculations. How fast can Fred entangle them and how fast can Ben move them without breaking entanglement? Then determine whether it'll actually be faster than one at a time buckyballs?"

Roger nodded.

Ben put a hand up and Ell nodded. "I'm just wondering," he said, "exactly how long are the investors going to put up with our lack of progress? Should we be taking any offers we may be getting for other jobs?"

For a moment Ell considered telling them that *she* was the only investor. Then she thought about telling them they *did* have a deadline after which they would be disbanded. That'd be the way it'd work in the real world. Mentally she shrugged, after all, there wasn't really any reason to stop working on it until Ell herself was ready to give up. With PGR Comm paying her a minimum royalty of 2.1 billion dollars a year, minus the 230 million a year she was funding NCSU and UNC with, and about 800 million in taxes, she had about a billion dollars a year in disposable income. Financing D5R hardly put a dent in that kind of cash flow. She didn't want to tell them that, because she didn't want people to know she was wealthy.

Rocket!

She looked at Ben a moment, then around at the others. "Our investors," she said, "have personally guaranteed me six months of salary for each of you should they abandon our efforts here at D5R. I hope that that's enough cushion that you'll be able continue to focus all your energies on achieving success, rather than working on backup plans?"

There were surprised nods all around the table. The meeting broke up shortly afterward.

***

It turned out that Gordon and his roommates lived south of campus in a small rented house. Ell's car dropped her off and headed out to find a place to park. She walked down a gravel driveway already hearing the heavy thump of the music. She'd arrived very late to her first ever "college party" so she wouldn't feel too awkward arriving when she didn't really know anyone. It looked like she'd been successful; the front porch was crowded with people swaying to the music. People spilled out into the yard, most of them holding a cup in one hand. Ell slowly worked her way through the crowd.

A young Asian man staggered into her. For a moment the multiple attempted kidnappings she'd suffered at the hands of Chinese nationals leapt to the forefront of her mind. Then the red faced young man smiled widely at her and held up his beer, "Heeyy! You're pretty! I'm Joe Chan. Can I be your boyfriend?" He swung his hands to point at himself with both thumbs, spilling some of his beer.

Ell grinned at him, "You can be my friend."

Laurence E Dahners

"Heeyy!" he raised his arms. "And I'm a boy! Tha' makes me a boyfrien', right?"

Ell laughed at his cheerfully good-natured drunkenness, "A 'friendly boy' at least. A friendly boy who's had too much to drink, I think."

"You're a poet! But you're right. You should help me maintain my balance." He put an arm over Ell's shoulders, "If you help me walk without falling I'll introduce you to the band." He waggled his eyebrows proudly, "I know 'em all."

Ell rolled her eyes, "OK, I'll hold you up." She looked toward the window, surprised that people staying in a little house like this could afford a live band for their party. "Take me in and introduce me."

"All righ'!" Joe said enthusiastically, starting toward the porch steps, "Gangway, pretty lady comin' through!" He began crowding his way through the people on the stairs shouting all the while.

Ell worried someone would object, but they all grinned good naturedly at Joe, many shouting good natured taunts, "Oh no, Joe's fooled another one."

"Give it up Joe, she's too good lookin' for you!"

"Look out little lady, he's a devil in disguise."

Joe drew himself up, "Ignore those small minded people, remember... I know the band!" He clumsily maneuvered her in the door.

The house had a surprisingly large front room, crowded with even more people. The band was set up at one end. The people were swaying to the loud music. Perhaps you could call it dancing, though packed so tightly, it was a little hard to tell. Joe said, "Let's dance!" Or at least that's what Ell thought he said. He took his arm off her shoulders and turned toward Ell. Assuming a wide stance, he began moving jerkily to the music.

Rocket!

Ell turned toward Joe and began swaying and shuffling her feet in a minimized version of the line dance she'd learned in Las Vegas. Joe smiled happily at her, then bumped into the woman behind him. He turned to apologize to her and Ell stole a glance at the band. They were mostly hidden by the crowd since they weren't up on a stage, but a small gap in the crowd revealed Gordon.

He was actually part of the band and was standing behind a microphone! He saw her too. Grinning widely, he leaned to the mike and started singing the next verse. Ell realized he was the lead singer!

He's really good! she thought.

Joe leaned close to her, Ell put up a hand to steady him. The song was winding down he shouted, "What's your name?"

Ell shouted back, "Belle. Belle Donovan."

Joe's eyebrows shot up. "Gordon's friend?"

Ell shrugged. "Gordon invited me."

Joe turned vaguely toward the band and bellowed, "Gordo, Belle's here!"

Gordon's voice came over the PA system, "OK folks, last song before we take a break! I give you Belle... Bottom Blues!"

Ell rolled her eyes. She should have known!

A rough, distorted, bluesy guitar lick started up. Joe resumed swaying so Ell did too. A commotion from her left proved to be Gordon pushing through the crowd while still playing the guitar. Behind him a guy was carrying the microphone on its stand. Ell raised her eyebrows at him as he stopped in front of her and waited for the guy to put the mike down. He leaned to the mike, raised his eyebrows, and began singing, "Belle bottom blues..."

Laurence E Dahners

Like the rough mildly distorted guitar, he sang with a gravelly voice. Ell thought he sounded great. When the song was over, he pushed his guitar around behind his back on its sling, grinned at her and said, "I see you've met my buddy Joe Chan?" Gordon gestured at Joe who staggered a little. Gordon put a hand out to steady him.

Joe said, "Oh yeah!"

Ell grabbed Joe's other shoulder to keep him upright, "Yep. I think Joe's had enough to drink for a while." She turned back to Gordon raising her eyebrows, "Are you ever gonna ease up on my name?"

"Oh no!" he said, mock seriously. "You challenged me with that, 'I'm sure I've already heard all the 'Belle' jokes you can possibly think of' line. I spent hours learning Bell Bottom Blues for you, you know?"

"I liked it. Even if you *were* hassling me with it."

He raised his eyebrows, "What's not to like? A blues standard, played by an awesome guitarist, sung by an amazing singer!" He frowned, "Of course you liked it!"

"Astounding modesty too!" Ell laughed.

"Hey Joe," Gordon said, "We need to get this girl a beer. She's too sharp for us when she's sober!"

"Yeah! But don' gi' me another one, or, I'll be, too drunk, to im-impress her with my sc-scin-tillating wit."

Without the band playing, the crowded room was emptying out. People filtered out into the yard where the keg was set up. Ell and the guys went out into the crisp spring evening. Someone had started a small fire in what appeared to have been a brick planter in the middle of the patio. Ell said, "I'd like a Coke, not beer."

Gordon looked at her and said, "A rum and Coke?" He winked, "Remember, we're trying to dull your resistance to our sharp wit." He waved to a table, "It's over there."

Rocket!

Ell made her way to the table and got herself a plastic cup full of ice. She poured Coke into it.

Gordon shouted at her from the keg, "I'm watching you. Don't forget the rum!"

Ell picked up the rum bottle and pretended to pour some into her Coke, then headed back toward the fire. Part way there she was stopped by a large guy with a beer in one hand. "Hey girl! What's your name?"

"I'm Belle." Ell glanced past him, looking for Gordon and saw Joe unsteadily coming her way. She was beginning to regret this Belle disguise. The platinum blonde wig seemed to attract too much attention. To become "Belle" she put on a heavy makeup with a slightly lumpy texture to make it seem like it was trying to cover a case of acne. She also tucked prosthetic lumps between her gums and cheeks to give herself slightly puffy chipmunk cheeks. As opposed to her "Ellen" and "Raquel" disguises she wasn't wearing a nasal prosthesis.

The "Ellen" disguise with the large nose and fat pants made from silicone had rendered her pretty unattractive. In that disguise men had *never* accosted her. In fact, they seldom even gave her a second look. As "Belle" she looked different enough that she wouldn't be recognized as Ell, but she was still getting some unwanted attention. She wondered if she'd unwittingly made herself look better than her natural state.

She wondered if she should have used fat pants for "Belle?" She'd wanted to avoid the extra time the pants required while changing into her disguise because she changed in and out of the disguise three mornings a week for her Astronomy class. But really, she could have changed in the car during transit without that much trouble.

The big guy said, "I'm Vic. Are you a student at the 'U'?"

"Part time."

He nodded, "I'm on the football team." His eyes said she should be impressed. "Vic Galtieri."

"What do you study?" Ell looked over at Joe who'd unsteadily come around Vic.

Joe cheerfully said, "Belle!" and reached out toward her.

"General studies." Vic said to Ell, then he turned slightly toward Joe, "Get lost."

Joe turned to look blearily at Vic.

Ell said, "Joe's a friend of mine."

Without looking back at Ell, Vic growled, "Joe's a drunk who's gonna go sit down until he's sober enough to walk."

Joe turned back to Ell with his big grin still plastered on his face, "Maybe he'sh right Belle, you wanna help me go sit down?"

Narrowed eyes on Joe, Vic said, "No, she's gonna stay here. She and I were talkin'."

Sighing inside, Ell reached out to steady Joe. "Vic. I can decide for myself what I'm going to do."

Ell saw Vic tense and his hand start to rise. She dropped into the zone a little.

Vic said, "This *drunk* can sit down right here then." His hand rose.

Realizing that Vic intended to shove Joe and knock him down, Ell sent her hand up underneath Vic's. She wondered if she could push his arm up just the right amount. She didn't want to hit his arm hard enough to hurt him like she had her step-dad Jake; she just wanted to push it up enough that it didn't hit Joe. It was a *big* arm. She went deeper in the zone and watched her hand settle under Vic's meaty distal forearm. She pushed upward gently and then a little harder when she realized it wouldn't be enough to move an arm the size of Vic's. Vic's hand slid up and over Joe's shoulder. Ell's hand rotated to settle on Joe's shoulder, steadying and turning him away from Vic.

Vic stumbled when his hand didn't meet the expected resistance. Ell realized that Vic was pretty drunk himself, though it didn't show on him like it did on Joe. Ell started to guide Joe toward a bench keeping an eye on Vic over her shoulder. Vic staggered a step or two, then turned back toward them. *Damn, why can't he just leave us alone!*

Gordon appeared behind him, "Hey Vic," he started.

"Butt out Gordon." Vic rumbled, shambling after Ell and Joe.

Gordon started to reach out for him, "Vic, calm down! You know how you get when you're drunk."

"I *said* BUTT out!" Vic reached out one big meaty hand and shoved Gordon. Gordon staggered back, stumbling into an azalea bush and losing his footing. Vic resumed stumping after Ell and Joe.

Ell turned Joe and sat him down on the bench. He grinned up at her. "Heeyy Belle," he drawled, seeming to be completely unaware of the high tension situation around him.

Vic lumbered up and reached for Ell's arm, "Let's get outta here Belle."

Ell moved her arm so he missed it, "No! Vic, I'm sorry, but you're acting like a jerk. I don't want to go anywhere with you."

He narrowed his eyes and reached again, "Come on! You'll like it!"

Ell moved her arm to dodge his grasp again, Gordon was coming up on Vic's other side. She wondered what she could do to get this situation back in control. *How did it escalate so quickly?* she wondered. *Are all college parties like this?* Or was there something about her that brought out the worst in people?

Gordon said, "Vic! Leave her alone!" and reached for Vic's arm.

Ell'd come most of the way back up out of the zone. Now she pushed herself back down into it. *Crap!* She saw Vic tensing as Gordon touched his arm. *He's going to hit Gordon!* Vic's hand formed a fist and he began to turn toward Gordon, muscles bunching as he built a full roundhouse punch. *My God! If that punch hits, Gordon's going down hard!*

Ell moved with Vic, reaching up again to slap the bottom of his forearm and deflect the punch up above Gordon's startled face.

Gordon's expression showed that he realized how badly he'd underestimated Vic's current state.

Vic's knuckle grazed Gordon's forehead, knocking his head back a little, but then Vic himself, unbalanced by the miss, lurched forward and stumbled into Gordon. They went down in a tangle of limbs, Vic bellowing with rage.

Ell stepped closer, studying the debacle in front of her. Vic was coming down, his waist across Gordon's ribs, Vic's upper body to Gordon's right. Gordon's arms were flailing out, trying to slow his descent and keep his head from hitting the ground.

Ell reached out for Gordon's right hand with hers, reaching into her purse with her left hand. When she had a good grip on Gordon's hand she leaned back, pulling hard, trying to help keep his head from hitting the bricks, as well as pulling him out from under Vic.

As the two men crashed to the ground, Ell's pull slid Gordon somewhat out from under Vic, but not completely. She leaned to her right, trying to roll Gordon out from under him.

As she'd feared, the thrown punch having failed, Vic began to surge back, now ready to wrestle.

Ell leaned forward, stretched out her left arm and gently squeezed a small shot of pepper spray into Vic's face. Then she surged back to resume pulling on Gordon's arm.

Vic's arm that had been snaking into a wrestling hold around Gordon's torso, stopped and began pulling back to grasp his own face in agony.

Gordon rolled the rest of the way out from under Vic, got his hands under him and heaved himself to his feet, prepared for fight or flight. His eyebrows creased as he looked at Vic. "What happened to him?" Vic was scrubbing at his eyes and coughing violently.

"Pepper spray," Ell said quietly, looking around at the crowd that'd begun to stare. Barrett and Randy from her security team were just turning to fade back into the shadows, realizing they weren't needed. She leaned down to Vic, "Sorry Vic. Let me help you get into the bathroom to wash your face."

Gordon said, "Whoa! Remind me not to piss *you* off!"

Vic coughed again, he must have been taking a breath when Ell shot him with the spray. "Wha' ta' Hell happen'!?" He coughed again but pushed himself to his feet and let Ell start leading him toward the house.

Ell turned to Gordon, "Gordon. Where's the bathroom?"

Gordon shook his head, "I wouldn't go in there with

him if I were you Belle. He's an *animal* when he's drunk. I wouldn't have invited him but he *promised* he'd stay sober."

Ell rolled her eyes at Gordon, "He's hurt, we gotta help him get in there to get this stuff washed off of him."

Gordon shrugged and reluctantly said, "This way." He stepped into the lead and Ell guided the sobbing Vic after him.

~~~

When Ell got back to the farmhouse that night she found Steve waiting up. She said, "Hey, you're not on duty."

"No, but Barrett called to let me know what happened. You're a one-woman calamity zone!"

"Hey! *I* didn't start anything! It was a drunk guy that apparently *likes* to get into fights!"

"Drunk guy getting in a fight over a woman. You! You really should stay away from those kinds of situations!"

"I didn't do anything to get the guy started! He was just spoilin' for a fight!"

Steve rolled his eyes. "Yeah, sorry. I know it wasn't your fault. I just don't want you getting hurt is all. You really shouldn't be going to these kinds of wild parties. At least not looking so good. Pretty girls attract aggressive guys."

Ell gazed at him for a moment, "Hey Steve. I know it's a weird dichotomy, but, even though I'm your boss, I *am* just a kid you know. I need to get out and live life a little don't you think? That's half the reason I'm taking that astronomy class—so I can spend some time with kids my age."

Rocket!

Steve looked up at the ceiling, then drew a long suffering sigh. "Yeah, yeah. I get it. I just don't like it."

She grinned at him, "G'night Dad."

Steve rolled his eyes, "I'm not your Dad," he growled, "if I were, you'd be better behaved!"

She blinked her eyes up at him, "Yes Daddy."

"Oh Hell, who am I kidding? You'd have me wrapped around your finger."

Chapter Five

Ell looked around the table at her D5R researchers. Another meeting, another set of failed results. "Roger, what about your idea to use nanotubes for an intermediate path to making our ports?"

He shook his head dispiritedly, "We entangled some nanotubes, but they have to be moved even slower than buckyballs if you don't want to break the entanglement. It would slightly speed up the creation of a 10mm port from doing the whole thing with buckyballs. But each port would still take months. Sorry."

Ell tried not to let her disappointment show. "Any other ideas?" she asked trying for a perky tone.

Stavos said, "We should go out."

Ell tilted her head, "Out?"

"Yeah, socialize. Get to know each other away from here. Think about something else besides work."

Ell's first thought was surprise that he thought of this as work, doing what you loved. *Well, what I love,* she thought. Though she loved trying to figure this out, maybe the rest of the team really did think of it as a job? She knew first hand that research was fun when you were getting results—not so much when positive results were few and far between. In fact, maybe she liked science, not slogging away at the research end of it.

"Sounds good!" Ell said, trying to keep some sparkle in her voice. It frequently surprised her to be nineteen and have these older people looking to her for leadership, but she recognized that she was their leader, no matter how unexpected it might be. "What do you suggest?"

"Sports bar, tomorrow night."

Ell looked around the table, seeing ambivalence, or at best small amounts of enthusiasm, but she didn't have any better ideas. "OK!" she said keeping an enthusiastic tone, "Tomorrow night. Ben to pick the bar, D5R to pick up the tab, fun to be had by all!"

***

Washington D.C.— Critics of NASA are lining up to say "I told you so." NASA's decision to move quickly to the ill-fated Vulcan 5 rockets has proven disastrous, but there is little evidence that the critics actually warned against it. Steven Esklund has begun demanding that the ancient International Space Station be abandoned as soon as the current astronauts have been safely rescued. "It's been up there far longer than its expected lifespan anyway. We have no business putting people up into harm's way when they're just doing things that could have been done by robotic entities."

"The new PGR chips make remotely operated telepresence the obvious method to further space science..."

Allan, Ell's AI spoke in her ear, "You have a call from Phillip Zabrisk."

"Put him on! Phil, how are you doing?"

Phil chuckled, "How am I doing? Ha! Asks the woman who's single handedly destroying my intended career as an astronaut?"

"What?! How do you figure that?"

"Haven't you been hearing all this talk about remote controlled robotic astronauts using those PGR chips that are based on your theory? Then they won't have to keep sending expensive astronauts into dangerous locations?"

"Oh!" Ell thought furiously, then said with a chipper tone, "But a remote telepresence astronaut can be over six foot three can't he?"

"You're so behind the times! I took Denson's advice to slouch and convinced NASA I'm six foot two and a half, not six foot three and a half."

"Oh." Ell said in a small voice.

"And, I *don't* want to fly my spaceship from a cubicle! No girl's gonna go all googly eyed over that!"

"Sorry." Ell said contritely.

Phil laughed, "Oh hell, it isn't your fault. Besides, telepresence or no, I can't believe they won't be sending people up there again once they get this Vulcan 5 snafu straightened out."

"So, did you get accepted by NASA?"

"Well I haven't been rejected yet. I'm hoping to find out before graduation."

"Oh! That's right, when exactly is your graduation?"

"Wednesday, two weeks."

"Hey, could I get a ticket?"

"Sorry, they're all gone."

Disappointed, Ell said, "Oh."

"However there's a spot reserved for one 'Captain Donsaii' on the reviewing stand. Something about her being a special friend of the graduating class."

"What?!"

"Yeah, the class figured that Ell Donsaii should be

there for the graduation of her class, even if she was too uppity to graduate with the rest of us. I got elected to ask you."

"Hah! I'll be there. 'Uppity' and all."

"They want you to wear your uniform. Since you're still in the reserves you're entitled to wear it."

"Oh! I'll have to get it out of storage. Have your AI send me ticket codes and the rest of the info."

***

Ell walked into Bailey's for their D5R "social hour" and looked around.

A pretty hostess asked, "Hello Ms. Donsaii. Would you like a table?"

Ell heard her name and saw Ben Stavos waving from over near the pool tables. She thanked the hostess and headed over to where he was sitting. She hopped up on one of the barstools around the tall tables Ben had sequestered. She grinned at him, "Is it just you and me?"

"Naw, Eddy just came in, Sheila's in the bathroom, Brian promised he'd be here. Don't know about team ring ding though."

Ell had noticed a little rivalry developing between the team trying to entangle tori and the team trying to make rings out of the buckyballs. She wasn't sure whether it was good or bad, but it was crazy to pretend it wasn't there. "Are all the ball busters going to be here?"

"Hah! 'Ball busters!' I like that! I think they'll all be here."

The waitress came by and Ben ordered a Guinness.

Ell ordered a Coke. "What!" Ben said, "Are you a teetotaler or something?"

Ell grinned at him, "Uh, Ben? Underage? Are you trying to be a bad influence on me? Lead me into a corrupt life of drunken debauchery?

His eyes widened in startlement as he remembered just how young his boss was.

Eddy ordered a wheat beer and Sheila a glass of Merlot.

More and more of D5R's team filtered in and ordered drinks, then nachos and wings. Everyone seemed to be in high spirits. A good-natured teasing developed between the "Ring dings" and the "Ball busters." Ell surveyed the happy crowd and decided that the social hour had been a great idea. She leaned closer to Ben and said, "Hey thanks for suggesting this. Think we should do it regularly?"

"Sure, maybe every couple of weeks?"

Ell nodded, "OK."

"Hey," Ben proclaimed, "Team 'Ball buster' challenges team 'Ringa ding' to a game of darts! You guys up to the challenge?"

Fred Marsden raised his glass, "You bet!"

As the two teams wandered over to the dart board Ell scooted down to sit with the admin folks who'd conglomerated at the other end from the science team. They were a pleasant group and several of them were happily becoming inebriated. The woman next to Ell asked if Ben Stavos was married. She grinned when Ell said he wasn't and got up to walk unsteadily over and watch the dart game.

Their machinist, Brian Short, moved over to sit next to Ell. "Uh, Ms. Donsaii?"

Ell turned to him and raised an eyebrow, "I thought

we were informal Mr. Short?"

He grinned sheepishly, "Uh, 'Ell' then. I've got a crazy idea that I'm too embarrassed to bring up in the group meetings."

"Why not?"

"Well... you know... I only finished high school. So I don't want to suggest stuff to you big brains."

Ell raised an eyebrow, "Smart doesn't *have* to go to school. I'm amazed by the way you make those machines sit up and beg!" She shrugged, "Anyhow, what's your idea?"

"Well I've been wondering if the entangled buckyballs really have to be precisely placed? You can make 'em by the millions right? What if you just made huge quantities of them and sprayed them into a circle, like with an inkjet printer or 3D fabricator? Could they work even if they weren't precisely arranged into a circ..." He paused as Ell's eyes widened.

Prickles ran over Ell's scalp as she said, "Oh, my, God!" Her eyes focused off into the distance. "That might work." she mumbled.

***

Ell was early to Falcon stadium for the Academy graduation. The rental car deposited her near the gate and then took itself away to park in the big lots nearby. The code Phil'd sent got her through the gate and she walked out into the stadium reminiscing about the two years she'd spent at the Air Force Academy. She made her way to the reviewing stand. As she approached a 3rd class cadet saluted and said, "I'm sorry Captain, this area's reserved for graduation officials."

Laurence E Dahners

Ell returned the salute and said, "Thank you Cadet. I'm told that I'm actually supposed to be one of those officials."

The cadet's eyes widened and darted down to Ell's nametag. She drew herself up and saluted again. "Excuse me! Captain Donsaii, it'd be my honor to escort you."

The cadet conducted Ell up the stairs. As they approached the podium area Lt. General Ammonds, the commandant of the Academy saw Ell and interrupted his conversation to salute her.

The colonel who had been speaking to the Commandant turned to see whom he could be saluting. There weren't supposed to be any officers senior to a Lieutenant General at the graduation. His eyes widened as he saw a cadet and a female captain approaching and just dropping their own salutes. The colonel began his own salute after his eyes dropped to her left breast and recognized the Medal of Honor ribbon.

The Commandant grinned at Ell and said, "I assume you still have some friends in the graduating class. If you'll step to the podium with me, I'd like you to mark which of the cadets you'd like to present with their diplomas?"

Ell raised her eyebrows, "Really sir? I'd greatly appreciate that."

He lowered his voice, "I heard what you did for us in the recent China debacle and wanted to let you know how proud it made me. I often think back to the day you were brought to my office to determine whether or not we'd let you try out for the Olympics."

"Yes sir?"

"And now I wonder how there could ever have been any doubt. Of course, we didn't know you then ...like we know you now."

"Well, I appreciate your providing me that opportunity, sir."

He looked at her a moment musing, "Actually, would you mind handing out *all* the diplomas?"

"I'd be honored, sir."

When Ell turned she found Secretary of Defense Amundsen standing behind her. She saluted him. He said, "I *thought* that was you!" He grinned at her. "What are you doing back in uniform?"

"Um, Sir, this is the class I would've originally graduated with. They invited me to their graduation ceremony as a special guest. General Ammonds asked me to hand out the diplomas and I still have the uniform since I'm in the reserves …"

~~~

When the Secretary finished his commencement speech to the graduates he paused. Then said, "I have a real treat for you today. In a break from tradition this year, your diplomas are to be handed out by a celebrity." He paused again. "A celebrity and a former member of your class… An early graduate, who's already earned an early promotion to Captain… I give you Presidential Medal of Freedom and Congressional Medal of Honor winner… Captain Ell Donsaii!"

As Ell blushed, the susurrus of puzzled murmurs amongst the crowd crescendoed into a lusty cheer.

~~~

After the ceremony, Ell walked down the stairs from the stand and found Phil, Joy and Jason waiting with their families. She was introduced around. Because of their long military history Phil's family was especially enthusiastic about meeting her.

Phil and Jason's families had already made plans to go out to dinner together and they began to get ready to leave the stadium. Ell had Allan call her car and wondered somewhat despondently when the next flight back to NC would be. Phil turned to her and said, "Ell, I'm hoping you'll be my 'plus one' at dinner?"

"Sure!" Ell said with a big smile. She'd been pretty let down at the thought of flying right back after the ceremony.

~~~

At the dinner Ell turned to Phil and asked, "So what's the word from NASA?

"Oh they're really in trouble with this Vulcan 5 thing. No one can believe they got themselves in this situation with no backup system to re-supply the station!"

Ell glared at him, "You know what I mean! Did you get accepted?"

"Hmmm, let me check with my AI," he looked up at his HUD.

She poked him in the ribs, "You got in didn't you! You wouldn't be messing with me like this if you didn't!"

He grinned, still looking up at his HUD. "Hmm, Yup! Says here I head to Houston for training in July. After a well deserved break from the rigors of my life so far..."

She poked him again, marveling at how hard his abs were. "I can't believe you didn't already tell me. Spaceman Zabrisk! Will you still have time for me when you're a famous astronaut with googly eyed girls falling all over you?"

Phil's mother leaned toward Ell, "I think he'll always have time for *you*." She winked at Ell.

Chapter Six

Washington D.C.— NASA announced a deal with the Chinese to send supplies up to the Space Station on one of the PRC's "Crouching Tiger" launch vehicles. A special adaptor is being constructed to allow the Chinese capsule to connect to the Space Station's airlock. In view of past animosities, many have expressed surprise that the Chinese are willing to help in this situation, no matter how desperate...

Ell's flight from Colorado landed in Raleigh late in the evening. The seven members of her security team who'd gone to Colorado with her were met by a pair of their own cars, but Ell asked Steve to ride with her to talk about how the team was doing. "Are they happy? Do they like the farm and their houses?" Ell had bought the team a few houses in the neighborhood next to the farm. Only the ready team actually slept in the little outbuilding next to her house. To get a couple of those houses she'd used her tactic of offering the homeowners a price well above market value.

"Oh yeah! Everyone seems to be really happy. This is pretty much a dream job for security people like us. You don't do crazy stuff or even travel very much. You pay well and provide great benefits. Providing housing is unheard of, let alone excellent housing like you've gotten for us. It might be a problem if some of them get married and their spouses want to live somewhere else, but right now all of them are really delighted to be part of your team."

"Great, it seemed like this trip to Colorado would be a real hassle for..." Ell put up a finger indicating an interruption.

Allan spoke in her ear, "Five persons have entered the D5R facility. The guard shack guard's ID key was used to open the door. They've divided up, four going to the research area and one to your office."

Ell told Steve what'd happened as she took the car off AI control. She immediately accelerated far above the speed limit. She was momentarily grateful for the modifications Steve had made to her cars, overpowering them and allowing her to break out of the AI's safety controls.

Once he reviewed Allan's message Steve said, "Damn!"

Ell said, "Have the team from the airport speed up and ask everyone on the team whose here in North Carolina to head to the D5R facility too. Allan, please call the police to the facility too." To Steve she said, "Do you think we can trust the guard company?"

"Yeah, I'm contacting them now. How did *Allan* detect the intrusion?"

Ell took the freeway exit at a high speed, passing cars that were under computer control by driving on the paved shoulder. "I asked him to monitor the facility. He's tied himself to the building's AI and keeps an eye on anything out of the ordinary that happens. The gate guards aren't supposed to be at the building so that drew his attention. He can pick up the intruders' activity from the microphones on the various AI systems here and there in the building. He's tapped into all of them."

Rocket!

She snorted, "The intruder in my office is using some pretty sophisticated software to try to break my office AI. Fortunately, even if he does successfully break in, the office AI really doesn't have any secure information on it. Anything I care about's actually stored on Allan." She paused a moment to listen to Allan, "The people in the research area seem to be taking photographs of our equipment. They're presently trying to send them out over the net, but Allan activated the building's net jammer. It looks like none of them have PGR chips since they're trying to transmit using cell technology."

Ell made a corner with the tires squealing and accelerated down the driveway past the empty guard shack. As the car skidded to a stop near three strange cars in front of the building she said, "You coming in with me?"

"Of course!" Steve said slamming his door open and running toward the door. Somehow he wasn't surprised to find himself falling far behind her. *My God, the girl can run!* The door had opened itself as they pulled up. Steve was momentarily concerned that someone inside was exiting, but apparently it was just Allan activating the building's automatic doors. When Steve entered the building he had to ask his AI which way to go to reach the research area because he'd never actually been inside before. Based on the premise that she could protect herself—and only needed the team to rescue her from being kidnapped if someone successfully trapped or drugged her—Ell's policy was to keep Steve and the rest of her security team nearby, but not actually visible.

~~~

Manny left Ell's office and entered the research

area, "No joy! The security she's got on her desk AI's way beyond what I can crack. You guys about done in here?"

The other four men were wandering around inside the facility filming everything they could lay eyes on. He could easily tell where they were as each of them had a high intensity light source to provide good images for their video.

Jeff said "I think we've got it all, but I'm gonna pry this one open so we can get images of the inside, it's been modified…"

A sudden voice cut through their chatter, "Stop right where you are!" The room lights came up. In the suddenly frozen tableau they saw Ell Donsaii just inside the door to the big room.

Manny recognized the Donsaii girl. Alone. He'd been offered even more money to kidnap her, but he'd backed out of that deal in a hurry when he learned about the security team that followed her around. There were SEALs on that team! But, right now, she was here all alone and he had five guys.

On the link to his team he said, "Guys, we don't need the computer files if we've got her. Grab her and let's get out of here!"

The two men nearest to Donsaii lunged at her.

To Manny's surprise she didn't back up. Instead, it seemed like she flickered between them. A couple of meaty thuds sounded and the men staggered, then grabbed their faces. One dropped to his knees.

A "pop" sounded and Jeff dropped like he'd been clubbed.

Manny recognized the "pop" as the sound of one of the new Tasers firing a dart. He reached for his Glock.

The lights went out and Manny heard another pop.

Rocket!

His muscles spasmed and the floor rushed up to smash into his face. In agony, he wondered whether Torain would get away. If he remembered right, Torain'd been over by the far exit...

~~~

As soon as the woman shouted, Torain bolted from the main room and started running down the hall to the rear exit. As he slammed out the exit, he heard the alarm go on. He supposed the exit wasn't supposed to be used except in emergency. He didn't even consider trying to run around the building to their car. Instead he sprinted for the woods. He should be able to lose himself in the office complex on the other side of them. Glancing back, he saw the woman come out the door. An excellent sprinter, Torain wasn't worried she'd be able to catch him. He concentrated on covering the rough ground without breaking an ankle.

To Torain's astonishment something smacked his right foot into his left and he found himself sprawling forward into the grass.

As he started to scramble back to his feet he saw Donsaii jogging back towards him.

She'd passed him! After a moment of complete disbelief and denial he realized she'd not only caught him, she'd kicked his foot to trip him as she'd passed! She said, "I've got a Taser on you so just lie still. I'd rather not shoot you with it... they hurt."

Stunned he watched as she squatted down and switched off his AI, then pulled it out of its case and disconnected the battery.

"Who sent you?" she asked.

***

Wang slammed his fist down, "Two minutes of video! Two minutes, seventeen seconds to be precise! That's all we got between when he left the jammer field and when she turned off his AI! And what do we see on it? The machine shop! None of their tech, not a single picture of a single instrument! We invested three hundred thousand dollars bribing the guard and hiring those idiots and that's all we get?! Pictures of their machine shop?!"

"Can they be traced back to us?" the man across the table rumbled in Mandarin.

"Not a chance."

"There'd better not be."

***

Washington D.C.—NASA admitted today that they've had the astronauts at the space station restrict themselves to two-thirds rations. They've also had them stop exercising or exerting themselves in an effort to decrease oxygen consumption — "as a precaution in case the Chinese mission to the station encounters problems..."

~~~

Ell looked around the table at their 10 AM morning meeting. After talking to the police and cleaning up after the break in she hadn't gotten back to the farm until 4AM. She'd slept in until 7 in order to get her customary 3 hours of sleep. Allan'd brought her up to date during her drive back to D5R. She cleared her throat, "The men inside the building had been paid a *lot* of money. But it'd been put in offshore accounts. Once they moved the money to their own accounts, those offshore accounts were closed. So far the police can't trace the money. The men had never met their handlers wearing their AIs so no records there either. They *claim* their handlers were disguised when they met them.

"Though the gate guard claims he was attacked, the nervous twitches on the last few moments of his AI record suggest that he was trying to avoid looking behind him so that they *could* sneak up behind him. They held a gun to his head and made him say, 'Open the door.' Then they tied him up and carried his AI to the front door so it could handshake with the AI inside. They opened the door using the recording of him saying 'open the door.' The guard's AI wasn't a very sophisticated model so it didn't detect the stress in his voice. In actuality however, there wasn't all that much stress, which suggests that he expected the entire thing.

"The gate guard hadn't moved any large sums of money into any onshore accounts, so we don't have proof that he was bribed." She sighed, "The police think it was a large corporation undertaking some industrial spying. On the other hand, it may have been the Chinese working with local assets, they've attempted to kidnap me several times in the past."

Stephen Black, one of Fred Marsden's assistants, had been getting more and more wide eyed. He exclaimed, "My God! This is crazy! What the Hell would have happened if one of us had been here working late when those guys broke in?"

Ell sighed, "I don't know. Hopefully nothing since they were apparently here after the tech, not the people, but we can't be sure."

Black said, "Why would they want our tech? We haven't discovered anything! All we have here is equipment you can buy from most scientific suppliers!"

"You're right of course. They may be hoping that we've had more luck than we have." She looked around the group, then said, "D5R's investors realize that most of you hired on with no intention of getting into anything that might be dangerous, so D5R has asked me to offer you all the opportunity to exit your contracts. With a half year's salary bonus as thanks for your work so far. Of course, I would personally like it if you stayed on, but this wasn't what you signed up for."

Black said, "A half year's pay? For doing nothing? I'm taking that!" He got up and started for the admin offices. Carol got up too. "Sorry Ell, but I want out. I've got kids to worry about." She got up and followed Stephen.

Ell had begun to despair. *Is everyone going to leave me?!* She looked around the rest of the group. They all looked pretty calm. "Anyone else want out?"

They all shook their heads.

She smiled, "Thanks team. I'm glad we still have you aboard. You'll find a danger bonus of three month's salary in your next pay deposit, just for staying around."

The team all looked at one another in surprise, then Viv led a small round of applause.

"Now," Ell raised her eyebrows, "what can you tell me about the progress you made while I was in Colorado? Have we successfully entangled tori? Can we assemble buckyballs at speed yet? Is Brian's idea of spraying buckyballs all around the opening going to work?"

Ben grimaced, "No joy on the buckyball assembler. It

looks like we might, with further optimization, get the assembly of a 10mm port down to 3 months. Not very good."

Ell shrugged, "If that's all the faster we can make them, then that's how we'll have to make them. It'll just make them a lot more precious than I'd hoped." She looked at Marsden.

Fred just shook his head disconsolately. "Can't seem to get full tori of any size to stay entangled when we separate them, sorry." He said, "I'd say, 'so far,' except I don't have any other ideas to try." He shook his head, "Maybe one'll come to me, but I doubt it."

Brian said "I've put together a micro-sprayer jet and Fred's provided an entangler that can supply entangled buckyballs at an extremely high rate for the jet. The jet's turbulence should separate entangled buckyball pairs as it sprays the edges of two disks. Those disks will become the two ports. The jet sprays the touching edge of the two disks while the discs rotate their edges together under it. We'll have lots of entangled pairs landing with both members of the pair on one port instead of one member on each port like we want. Also Fred thinks the turbulence will break the entanglement of about seventy percent of the pairs. But, if you're right that it might work, as long as we have a *lot* of correctly separated pairs, they should function since we'll be putting billions of entangled buckyballs per mm on the edges of the disk-ports. We should be ready to attempt a test run this afternoon."

"Great! Think positive!"

~~~

That afternoon Ell watched as the inkjet Brian set up sprayed buckyballs, looking for all the world like soot, onto the edges of two 5mm diameter metal disks as they rotated beneath it. Ell's stabilizing field was already established on the disks so any pairs that were correctly entangled when they landed should stay entangled. Between pairs that both landed on one disc and pairs that lost entanglement they only expected about 3% total efficiency but they were spraying so many that Ell still thought it might work.

She couldn't think of a way to *calculate* whether or not it would.

After a couple rotations under the sprayer the edges of the disks looked black. Brian turned off the jet and popped them off the machine, handling them carefully so as not to break the circuits maintaining the fields. Ell shifted the field strength so it'd energize a port. In theory it should have taken about 60 watts to energize a 5mm port, but due to inefficiencies, Ell had to pump in about a hundred watts. As Brian moved one port around, Ell looked into the other one. With rising excitement, she saw what appeared to be shifting light patterns in the stationary port she was watching. Brian turned his port down toward the floor and Ell put a drop of water onto the port she was holding. She held her breath.

Water dripped out of Brian's port and onto the floor! A cheer went up, then vehement applause and even a couple of shrieks. Ben was hopping up and down. Ell gave a couple of fist pumps then said, "Allan, ask Sheila to break out the champagne! Invite everyone at D5R in for a celebration!" She turned to the group, "Hook it up to the piping and let's pour some more stuff through it!"

The disks were inserted into pipes that had been designed to fit them in so liquids and gasses could be put through the ports under pressure.

Before the pipes were pressurized Ben insisted on pouring a dollop of champagne through the port. He drank it with great relish.

Brian inserted another set of disks in the printer and set them to being "inked" as the group was calling it now. They closed off the pipes and blew pressurized air and water through them, Fred managing to turn the jet of pressurized water onto some of the "ball busters." Then Ell insisted on holding the hi-jinks a minute or two so she could try sending liquid oxygen and then liquid hydrogen through the port. She held her breath, worrying that the ultra-cold would destroy the port, but it held up! The port was heated by the waste heat from generating the field, so vapor rose from the warmth. Nonetheless, the liquefied gases transited the port without damaging it. Seeing this made Ell's heart pound. "Brian, can you bring out the components of the side project I've had you working on?"

Brian nodded and headed back to his machine shop. A minute later he returned with a box of components. He set it on the table.

Excitedly Ell started picking up the parts in the box and laying them out on the surface of the big table. The happy babble around her quieted as one by one the team members turned to watch her lay out a number of metal tubes. She heard them speculating,

"What is it?"

"Bunch of tubes. Some kind of plumbing project?"

Ell laid a pointed cap at the left end and a conical device at the other, "A rocket?" someone asked.

Ell grinned up at them, "Yep, a rocket."

Ben said, "Why a rocket? I thought we were going to *replace* rockets with instantaneous transfer of materials

Laurence E Dahners

through ports to satellites and to the space station?"

Ell smiled even more broadly, then lifted an eyebrow. "Well, *first* we have to get our ports up to orbit where we want to transfer those materials, right? And before you say we can just send them up on the rockets that already go up there, think about why those rockets are so huge?" She looked around the group. "Right? Because they have *to carry so much fuel*! For the first part of the mission they're mostly *just launching* fuel for the next part of the mission. It's *horribly* inefficient!"

The group stared at her as they pondered her words.

Fred scratched his head, "Are you thinking this little rocket," he waved at the parts on the table, "because we can port fuel to it, could make it all the way up to orbit?"

Ell waggled her eyebrows, "All the way to the International Space Station!"

Eyes widened around the group, someone said, "Then we could 'port' them supplies!"

Ell said, "Yeah! So full speed ahead! I want to prepare a rocket that can get to the Station and deliver ports that we can use to supply the astronauts. If the Chinese fail their supply mission, we need to be ready to be their backup." She turned serious and eyed her people, "I'm sure you guys know that if the Chinese fail to deliver supplies, the folks on the station are going to be in serious trouble. All their other backups have already failed. Like Epaulding said, 'they're having the perfect storm of problems.'"

"This is one of the most important things we may ever do and D5R's prepared to pay you guys triple time for any overtime you have to put in to make this work.

"Now, Brian machined this motor from specs off the

web. It's designed for a model rocket that's supposed to burn hydrogen-oxygen and you'll note that I've already determined that liquid hydrogen and oxygen will go through without destroying our ports. So far, my plan is for us to figure out how to install one port into the hydrogen chamber and one into the oxy chamber of the rocket. We need someone to figure out how to be sure the airspace above us is clear. We need someone to work on calculating when to launch so that we have a short track to reach the Space Station. We need someone to work on what kind of ports we should install in the body of the rocket in order to supply the astronauts needs. Also, how the astronauts could get to those ports. Also, what adaptors the ports should have on them to be able to deliver oxygen and water etc. to the Station's systems. Brian, we need you to build a test stand for our rocket's motor so we can be sure it'll produce the expected thrust and that it'll withstand long enough burns to get into space. We need a power source built in to the rocket that can energize the ports. Can anyone think of other things we need to do?" She looked around.

Fred said, "I can put the ports into the chambers."

In a mad scramble people enthusiastically signed up for the tasks Ell had outlined and thought of others.

~~~

Ell said, "I'm sorry, Mr. Braun, but I'm not ready to tell you why we want to hire a rocketry expert until and unless you take the job. For the moment it's *very* confidential, and in fact *would* be confidential for some time after you took the job. I've made a good faith deposit to the account we agreed on so you can be confident of one year's salary if you take the job." She saw him glance up at his HUD to confirm the deposit.

"OK, Ms. Donsaii," he said with a little exasperation, "I'll take the job and I'll agree to the confidentiality clause. Now do I get to talk to your boss?"

She grinned at him, "You're talking to the boss."

He looked askance at her, "Come on! I mean someone who understands your rocketry needs."

"That'd be me."

"Okaaay, when do you want me to start?"

"Right now. I want you to assume that we have a rocket motor capable of producing essentially the same thrust as a hydrogen-oxygen motor but not needing to carry propellant." She paused a moment for him to digest this. "We want to launch…"

He interrupted, sounding irritated. "I'm sorry Ms. Donsaii, but that just isn't possible…" he stopped when he saw her smiling enigmatically at him.

"I'm afraid you're going to find us doing several impossible things, Mr. Braun. For now, just make the assumption. I'm sure you'll immediately realize this means we can launch small rockets to orbit because we don't have to carry huge quantities of fuel. While you're on your flight here, we'd like you to be thinking about how to best put this capability to use."

His eyes widened, "You want me to fly out for an interview? I thought that was what we'd just finished doing?"

"No, we want you to fly out here to work. Today. D5R's paying you starting *now*. Therefore, we want you to immediately begin thinking about how to use these rocket engines."

"But then I'd just need to fly back to get my stuff packed up!"

"We'll have someone pack and move everything in

Rocket!

your house, after you've arranged housing here. They'll also sell your house in Florida for you, should you so desire. You just pack what you need for the first couple of weeks and start your trip here."

"But, but, I can't..."

"Don't tell me you can't. If you can't, you aren't the man we want to hire. We'll pay you double time, 24 hours a day until your stuff arrives from Florida, but we want you here *this* afternoon and working on the project this evening. We're under huge time pressures. My AI's found you a flight that leaves in three hours and made you reservations."

He looked stunned, then apparently gathering resolve he said, "OK. I'll be there." He signed off.

Ell looked up. Roger and Brian Short stood in her door. "We're ready to run the rocket in the test stand if you want to watch."

She jumped up, "Wouldn't miss it!"

As they walked out Roger said, "I've been looking into small rocket design. The engine you have on this thing is bigger than it needs to be?"

Ell said, "Yeah, but it's going to be running a *lot* longer than model sized rockets normally run. A rocket this size usually runs out of fuel in a minute or less. If you run them for very long the heat can melt or burn the nozzle, which is facetiously called an 'engine rich exhaust.'" she grinned. Our nozzle has ducts in it. The liquid hydrogen's supposed to run through the ducts to cool the nozzle before the hydrogen gets burned. Also, Brian made this nozzle from a tungsten alloy that should hold up to the heat for quite a while—but I figure we need to be sure. So we're going to run it a little below max efficiency so it'll stay cooler. We have temp sensors in it so we can turn it down or off for a while if it gets too hot, but I want to run this test using a long enough burn to reach orbit so we'll know if it can take it."

Brian had set up the test stand in the building's chemical reaction safety room. This was a preexisting room from the building's QemZ owners. It had thick concrete walls and excessive ventilation in case a dangerous chemical reaction went bad. The group stood outside the heavy glass windows as Brian fired up the motor. Even through the thick concrete they could hear the motor howling. Ell had Allan run it up to 100% then back off to 80%. Then she just let it run. The thrust was about 3% less than expected for the design they'd modified off the net, but the nozzle cooling appeared to be working. The thermal probe read within acceptable limits. Ell worried because the infrared cameras showed a few hot spots on the nozzle. After a couple of minutes everyone got bored. Some wandered away and others began chatting.

The sound of the rocket engine had faded to a distant irritation when it ceased with a bang. Ell looked back through the window into the room and saw the rocket nozzle had pretty much disappeared. Flames that were rising from the hydrogen port stopped as Allan shut down both ports. The small tanks containing the ports and the remainder of the tubing appeared to be intact. In a few moments Allan had the video of the rocket's last seconds playing on the screen outside the room. The video showed that the nozzle was white hot in several areas, then it disappeared between one frame and the next.

Brian looked up at Ell with a disappointed expression. "It lasted 3 minutes. Not enough to get it to orbit. It sure isn't as long as I'd hoped for."

Rocket!

Ell clapped him on the shoulder. "Probably pretty good for rocket amateurs, I'd say! But you're right, we've got to do better." She turned to the group, "And soon. Any ideas?"

Roger said, "Instead of using the liquid hydrogen fuel as a coolant, why not just add a separate port to send coolant through, that way you could send a lot more…"

Ell clapped a hand to her forehead, "My God, of course! We have to break old thought patterns. The ports change everything! We can put a water jacket around the engine and feed water into it. It could blow out the back as steam and add a little to the thrust! Or instead of hydrogen, we could burn something that doesn't generate as much heat or as much thrust. It won't matter because we can supply more of it for longer!" She looked up at the ceiling a moment, "I vote for burning hydrogen-oxygen that converts to steam and cooling with water which also converts to steam. That way our exhaust will only contain water and there won't be any concern about toxic products." She looked around the group, many of whom were nodding.

Vivian said, "Guys, you should look at your news feeds, the Chinese supply rocket's arrived at the Space Station, but they're having problems with the hookup…"

***

Emil Taussan turned white faced to the eager astronauts behind him. "The airlock won't pressurize!"

Dave Slager pulled himself forward to look at the display. "How can that be?! They flew the dummy airlock over to China from Houston. They tested it there and it mated just fine!"

Emil looked back at the pale faces, "I don't know. I think I must do a spacewalk to look at the connection and see if it can be repaired."

"No!" Jim Sasson said in a panicked tone, "You *know* we vent a little air with each EVA. We can't afford to lose any air now!"

"James," Emil said quietly, "we can't afford a failed connection to the supply capsule either. If we can't get at those supplies, we'll be in serious trouble." He didn't have to say, "We'll be dead," they all knew that already.

Sasson swallowed spastically. Then nodded his head jerkily. "First let's back it off and try to mate it again."

Emil nodded, "OK, that's reasonable. You try it, I'll start the oxygen pre-breathing so I can EVA."

***

Washington D.C.— NASA confirmed today that the Chinese supply mission had failed to make an airtight connection with the International Space Station. Emil Taussan, one of the astronauts, made an EVA to examine the problem and says it appears that the metal used in the Chinese to US adaptor has contracted differently in the cold of space than the alloys used by NASA. The misfit, though small, has prevented an airtight seal from being achieved. For a while there was hope that Dr. Taussan would be able to remove items from the Chinese capsule and move them to the Station airlock, but safety interlocks in the Chinese capsule prevent it from being opened into a vacuum. Taussan has moved the adaptor into sunlight in hopes it will heat enough to correct the misfit...

Rocket!

Sheila said, "Mr. Miller we need four machinists *today*!"

"Sweetheart, I heard you the first time. You just can't have me or any of my people today. We have commitments to other customers. I can free you up some people in about two weeks. Even when we're available, I'd strongly suggest you just contract us to make the parts you need and let us make them here on the machines we're familiar with."

Sheila had walked out to the research floor where everyone was desperately working on creating their rocket, "Just a minute Mr. Miller." She turned to Ell, "I can't get anyone to send us any machinists."

Without looking up Ell said, "Offer them $200 per hour, but they need to be here within the hour."

Wide eyed, Sheila said, "Mr. Miller, I've been authorized to pay $200 per hour."

A long period of silence greeted her, then Miller said, "Sorry, honey I don't believe that."

"I've just transferred $20,000 to your public account."

A pause while Miller checked the account then, sounding surprised, "OK, we'll be there tomorrow morning at 9AM."

"You'll be here within the hour or the deal's off."

***

Jim Sasson hung in front of the comm station. Normally, this was where he had audio-video chats with his wife and daughter. With the specter of his death hanging over his shoulder he didn't think he could hold himself together for a realtime conversation with them. He was, however, hoping to record something brave for them to watch after he was gone. Slager was expecting reduced oxygen concentrations in the Station's air to begin in the next ten to twenty hours. Low oxygen would start causing blackouts and drunken behavior so Sasson wanted to get the recording done before that happened. Idly he wondered why they didn't just do themselves in *before* they ran out of air. There was no longer any chance of rescue. He used a tissue to dab gently at the tears that had welled up and threatened to float away.

Dry, he reached out to switch on the recorder.

Rocket!

Chapter Seven

Cape Canaveral— People have begun to gather in a vigil for the astronauts on the Space Station. NASA has not provided estimates of how much longer the astronauts can last without resupply, but several "unofficial" sources predict they have days at best. NASA says it's still exploring all avenues for sending up another supply mission and for extending survival without resupply. However, India, China, Japan, Russia and the European Space Agency have all been queried. All have said that they do not have a launch vehicle that can be ready to go within...

Sheila said, "Ms. Donsaii, I have a Robert Braun here who says he's the rocketry expert you hired?"

"Great!" Ell straightened and turned.

Sheila grinned as she watched Braun's eyes widen when he came face to face with Ell for the first time. She found it amusing to watch the new hires as they realized just how young their new boss was.

Donsaii said, "Come this way and look at the rocket we have on the test stand. We're desperate to launch, but we'd really appreciate your advice! We're running oxygen-hydrogen in our current engine..."

She took him to a window where a rocket nozzle could be seen and heard through the heavy glass. Braun estimated it to be about an inch and a half in diameter. It had to be mixing propellants in a terrible ratio because it was generating a huge cloud of exhaust rather than the clear flame oxy-hydro should produce. Braun frowned. The engine was burning steadily, but didn't seem to be hooked up to any tanks or supply hoses. He looked again, trying to see where the tubing was that supplied it. As near as he could tell just the motor was bolted to the test frame. *Some of those bolts must be cannulated for the fuel runs,* he thought. "Uh, your mix must be off, oxy-hydro shouldn't be making all that smoke."

"Oh! That's steam. We're cooling the nozzle with water."

"Well, *that* won't work for a real rocket, you can't possibly carry enough water!"

Braun listened goggle eyed as Ell explained the ports. He interrupted several times to tell her that this or that wasn't possible.

"Mr. Braun," she finally said in exasperation, "*Look* at the set up! There *aren't* any tanks hooked up to it, yet you see the motor burning. Trust me on the port stuff. Assume that that part of our equipment works. *Please* stop telling me that something you can see with your own eyes is impossible. Please!"

Braun swallowed and nodded somewhat spastically.

"I'm sorry. I don't mean to be short with you, but the lives of the people on the Space Station may depend on your coming to grips with this stuff now, not later."

He nodded again and raised his eyebrows, "OK, I'll suspend my disbelief and do my own particular job. I'll just assume all this other stuff actually works."

Ell turned back to the window, "So this particular motor has been burning for," she looked up at her HUD, "thirty minutes now, and we're planning to use it or one like it on our mission but I'm uncomfortable with the fact that we can't see how the nozzle is heating behind all that steam."

"Can't you cut off the steam... and the fuel itself, just long enough to get an infrared picture?"

"Great idea!" Speaking to her AI she said, "Allan, please shut off the coolant, then the motor."

The rocket snapped off, the cloud of steam dissipated and a screen lit with an infrared image of the nozzle which glowed warmly but evenly. In regular light it was red, not white.

Braun raised his eyebrows and said, "That doesn't look bad at all. But may I make a suggestion?"

"Sure! That's what you're here for." She cocked an eyebrow at him and grinned, "As long as it doesn't include another lecture about how the ports won't work."

"No, no, I'm giving up on that," he said somewhat sheepishly. "But I'd like to suggest that using liquid hydrogen has a lot of problems that you could avoid. First of all, it's so cold that sooner or later you're going to have a problem with it freezing some part that breaks or plugs up. Second, the molecules are so small they leak out through anything and you'll have a fire. Third, as you've already seen, it burns really hot and melts nozzles. Fourth, it's expensive and dangerous to store.

"If your ports work the way you say they do, the upside of hydrogen being light and easy to launch provides little benefit. I think you'd be much better off burning RP-1 or kerosene."

"RP-1?"

"Rocket propellant number one. It's just purified kerosene. You could still cool with your water shroud, but you wouldn't have as many issues with overheating in the first place."

"OK, Allan resume the burn." The rocket engine fired back up, "Come on," she said to Braun, "Lets order some kerosene, then I want to review my flight plan with you."

"You've made a flight plan? To orbit?"

"Well, my AI and I have. I fed him the numbers and he crunched them. My AI's running on a supercomputer so calculating stuff like orbital mechanics is pretty easy for him. We want to launch to the Space Station in the next few hours. If it fails, we want to have time for some do overs before the Station runs out of air."

***

Everyone from D5R gathered outside the building to watch the launch. Ell had paid a premium to get fifty gallon barrels of kerosene delivered immediately. They'd moved the input port for the test stand rocket into the kerosene and run the test nozzle for a while. It didn't have the same thrust it did with liquid hydrogen, but it still had more than enough. So they moved the input port for the launch rocket into the kerosene as well.

The gate guard stopped all traffic. Their rocket—which was only twenty inches long by two inches in diameter—was clamped to a launching rail that one of the new machinists had built. The engine was being given one last test before launch. Even though it was about a hundred yards away on the far side of the parking lot, almost everyone had their fingers in their ears. Ell's military grade AI earpieces kept the sound down to a comfortable level for her, but she wished she'd thought to purchase earplugs for everyone else.

Allan spoke in their ears, "Sensors on the launch stand report that thrust is nominal for LOX-kerosene at 100% and at 80 %."

"Good, let's test the attitude thrusters." These simply consisted of ports behind nozzles arranged radially at the front and back of the rocket body. The ports were connected to a pipe coming out of the top of the big liquid oxygen tank out back behind the research facility. Energizing the port behind a nozzle blasted the high-pressure oxygen from the tank out through the nozzle, providing thrust to push the nose or stern around depending on which nozzles were energized. Paired counter jets controlled axial rotation.

Ell could see puffs of mist where the cold oxygen jetted out of the rocket here and there. A moment later Allan said, "All attitude thrusters are generating nominal thrust."

"Allan, are we still in a reasonable launch window to the station?"

"Yes."

"No aircraft overhead?"

"Yes."

"OK, folks," Ell called out to the group, "Here we go!" more quietly to her AI she said, "Proceed with... Wait!" She turned to the group, "We need a countdown! Who wants to do the honors?"

Ben Stavos shouted, "All together now! Ten, nine, eight..." everyone joined in by the time he got to the last six numbers, "three, two, one, blastoff!"

The launch was anticlimactic. Everyone was used to billowing smoke and slow liftoffs from years of watching launches televised from Canaveral. Even those who should have known better were surprised by the pop of ignition and brief screech as the rocket shot out of sight into the sky. Some of those watching feared it had simply exploded after the "pop" and disappearing act they'd witnessed.

Seeing her team looking worried Ell said, "No worries team, the launch was successful! You can see a faint steam trail going up if you look hard. Let's go back inside where we can watch the take from the cameras on the rocket."

An excited babble greeted this announcement and everyone shuffled back inside. Allan put the feeds from the cameras onto several of the big screens scattered around the main research room. There were cameras on four sides of the rocket and one in the nose transmitting back to D5R over a PGR chip. The camera in the front showed a red glow. As they watched, the upper right part of the screen turned bright red, the image distorted and shifted, then with a snap all of the images disappeared. A moan came from many throats at once. Ben could be heard cursing in the back of the room.

Ell's heart sank. After a moment to work the frog out of her throat she said, "Allan, what happened?"

"The PGR chip became un-entangled and telemetry was lost."

Ell relayed this to the room, "What do you guys think went wrong?"

Braun said, "It looked like the optics of the forward camera melted in the heat of atmospheric passage. What do you have protecting them?

"Of course!" Roger said, "The PGR chip and communication board's right behind the front camera. If we had a melt through there, it would have burned out the electronics right away."

Rocket!

Brian said, "The camera's behind high temp glass, but the seal around that glass might not be able to take the heat."

Ell closed her eyes, it sounded right to her. "OK, that sounds like the most likely source of failure to me. Anyone have a good solution?"

"We could travel up through the atmosphere more slowly?"

"That might work but would take a very long burn on the rocket nozzle. Even though it wouldn't even be at 80% the nozzles might not take it."

Fred said, "Cover the entire nose with high temp glass?"

Brian shook his head, "We don't have equipment to shape that kind of glass. We'd have to get it from an outside supplier and that'd be too slow for the Station."

"Can't we cover the nose with a tungsten alloy cap until the rocket gets up through the atmosphere?" Roger asked.

Fred said, "But wouldn't we lose orientation?"

Viv said, "We're already using GPS to determine location. We can use GPS for orientation too, at least until we're out of the atmosphere."

Ell frowned, "OK, we'll have to put a forward facing thruster that we can use to blow the cap off the end of the rocket once we're up there. Anyone see a problem with that plan?"

"What if the heat makes the cap stick so it won't blow off?"

"I think the heat'll make it expand so it'll get looser, but we'd better keep making plenty of rockets. OK team! Let's get on with finishing rocket number two with a cap and a forward thruster. Anyone not busy on number two, keep working on numbers three and four.

Number three we could send up slow and see whether the nozzle'll last through a slow launch and the camera'll tolerate the lower velocity. Set number four up for a 'cap' in case that looks like it would work, but we need to do something different."

Two hours later some of the group gathered outside to launch the second rocket. Unfortunately, once the rocket started its test Allan said, "The thrust vector's not coaxial to the rocket."

Ell asked hopefully, "Is the vector misalignment small enough to compensate with the nose thrusters?"

"No."

"Damn! Shut it down. The rocket nozzle's misaligned or something folks. Let's trouble shoot it." Inside Ell felt a little frantic at the thought that they seemed to be flailing around when the lives of the people on the Space Station could depend on their ability to launch a functional rocket. Nonetheless, she did her best to project calm assurance to her team—as if the minutes weren't ticking away.

When they got the rocket back inside it turned out that the nozzle was aligned with the body of the rocket. However, it was slightly off center inside the "water shroud." The steam blasting out of the water shroud as the water absorbed the heat of the rocket nozzle was asymmetric enough to produce the misaligned vector.

"OK, let's get the rocket engine from number 5 and mount it on number 2."

~~~

The switch only took thirty minutes. They mounted the rocket on the rail again. This time Allan reported thrusts were nominal and aligned. "Are we in a

Rocket!

satisfactory launch window to the station?"

"Yes, but it's closing."

Ell closed her eyes, "Is the airspace above us free of craft?"

"No."

Ell sighed and her shoulders drooped.

Braun said, "Wait, ask if we can still launch safely. Remember, you told your AI you wanted the airspace 'completely clear.' It might be that there is an aircraft but it's actually pretty far out of our path."

Ell checked and Allan confirmed that the aircraft in question was actually near the periphery of their immediate airspace and should be safe.

Ell had Allan launch without a countdown this time. They turned to go back inside.

When they got back inside the views from the camera were already black! Depressed, Ell said, "Allan, play back the minute up to failure please."

A video image popped up showing the familiar red glow. In fact, it looked exactly like the first failure!? "Allan, is this feed from the first or second launch?"

"First launch."

"Show the failure from the second launch please."

"The second launch has not failed."

Ell's eyes widened and then she slapped her forehead. *Of course! The cameras are black because they're covered by the cap!* "Are we high enough to remove the cap yet or is there still significant atmosphere?"

"The rocket is at 125 kilometers and thus above significant atmospheric drag."

"OK, pause thrust."

"Thrust paused."

"Fire forward thruster to remove the cap."

"Forward thruster firing."

They all eagerly watched the screens but they remained black.

In an agonized tone Ell said, "Is the forward thruster on full?"

"Yes."

She scrunched her eyes shut… "Fire the forward attitude thrusters in an alternating pattern, 1,3,2,4; each one for 50 microseconds and repeat the cycle times 3 keeping the forward thruster on full."

Behind her Ell heard Fred say, "What the hell will that do?"

Roger answered, "She's shaking the nose of the rocket around, like a dog trying to shake off its collar."

Nothing happened.

Ell closed her eyes in despair. "OK, let's try rocket number four that has a front thruster. We'll need to loosen the fit of the cap first though."

Fred said, "Wait! Try the rotational thrusters, maybe you can *twist* the cap off?"

Ell nodded, but said, "Brian, can you work on the cap for number four?" As Brian nodded and left she gave the directions for rotational thrusting to Allan. Long moments passed with no change. She sighed, "OK, plan C folks…" She paused as light blossomed across the screens and the front screen showed the cap tumbling away. "YES!!!"

Excited shouts filled the room. Stars whirled across the cameras with the Earth appearing randomly on different screens. The rocket was wildly tumbling.

Ell said, "Can you stabilize the rocket Allan?"

"Working" First the spinning stopped, then the tumbling came under control. Finally, three of the side cameras showed the black of space with steadily glowing stars. One showed the Earth below. Only blackness was visible in the nose camera at this point.

"Allan," Ell asked, "How are we tracking on our planned trajectory?"

"By GPS the rocket's on track. We need an additional burn to reach the station without an extended chase."

"OK resume burns to reach the station in the shortest possible time, but stay below 70% thrust if possible?"

"Calculating... The rocket can match orbits with the station in 50 minutes with burns under 70%."

"OK, up the thrust to 85%," she said with a grimace, worrying that the motor might burn out. "Proceed with that flight plan and put me in contact with Ed Candela at NASA."

Their earlier search for a NASA contact had come up with Candela. He was supposed to be a "can do" kind of guy. Ell hadn't wanted to talk to NASA until she was reasonably sure they had something to offer. She hoped they weren't too late.

Ell turned to the group, "Is number four ready to go?"

"Almost, Brian's milling the cap out a thousandth to make it easier to blow off. Do you want to launch it as soon as it's ready?"

"No. If something goes wrong with this flight we'll want to implement fixes before we launch. But let's put it on the launching frame and do our test burns. Same with number three for a slow launch."

Ell wandered over to stare out the window at their launch pad across the parking lot.

In her ear she heard, "Hello, this is Mr. Candela's assistant."

"Hi, this is Ell Donsaii. We believe we have a means

Laurence E Dahners

to resupply the Space Station. May I describe our plans to Mr. Candela?"

The woman sighed, "You and everyone else I'm afraid. We must have a million callers, each with their own sure-fire solution. Mr. Candela is in a NASA brainstorming session that attempting to put together a rescue at the present. I'm not authorized to interrupt it."

Oh crap! Ell thought, *this is going to be* just *as hard as I'd feared.* On the other hand, it seemed unlikely that she'd have gained any traction with people like Candela before she even knew that they *could* launch to orbit. "Is there anyone else I could talk to about our plans?"

"Sure, you can tell me."

Double crap! It seemed unlikely in the extreme that Candela's assistant intended to do anything but listen politely. However, Ell said, "OK. We've launched a rocket to orbit that's presently closing on the Station. We'd like to be able to communicate with the people on the Station so we can tell them of its impending arrival. They'll especially need guidance from us on how to make use of it."

There was a long pause, "Um, sure. Where did you launch this 'rocket' from?" From some of the irregular pauses in her response, Ell thought that the woman was struggling not to laugh out loud.

"North Carolina."

Another pause, "And what's it carrying?"

"Devices called 'transfer ports.'"

"And they would help the astronauts how?"

"They'll be able to deliver oxygen as well as water for the oxygen generators."

Ell could practically hear the woman's eyes rolling in her head as she said, "Sure, sure, I'll let Mr. Candela know as soon as I see him."

After she was disconnected Ell mused a moment then said, "Allan, connect me with the President Teller's Science Adviser Chip Horton."

She walked back over to the group watching the screens. There wasn't much to see from the rocket's cameras, so Allan had displayed a graphic of the rocket's trajectory and position relative to the Station. "Hey group, I'm running into trouble finding anyone at NASA that'll talk to me. Candela's aide shot me down. Do any of you know someone who even *might* know someone who could get us connected over there? We're looking for second and third order connections now. I know we went over this before, but we need more ideas. Braun, how about you? We need to be able to talk to the astronauts so we can tell them the rocket's coming and how to use it."

Many of the group got a far away look as they considered who they knew. Braun said, "I don't know anyone that'd be able to put us in contact, but my friend Ed Janssen works in Candela's division. I'll touch base with him and see what he says."

Allan spoke in Ell's ear, "Mr. Horton is in meetings at the White House regarding the Space Station. His AI refuses a connection. He's instructed his AI not to allow any interruptions until the ISS crisis has been resolved."

"Leave a message with Horton's AI that I have a solution for the Space Station problem and see if you can find a White House underling who'll talk to me." To the group watching the monitors she said, "OK, the rest of you who don't know anybody that might help us speak to the astronauts, come brain storm with me over here."

She walked over to one of the big stainless tables

that didn't have much on it and turned to the members of the team who'd gathered with her. "Let's brainstorm how we can communicate with the Station even if we don't have radio access. The first thing I've thought of is that we should have written a message on the outside of the rocket that they could read through the Station windows. It shouldn't be hard to have the rocket knock on the window, we just need to pulse the attitude thrusters with it next to the window. But how do we convince them to open the airlock and let it in? We didn't even put a radio on this one! As soon as we break up we should start working on launching another rocket, this time with a radio on board."

Brian said, "Rocket 3s ready. Vivian, if I open it up, can you install a radio? Someone could try to find out what frequency the capsules use to communicate with the Station?"

"I think I can do that." Braun said.

Brian said, "Viv, remember that whatever we put inside has to be less than 1 7/8" diameter." He thumped his forehead. "No it doesn't. I can insert a section in the rocket that has a bigger diameter if I have to." Brian, Viv and Braun turned to go.

Ell said, "Thanks guys." She turned to the rest of the group. "Any other ideas?"

Sheila tentatively put up her hand, "Is the thruster control good enough that the rocket could actually write something out?"

Ell frowned, "Seems like it'd be hard to recognize that it was writing if it wasn't leaving a trail. Let's keep that as an 'if nothing else works.'"

Roger said, "We have those LEDs on it for 'running lights,' maybe we could turn them on and off in Morse code."

Rocket!

Ell raised her eyebrows, "Good idea, can you look up the Morse code and figure out if we can actually turn the LEDs on and off?"

Allan said, "I have control of the lights and can use them to relay Morse code messages."

Ell said, "Roger, stay here with us. My AI says he can do Morse code with the lights already. Anyone have more ideas?"

***

Floating in the middle of one of the Space Station's modules, Dave Slager felt just a tiny bit drunk. He suspected that was because oxygen was starting to get low. A mildly oxygen deprived state made people feel and act drunk. When he'd checked the atmosphere a little while ago the oxygen had started drifting lower than normal. He assumed it was continuing to get worse.

He pondered the situation pleasantly. This drunken mood was better than the depressive funk he'd been in before. In fact, he kind of liked the frame of mind he was in. He stretched. *I hope the low oxygen has the same effect on the others. Maybe it'll help them through this countdown to death? I wonder if I should re-record that depressing message I did earlier for my family.* He heard a tap from over near the observation window. It repeated itself. Lazily he turned his gaze that way. *Huh, maybe the oxygen's really low?* He giggled. *Cause I'm seeing someone's model rocket outside the Station's observation window! Hah!* It bumped the window again to make another tapping sound.

Emil Taussan pulled himself into the module, "Hey,

I'm going to try to use the CRV, even with the damaged rocket nozzle. You wan' go wit' me?"

Slager turned toward him, "I thought the nozzle was destroyed?"

"Yeah," Another tap sounded and Taussan turned toward the window. He stared that way a moment, then turned back to Slager. "It's got a big hole in the side of the nozzle and a crack in the chamber. But maybe it'd generate enough thrust to get us low enough for atmospheric braking?" At another tap he turned toward the window again. Turning back, he shrugged, "What do we have to lose?"

Slager didn't point out that he'd already used the oxygen from the CRV's tanks to extend the Station's supply. Instead he said, "Do you see a model rocket in the window? Or something else?"

Taussan turned back to Slager, "I see a rocket too, about this long," he separated his hands a couple of feet, "with blinking lights." He grinned, "What do you see?"

***

Ell and the others watched in horror. On the screen showing the view from the rocket's side camera they could clearly see two of the astronauts inside the module. They looked drunk!

"Have they been drinking?!" Ell asked in dismay.

"Maybe? They're about to die for God's sake. Don't judge."

Braun said, "If the oxygen concentration's getting low that'd make them drunk."

"Oh, my God! What if we can't get them to open the

Rocket!

airlock in time?"

Ell said, "Sheila, please ask Brian and Vivian how much longer until they can launch the rocket with the radio?"

"If they're already low on oxygen, it might not get there in time even if it took off now."

Feeling desperate, Ell said, "Allan, make the rocket tap the window harder."

***

Slager's scalp prickled, "Tha's… tha's what I see too. Let's take some extra Oh-two and see if it's still there?" He reached out for the masks used to pre-breathe oxygen for EVAs. They were still hooked into the 100% source though it must be low because it fed the main supply. Slager and Taussan hung at an angle to one another in the module, breathing a little extra oxygen and watching the rocket tap their window. As they sobered up they recognized small puffs of gas were pushing the rocket to make it tap the window.

"Wow, it's *really* banging on the window now!" Slager said. "Hey, the lights are blinking fast-slow, think it could be Morse code?"

"Morse code?" Taussan's brows drew together. "Why not use the radio?" Taussan looked toward the comm center, confirming that it was still turned on.

To his AI Slager said, "Jimmy? Analyze those blinking lights for Morse code, can you read it?" He held the rocket centered in his field of view so the AI's video cameras would get a good reading.

In his ear Jimmy said, "Morse code translates the flashing as, '…you, understand, wave, if, you, understand, wave, if, you, understand, wave, if, you ...'"

Slager waved.

Jimmy said, "thank, you, this, rocket, can, deliver, oxygen, and, water, if, you, will, open, the, airlock, and, let, it, in, thank, you, this, rocket, can, deliver..."

Slager turned to Taussan and said, "Open the outer door to the airlock. That thing says it can deliver oxygen."

Taussan looked querulously at Slager, "Are you *crazy*?"

Slager shrugged and repeated Taussan's earlier question, "What do we have to lose?"

Taussan shrugged, pursing his lips, "Only a minute or so of oxygen." He started pulling himself toward the lock.

Slager watched the rocket puff its way out of view of the observation window in the direction of the airlock, then he followed Emil.

~~~

Ell watched the two men pull themselves out of the module in the direction of the airlock. She directed Allan to move the rocket over to the airlock where they all waited anxiously to see if the door would open.

A few minutes later a lusty cheer arose from the group when a slight puff of gas preceded the slow opening of the airlock door.

Ell pumped her fist and told Allan to fly the rocket into the opening.

~~~

Slager pulled himself up next to Taussan to watch through the window as Emil opened the outer door of the airlock. He was feeling drunk again now that they were away from the oxygen masks. Before the door had completely opened, their friendly little rocket sauntered in with a few judicious puffs of gas. Emil closed the airlock door behind it. The rocket promptly put its nose against a surface and began visibly blowing streams of gas out of all the little thrusters it had been maneuvering with. It wavered a bit before the thrust from the different nozzles was balanced out. A torrent of gas poured out of the big nozzle at the base, pushing the nose firmly against the bulkhead.

Slager turned to look wide eyed at Taussan. *If this's a hallucination, it's a weird one,* he thought to himself.

Taussan said wonderingly, "I haven' op'n the valve, but the pressure in the lock is risin'!"

Slager turned to gaze back through the window. As he stared at the rocket in the airlock chamber his AI, Jimmy said, "inner, airlock, door, this, rocket, is, releasing, pure, oxygen, when, pressure, is, equalized, you, may, open, inner, airlock, door, this, rocket..."

Slager turned back to Taussan, "My AI says tha' tha' toy rocket ish fillin' the lock with oxygen." Slager could feel his eyebrows crawling up his forehead.

Taussan said, "The preshure *ish* above station normal! Sensors *shay* itsh 99% O_2." He shrugged and again said, "Wha' do we haff to loosh?" He cracked open the inner airlock door and gas puffed into the station through it. *Cold* gas. Both of them backed away from the door. Taussan opened the door wider and a minute later the rocket came through the door with a few judicious puffs, then resumed blowing cold gas out of multiple nozzles.

They stared dazedly at the rocket a few minutes.

After a while, Slager realized he was feeling soberer. *More sober?* he wondered. To his AI he said, "Jimmy, ask the crew to come down to the main module."

When he turned to stare at the little rocket, his AI said, "communication, working, on, better, communication, working, on, better, communication, working ..."

~~~

Ell was out back of D5R at the big LOX (Liquid Oxygen) tank. She'd closed the valve to the pipe where their ports were located. "I can't believe I didn't think harder about communications!" she said exasperatedly to Brian as she pulled out the port module for one of the thrusters. Holding it up she said, "Allan, energize this port." Then she moved it closer to her lips and said, "Hello? Can you hear me?" If she was right, the sound of her voice would go in through the port and out through the thruster nozzle on the side of the rocket. It wouldn't be loud, but hopefully the astronauts would be able to hear her. She repeated herself.

~~~

Anya Stolchya pulled herself into the main module. She hoped Slager hadn't called them down there for some morbid final speech. The low oxygen concentration made her clumsy drunk and had given her a splitting headache. She wondered if Slager had intentionally dropped the oxygen concentration to make everyone a little drunk.

Maybe feeling drunk would be good for the rest of the crew, but Anya was a maudlin drunk. She'd been sobbing non-stop. Besides, she wanted to meet her maker in a sober state of mind. Dying drunk seemed the rankest of cowardice to her. She wiped her eyes with the back of a hand before clumsily pushing off for the opening.

As she pulled herself slowly into the module, she noticed with some surprise that her headache had faded. Briefly, she wondered why. *Hmm, I don't feel drunk anymore!* She looked around. The rest of the Space Station crew had reached the main module before she did. Dave Slager hung in the middle of the group holding a two-foot-long tube that looked suspiciously like a large model rocket. It even had some areas of blackened soot on it, as if it'd been launched.

Anya narrowed her eyes. A hissing sound came from the device as if it were leaking gas. Slager was staring at it like a mother might at a new-born babe. She wondered if it might be some kind of oxygen tank Slager'd found? If so, the extra oxygen could be responsible for her headache going away. Well, she thought dismally, if that were the case, it wasn't big enough to last them very long.

A tinny voice came from the tube. "Hello? Can you hear me?" It sounded like a little girl! The voice repeated itself.

Slager's eyes widened. After the first repeat he leaned toward the device and said, "Yes. We hear you. Who's this?"

"Great! Sir, this is Ell Donsaii. Can you unscrew the screws down the sides of the rocket? There are screws down two sides. If you remove them, you should be able to open it up… I hope to God you have a screwdriver up there?"

What the hell? Ell Donsaii the gymnast? Or someone else? Slager wondered to himself. Wasn't there a physics paper by someone with a name like the gymnast's that caused quite a stir? Nonetheless he snorted, "We have screwdrivers." He looked to Taussan who unzipped a pouch on his coverall and pulled out a multi-tip screwdriver. Slager showed him the ordinary Phillips head screws inset down one side of the rocket and Taussan put on the correct tip. Slager positioned the rocket between his knees, careful not to cover the little ports that were still gushing freezing cold oxygen. He began unscrewing the screws. "We're unscrewing it," he said.

Slager wondered briefly at the fact he was following this unknown person's instructions without question. He reminded himself that this unknown person had apparently just saved his life. *For a little while anyway.*

Anya said, "Vat in all da hells is dat ting?"

Shrugging, Taussan turned toward her, "We don't know. It just showed up and started tapping on the window." He jerked a thumb toward the observation window.

Anya said incredulously, "And how did it get in here?"

"We opened the airlock and it flew itself in."

Anya blinked slowly several times, "Are you crazy Emil? You don' even know what it eez!"

Taussan smiled lazily and expansively shrugged his shoulders, "What did we have to lose, Anya?"

Anya blinked owlishly at Taussan several more times, then pivoted her head back to watch Slager unscrewing the last few screws. "How did it get here?" she asked musingly, not really expecting anyone to answer.

The last screw came out and Slager tried to pull the two halves of the rocket apart. They wouldn't come. He pulled the Phillips tip off the screwdriver and chose a blade screwdriver tip which he stuck into a crack between the two sides. He pried and twisted. The cover popped off and sailed lazily across the module. Anya caught it.

Slager'd been expecting to see a little tank. Instead he found himself looking at a row of nozzles with different thread fittings on them! *What the hell!* He said, "The cover's off."

The little voice said, "Sorry sir, it's hard to understand you. I hear people speaking in the background and can't understand them at all. I think you have to put your face near the nozzle for me to hear."

Nozzle? He thought. It did seem like her voice was coming from one of the nozzles that had been outgassing oxygen earlier. But why *communicate* through what appeared to be an attitude thruster? He pulled the rocket closer to his face and said, "The cover's off. I see a row of threaded nozzles."

"Yes sir! What do you need the most? Water? Food? Oxygen?"

Slager pulled his head back in astonishment, torn between wanting to ask questions and wanting to get at whatever this thing had inside it. His forehead creased as he realized it had already blown far more oxygen into the station than he would ever have believed it could contain. "Water," he croaked. The mere question had made him feel parched. The Station's oxygen generators hydrolysed water to make oxygen, so the fact that they were running out of oxygen meant they'd already run out of water. They'd been on low water rations for quite a while, trying to conserve it to have enough oxygen.

"OK sir," the tinny little voice said, "We're set up to deliver water through the nozzle that looks like an ordinary hose bib. We don't want it to spray water into your module so we'll wait for you to hook it up to something to contain the water. We didn't know what kind of connection you'd normally use to fill your tanks? If the hose bib won't work, we can put water through one of the other nozzles?"

Taussan frowned. There couldn't be more than a half a liter of water in the cylinder. He pulled out a medium sized plastic bag with a drinking nipple on one end and an opening on the other. They were normally used for drinking liquids so that the liquids wouldn't spill into the weightless environment of the station. He slid the opening over the hose bib and used his fingers to close the opening around the bib. Moving his face closer to the rocket he said, "OK, turn on the water."

Water began blasting out of the hose bib, like a household spigot suddenly turned full blast. His bag, almost immediately full, slipped off the bib as he shouted "Stop!" A spray of small drops and one large globule floated away from the rocket into the free fall environment of the module as the astronauts choked out laughter and amazement. Taussan sealed off the bag and grabbed another. The other members of the crew fell to catching and sucking up free floating drops with their mouths, though Anya pulled her straw out of her pocket and stuck it into the big globule. Seeing her sucking it up, Slager pulled out his own straw and stuck it in a substantial globule floating by his head. He drank to his heart's content. As the laughing died down he could hear the small tinny voice from the rocket saying, "What happened! Are you OK?"

He pulled the rocket nearer and said, "Yes, yes, we're fine. We just didn't think there could be *that* much water in this thing." He eyed the huge globule Taussan had inserted his straw into. That globule alone certainly consisted of a larger volume of water than the rocket could've contained! "How did you do it? Water's supposed to be incompressible!"

"Sorry sir! Did we make a real mess up there?"

"Yeah, well, we've got a lot of experience with weightless messes." He saw Jim Sasson uncoiling a small vacuum hose to start sucking up the floating water. "Please. How did you get that much water in this thing? As near as I can tell you're breaking some physical laws."

The tiny voice said, "Oh, sorry sir. The water isn't *in* the rocket." All the astronauts fell silent to listen to whatever her explanation would be. She continued, "The hose bib has a 'port' behind it that connects it to a big tank of distilled water down here in North Carolina. You *do* need distilled water for the oxygen generators right?"

Confusion crossed the expectant faces hanging at all angles around Slager. He blinked several times. "Port?" he said, *did she just say that that bib is connected to a tank in North Carolina?* "I'm afraid we didn't understand that last part?"

"It's like the PGR Comm chips sir. It's a quantum entangled port that connects the bib you have there, to a water tank here in North Carolina, through the same 5th dimension the PGR chips use. Kind of like a sci-fi wormhole."

A confused and excited babble exploded from the surrounding astronauts.

Slager's brows drew together, he pulled the rocket close as if he were speaking into a microphone. "Did you say 'Ell Donsaii'?"

The tinny voice replied, "Yes sir."

"The physicist, not the gymnast?"

"Physicist, gymnast—same person sir. Though I only have an undergraduate degree in physics."

"You're... You're the girl that won the Olympics?"

"No. No sir. Only a few gymnastic events sir."

Sugi Nishikawa thumped Slager's shoulder, "She said she could send us food! I'm starving!"

Slager, feeling like his head was spinning, relayed the request.

"Yes sir. We can send food. But we aren't very well prepared for it yet. It needs to be something we can push through a 10mm diameter hole that won't get loose and float around up there. So we're thinking pasty foods? I brought in a couple of big tubs of peanut butter? If you have suggestions for other foods we can put through without messing up the station I can send someone out to buy some."

Sugi said, "I'd *kill* for some peanut butter right now!"

The tinny voice said, "Yes Ma'am, I heard that. Here comes some peanut butter."

To the astonishment of the group of astronauts, the end of what had looked like a "stubbed out" pipe in the row of nozzles turned dark as the people on the ground activated the port on the disk covering the "stub." Then it turned brown as peanut butter started extruding from it in fits and starts—as if someone was pushing it in the other end with a spatula—which they were.

Sugi darted a hand out and snatched a finger-full. She stuck it in her mouth. "Mmmm," she moaned.

132 | P a g e

Rocket!

Chapter Eight

The vid crews were setting up cameras in the Oval Office. One of President Teller's staff came into his study and handed him a slate with the script for his speech opened on it. Teller turned to NASA Director James Epaulding and said, "Do we know for sure that they're dead yet Jim?"

"Uh, no sir. Telemetry showed the oxygen concentration started falling about sixty minutes ago. That tells us that the generator had run out of water. Even though the Station holds a pretty large volume of air, they can't have long to go. It's possible that they might have some 'oxygen candles' or pressure bottles in the emergency locker that we don't know about."

"You don't have them on the line?"

"Uh, no sir. That seemed like it would be pretty morbid. The Station crew expressed a desire for privacy in their final moments. They did record some brave final words to be shared with the world after they're gone."

The President gusted a huge sighed, "Crap! What a terrible thing." He shook his head for a moment, then looked over at his Science Advisor, Chip Horton, who nodded gravely. "How'll we know for sure?"

"Telemetry will show us when the oxygen level's too low to sustain life. We expect that to be within the hour and well before your scheduled broadcast. Let me check what it is now." He looked up as he spoke to his AI. He frowned,

"What?" Teller said.

Horton turned to the President, "The oxygen level's back up. In fact, right now it's higher than normal. They must have had an oxygen candle or a pressure bottle or some other backup supply we didn't know about. It's boosted their levels for a while. We may need to reschedule the broadcast."

The President's secretary whispered "OK" and looked up at the ceiling as she listened to a message through her AI. She blanched and darted a glance at the President. "Sir... Dr. Slager... the, uh, Space Station commander is asking to speak to you."

Teller's stomach roiled. He reached into his pocket for a Tums. Talk about *Dead man walking*, he thought. He didn't want to talk to a man who was about to die any more than the next person. He grimaced; *I didn't take this job so I could shirk the tough stuff.* "OK, put him on," he said, suppressing another sigh.

"Mr. President?" He heard a voice say.

"Yes Dr. Slager? I'd like to express my sympathies in these bleak hours."

"Tell Chip Horton he really ought to answer his calls! Can you shift us to a video screen so we can have a real conversation?"

"Do as he asked, Cindy," Teller said to his AI. The large video screen on the other side of the study popped to life showing the eleven current astronauts floating in the main module, their weightlessness evident in the way they were all oriented differently. Teller noted with astonishment that they all looked like they were in good moods. Slager, right side up and close to the camera actually had a huge smile on his face. Teller said, "What's this about Chip's calls?"

Slager raised an eyebrow, "He's had his AI blocking all calls except those from NASA for hours now." Seeing

Horton near the President he said, "Hey Chip, you know a young lady named Ell Donsaii?"

Horton glanced at Teller and Epaulding in puzzlement, then back at the screen. He wondered if the astronauts were drunk from oxygen deprivation. Were he and the people in the President's study about to watch the astronauts die on screen? To Slager he said somberly, "Yes I do. Brilliant young woman."

"You don't know the half of it. Says you promised her she could call you *any* time but she's been locked out by your AI for the past few hours. Couldn't get anyone at NASA to listen to her either Jim," Slager said, focusing on Epaulding.

Horton said, "Uh, OK Dr. Slager. What does she..." *Need? Want? Have to do with why you're calling?* Horton couldn't imagine what Donsaii had to do with the Space Station and the dying astronauts. He did remember her talking about satellites and her technology a little back last year. But, much as he respected the young lady, her claims had seemed pretty outrageous. He frowned as he realized he'd mostly erased that conversation from his memory.

Slager looked at him exasperatedly, "Chip! Tell your AI to connect the young lady into our conversation!"

"Uh, OK."

A window popped open on the big screen. It moved Slager and the other astronauts to one side. The slender young lady on the screen was in three quarter profile and was evidently speaking into some kind of small microphone she was holding in front of her mouth. A number of other people were in the background. She was saying, "Dr. Slager, please! I don't need to be part of your conversation with the White House! Just ask NASA to let us connect to you over an audio-video channel so we can hear better and *especially* so we can visualize the connection problems you're having..."

President Teller cleared his throat, "You're already part of the conversation with the White House Ms. Donsaii. Dr. Slager feels it's very important that we speak with you?"

"Oh!" She turned to face the camera, which evidently was on a screen beside her, because her eyes seemed to take all of them in. She blushed and visibly came to attention. "Excuse me sir. I'm just trying to help..." her voice trailed off.

He shook his head. "Do you need something?" *And just why do you have a crew of dying astronauts on the Space Station putting your calls through for you?* he wondered.

"Um, yes sir. We need an audio-video channel to the Space Station so we can troubleshoot their port hookups..."

Epaulding had turned to the President, "Sir, perhaps I could take her call about a 'channel to the Station' down the hall while you talk to the crew?" He raised his eyebrows and jerked his head to the side.

Slager barked a laugh, "Jim, do *not* try to pawn this young lady off. She's just saved the Space Station for you!" His voice rasped, "She's saved all our lives too, for which we'll be forever in her debt."

President Teller felt the hair stand up on the back of his neck.

The astronauts hanging around Slager chorused, "Hear, hear."

Rocket!

PART TWO

Chapter One

President Teller drew a deep breath and looked Ell in the eye. "Ms. Donsaii, your country once again finds itself in your debt."

"Sir, we just got lucky that the ports actually worked. Once they did it was an easy step to realizing they might help the crew of the Station. These people around me are the ones that made it all work. I can't emphasize enough what a great team they've been. They willingly put in exhausting hours once it became evident that we might be able to help the astronauts."

Teller thought to himself. That's the mark of a great leader! Spreading credit to her team. Others would have claimed it for themselves. Out loud he said, "What can we do for you?"

"Oh! We don't need anything... But... if you don't mind..."

"What?"

"It would be helpful if this technology and our role in the rescue were kept confidential for a while?"

"My goodness! Why?"

"We don't really understand what we're doing very well yet and have only just applied for patent protection. I'm afraid if this becomes public right away we'll be besieged with attention that'll prevent our achieving a better understanding of what we're doing and what the safety issues might be."

Teller shrugged and his eyes swept the room. "OK. *We'll* keep it a secret for now." He looked at the screen where the astronauts were still visible. "Dr. Slager, would your people also be willing to keep the secret for a while?"

Slager glanced around at the other astronauts, "I think we'd be willing to do almost anything *that* young lady asked of us?"

Heads nodded all around the Station.

***

Cape Canaveral— People who'd gathered here for a vigil honoring the dying astronauts expressed ecstatic relief when the news broke that a clandestine relief mission had finally succeeded in extending the survival of the astronauts on the Station. Speculation as to the nature of the undisclosed relief mission is rampant. The most commonly accepted view is that the Department of Defense launched one of its "black" experimental craft with...

Holding up his hamburger, Ben called out, "Brian, you should give up your career as a machinist. Just open a restaurant and start raking in the cash!"

Brian lifted his spatula in salute. Reaching back into the grill to turn a couple of pieces of chicken, he said, "You should give up the micromanipulation career and start blogging as a restaurant critic." He grinned, "You know great food when you taste it."

After Friday's rescue of the Station they'd spent a tumultuous Friday evening and Saturday morning straightening out how to supply the station properly with water. This had culminated with the launch of another rocket which took up two of their new 50mm diameter ports. Then they passed the correct fittings and hoses to connect their hose bib to the Station's water holding tanks through those ports. At about two inches the ports were plenty big enough for the hoses.

They'd also sent through a bunch of PGR chips so the astronauts could be directly connected to the net through their AIs. With them connected, D5R could easily talk to the people on the ISS. Once the crew of the station was temporarily safe, Ell insisted that everyone at D5R go home Saturday afternoon to get some well-deserved rest.

Then to celebrate, Ell had invited the D5R team out for a Sunday afternoon cookout at her farm. She'd asked Amy to arrange a caterer, but when Brian found out she was using a caterer he'd pitched a fit, insisting that it was an insult to his skills as a grill master. They'd compromised by having Brian grill the meats and getting the caterer to bring everything else.

He certainly had grilling down to an art.

Ell had eaten a hamburger, a drumstick, some potato salad and was dishing herself some blackberry cobbler with ice cream. Ben said, "Whoa, little lady! You keep eating like that and you're gonna be as big as Brian."

Roger laughed, "She's been eating that way as long as I've known her. Don't know where she puts it all."

"I used to think she must be bulimic." Amy said.

Ell rolled her eyes, "I just have a fast metabolism guys."

Viv asked, "Are you one of those exercise freaks who runs ten miles before breakfast every day?"

"Oh, no way! A mile's about my limit. I do some

martial arts with the guys." she said, nodding toward the other end of the porch where the majority of her security crew were sitting with their plates. "But I don't get nearly as much exercise as I should."

Mary from Ell's security team turned her head and quietly said, "She may not get much exercise, but she kicks all our butts when we spar."

Ben glanced over at Steve. Six foot two inches of hard muscle Steve, who moved like a big cat. "All? Even Steve?" he quietly asked Mary.

"Yeah, even Steve." Mary grinned, "Really pisses him off to get beat on by a girl."

Ben looked over at Ell, then, at Steve. He turned speculatively back to Mary. "Remind me not to pick a fight with her! Does she beat you guys with some kind of gymnastic moves?"

"Not really. She's just faster than anyone has a right to be."

Ben turned back to Ell, "Why do you need a security team Ell? Especially if none of them are as good as you are when it comes to hand to hand combat."

Ell shrugged. "I've been kidnapped a couple of times. Once they drugged me, once they Tasered me. These security guys are gonna rescue my butt if it ever happens again, right Mary?"

Mary smiled, "You bet your left bunny!"

Ell said, "That's a huge part of why I asked the President to suppress our role in the whole Space Station thing for now. I don't want more notoriety bringing people like the Chinese down on my head again."

Janey leapt down off Randy's lap and ran up to Amy, "Mom, can we have ice cream now?"

"Did you eat all of your salad?"

Rocket!

"All but the tomatoes, you said I didn't have to eat them."

Amy rolled her eyes, "OK."

Janey ran back to her brother, "Mikey! We can have ice cream now!"

Roger rocked his chair back on its back legs. "Ell? What's next for D5R? Now that you've conquered space?" He grinned at her.

"Now that we've conquered low earth orbit you mean?"

He shrugged, "Mostly *you*. And 'low earth orbit' is still space. What's next?"

Ell's eyes swung to take in her people sitting nearby. She lifted her chin interrogatively, "What do *you* guys think we should do next?"

Fred said, "Well, so far we've only temporized the problem at the Space Station by providing them supplies. We need to figure out a way to get them back home. Or at least send them up a replacement nozzle for their Crew Recovery Vehicle."

Vivian said, "Why don't we just send up a huge port and have them step through it to come back home?"

Ben's assistant John frowned, "What if going through a port isn't good for you?"

Roger said, "Check your displays."

Everyone looked up at their HUDs. Roger piped them video that showed a number of objects squiggling against a clear background. Ell frowned, "What are we looking at Roger?"

"I put a drop of pond water through a port. It's under the microscope."

"So?"

"So, those are protozoans swimming around, looking perfectly healthy after a port transition."

"Hah! Cool. But we need to try it with multicellular animals."

Roger reached in his pocket and pulled out a small vial, setting it on the table. He grinned, "Way ahead of you."

The group leaned forward. An ant was crawling around inside the vial. Ell said, "You put that ant through a port too?"

"Yup, just stepped outside D5R and scooped him up."

"Worker ants are female."

Roger rolled his eyes, "Scooped *her* up. She was pretty excited after I dropped her through the port, but she seems fine now."

Ell said, "Cool! There's a small problem sending people through though."

Roger raised his brows at her.

"You know that we're powering the fields for the 10mm ports with about 300 watts?"

Heads nodded.

"Theoretically, the minimum would be about 248watts for a ten-mm port. The minimum energy requirements for a one-meter diameter port—one meter being big enough to send a human through lengthwise—would be four orders of magnitude larger or about 2 and half *million* watts. That's the power consumption of 2000 homes, i.e. a small town."

Eyes were wide as they digested this.

"Also, as Vivian noticed the other day, the ports draw a lot more power when we're sending something through them up to the Space Station. That's because the station's about 230 miles high. That fact that we're raising a kilogram up to the ISS means we have to add about... One kilowatt hour of electricity to provide that potential energy. *And*, the ISS is traveling somewhere around eight kilometers per second relative to us and so we have to inject about… nine kilowatt hours to provide the kinetic energy. We may be getting a free lunch in crossing the distance, but we don't get a free lunch in changing the altitude or velocity. Sending a seventy-kilogram person would require about 700 kilowatt hours to provide the potential and kinetic energy. That's in addition to the 2.5 megawatts to hold the port open."

Roger whistled.

Fred had narrowed his eyes at her, "Did you just calculate those energy requirements in your head?"

Ell shrugged, "The kinetic energy formula's simple. One-half mass times velocity squared."

"In your *head*?"

She shrugged again, "Yeah." Then at their wide-eyed looks, "Really, it's not that hard."

He snorted.

Ell said, "And remember, there'd be some waste energy in the form of heat. That could make a port that size pretty hot to pass through. So even though a meter's a bigger port than you'd need to pass most people through lengthwise, the person would probably need to be protected by something to shield them from the heat. Person plus shielding may add up to more than a meter in diameter."

Roger said, "Those *are* some pretty significant problems." He grinned, "But they don't sound insurmountable. They use a lot more power than that for all kinds of industrial operations. If you don't mind, tomorrow I'm going to try sending a mouse through a 50 mm port?"

Ell said, "Oh yeah, I think that's a great idea. We

definitely should figure out what the possibilities are. However, I think we'll find that the energy costs to launch one of our rockets to orbit might be lower than the energy cost of a big port."

Braun said, "Ms. Donsaii, I know I'm kinda new to this group but I'd like to put in my two cents?"

Ell grinned at him, "This whole group is pretty new Rob. We don't stand much on precedence or ceremony. Tell us what your 'rocket scientist' brain's thinking?"

"Well, I might be biased by my skill set, but I really want us to build a rocket that can move people, not just ports. We need to go to the Moon, and Mars, and, and *Venus*! We should start with little rockets like the ones we've been building. We can send them to those places with cameras and maybe some manipulator arms."

"Wow!" Ell grinned at him. "Rob, you're making it sound like you might believe the ports actually work?"

He rolled his eyes, "Somebody rubbed my nose in it!"

Ben said, "Don't forget we've also got to visit the asteroids! Maybe bring one back to earth orbit for raw materials."

Ell looked around the group. "Well, I think those are great goals. However, I think we all need to recognize that none of you originally hired on to explore the universe. You hired on to build ports and despite some frustrations on the way to it, that goal's been achieved." She raised her eyebrows at the group. Ell saw a mixture of emotions crossing their faces, ranging from satisfaction to apprehension that she might be about to shut down the company.

Suddenly Ben Stavos stood and raised his beer in the air, "Hell yeah we did! Gimme a hooah!"

To Ell's amusement, the rest of the crew she'd

assembled at D5R came to their feet hoisting their own glasses and cheering.

Fred Marsden said, "To the ball busters!"

Ben said, "Back at you ring a dings!" Then he pointed his beer at Brian Short, "And to Brian. The man who had the real breakthrough!"

Ell raised her Coke with the rest of them, cheering heartily.

When the group had settled back down Ell said, "OK, next. You guys all hired on for a salary and hopefully for a chance to do some cool science."

Many of the group raised their glasses again.

She continued, "How many of you read your contract carefully enough to know you've got some shares in D5R?" She tilted her head, "*Or* remember me telling you that?"

Eyes widened and people looked at each other. Fred said, "We do?"

"Hah! I knew it! None of you thought this port stuff had a snowball's chance did you? So you either didn't read about your shares, or skimmed over that part of your contract. Or forgot what I said about it. Well, all of you have shares, so all of you *should* care about what we do with *our* intellectual property." She raised her eyebrows at them. "Right? The way I see it, we have some choices. One, we could just license the technology to NASA or the highest bidder. Two, we could build our own company to explore space and do all the things Rob and Ben suggested a little bit ago. Three, we could explore a little ourselves, then license. What do you guys think?"

There was a lot of looking at each other, staring at the ceiling and quickly whispered conversations. Fred stood and spoke, "I think option one's 'get rich quick.'

Option two's 'get *really* rich slowly.' Option three's somewhere in between. But hell, *I* want to be at the forefront of some of these explorations, I vote for number two with the option to go for number three."

A tumultuous, "Hear, hear!" followed Fred's assessment.

Ell grinned at them, "OK, we keep it to ourselves for now. Next, do we expand to become a huge company that gets us out there into space fast, or do we stay small for at least a while?"

After some occasionally vociferous discussion they decided to stay small for at least a while longer. They'd just contract out the production of large components they couldn't make in the machine shop.

***

John Clarkson closed his eyes and contemplated the best spin to put on the news. He always felt like he was walking on eggshells when he spoke to the Chairman of ILX. He opened his eyes and spoke to his AI, "Place a call to David Dennison." He closed his eyes again while he waited.

"What's happened now?" Dennison's gravelly voice demanded without preamble.

"Good news Mr. Dennison. Someone successfully resupplied the Space Station."

"Really?! That's great!" Clarkson could almost hear the wheels turning. Initial relief that ILX wasn't going to get slapped with wrongful death lawsuits by the astronauts' families. Then suspicion regarding a possible competitor. Dennison was absolutely ruthless about competition. That'd gotten him where he was and no one was going to change him. "Who?"

Clarkson could hear the narrowed eyes behind that "who?" He tried not to sigh. "No one seems to know at present sir. Might have been some secret defense department launch."

"Find out. Our people at NASA need to…" Dennison ground to a stop before he said something on record about the people at NASA who were on ILX's secret payroll. "Find out."

***

Sheila walked outside at 7:30 AM Monday and saw the taco truck pulling up outside D5R like Jose had promised. She walked out to move the cones she'd set out to keep anyone else from parking right in front of the door. The truck pulled into the space she'd saved for it and a young man got out. "Jose?"

"Yes Ma'am."

"I know it'll take you a while to get set up, but I'm hoping to take some samples and a couple of menus inside so people can place orders?"

"Just a minute." The man shuffled some papers and pulled out a small stack of menus, handing them to her.

"Thanks. We're still good on our agreement that you'll put whatever ingredients in the burritos are requested?"

"Oh, yes Ma'am, and I bought premium ingredients like you asked. You really going to pay double the menu prices?"

"Yep, but that's for steak and fresh tomatoes, not hamburger and tomato sauce etc. right?"

"Sure," he nodded, "I got nothing but premium

ingredients today."

"OK." She handed him a metal ring. "This ring is one and seven eighths inches in diameter. Everything you make has to fit through it, right?"

"Ma'am, are you sure? The burritos'll have too much tortilla and not enough filling. They'll be better if I make 'em bigger."

"Jose, we talked about this last night. They've *got* to fit through that ring because we have to pass them through a hole a tiny bit bigger than that. Tear your tortillas in half or something. We want good burritos but they *have* to fit!"

"OK," he said dubiously. She could tell he thought she was out of her mind, but reminding himself that the customer was always right. He tilted his head, "Are you feeding a prisoner through that hole?"

"No!" she laughed, "But it's a secret that we're passing the burritos though the hole, OK?"

Jose shrugged, "OK."

"Do you have the sample burritos like I asked?"

"Just a minute." He lifted a side panel that made an awning, slid open a window then walked around to the back of his truck and got in. He stepped up to the window and set out the ring and a couple of burritos. He tried squeezing one of the burritos into the ring but it was obviously too big. He sighed, "You're sure you can't make the hole bigger?"

She rolled her eyes and nodded. "Maybe someday."

"OK, just a sec." He unrolled the burrito, scraped off some of the filling, tore a strip off the tortilla and rolled it up smaller. This time the ring slid over it. He laid it on a piece of paper and rolled it up, handing it to Sheila. "OK?"

She picked up the ring and slid it over the burrito

and paper. "Yep. I think your salsa's a little watery though. These shouldn't be sloppy at all, OK?"

"OK," he said, again sounding dubious. He took the two burritos back and put them in the microwave to warm them up. "They're gonna want more to drink with dry burritos. I sure don't have any cups that'll fit through your ring." Jose raised an eyebrow at her.

"Hmmm, I'll have to ask about drinks, but we may not be able to use them." Sheila took the two burritos and headed back into D5R.

~~~

Ell'd been working out some issues with connecting the astronauts, through PGR Comm's servers, to the rest of the net and world when Sheila came in with the two burritos and set them next to her. She glanced at them and then said, "Dr. Slager, I believe we have a treat for you. I'm going to activate one of the 5 cm ports and push something through to you."

Ell had Allen energize the port and she slid the burrito through it.

Slager grabbed it as it floated out his end, noting the warmth. He unwrapped the end and the smell broke out into the module. "Whoa! A hot burrito?!"

Taussan turned toward him, eyebrows lifted. "Really?"

The second burrito floated out. Slager passed it to Taussan then took a bite of his, "Awesome!" he mumbled around a mouthful.

Ell said, "We have a taco truck outside D5R ready to make burritos to order for you astronauts as long as I'm right that you're able to eat burritos when you're weightless?" She picked up the menu, rolled it into a tube and slid it through the port too. "You can pick from the menu, but the guy's agreed to roll anything you want up in a tortilla."

Slager looked at the end of his burrito, "Whoa, fresh tomatoes in this! Awesome! It's been sooo long since we've had anything fresh!" He turned and bellowed to the Space Station in general. "Hey! A taco truck's pulled up outside, come place your orders!"

Sheila turned to the grinning Ell, "Jose's making the burritos a little dry so that they won't squirt or dribble juice out into the Station. He suggested that they'd need more to drink with drier food. I can't think of a way to make a coke fit through this size port though."

Ell frowned, "Ohhh, they don't drink carbonated beverages in space anyway. Without gravity you can't burp out the carbonation and all the little bubbles just travel through your intestines. Maybe lemonade?"

A female voice in the station background said, "Oh yeah! I'd love some fresh lemonade. Could you send a hose through and we could fill some drink bags with it?"

Ell frowned, "Maybe? I'll talk to the guy."

Ell went out to talk to Jose. After a bit she and Sheila came back in with his soda dispenser set up without its carbonation tank. It had a water line and a syrup dispenser that dispensed several different syrups for different flavors of soda. It also dispensed un-carbonated lemonade, limeade, several juices and tea.

Sheila went back out to the truck with the astronauts' burrito orders. Ell hooked up a water line and fed the dispenser nozzle through the port tube. The nozzle was a tight fit for the 50mm port. Ell shoved and wiggled it into the tube leading up to the actual port on her side. For a moment she thought she'd have to pull it back out and shave off some of the plastic, but then it suddenly slipped through the port.

Rocket!

Ell felt a terrible burning, stinging sensation as the finger she'd had been pushing it with plunged momentarily through the port behind the dispenser nozzle. At first she thought her finger had struck something on the other side that had injured it. Then she realized that the finger'd crossed the port interface into the Station.

Something about crossing the interface had caused the burning. When she pulled the finger back out it continued to burn for a moment, even though it *looked* completely normal. Ell shook and rubbed the finger a few times while the burning sensation slowly faded away. *Hmmm, if it always feels like that going through a port, it wouldn't be very pleasant to travel that way,* she thought. *Maybe that's why Roger's ant was so excited?*

Roger'd arrived and he, Ell, and Sheila watched the take from Slager's AI video camera as the delighted astronauts filled drink bags with lemonade, fresh orange juice, and tea. One even took a bag of flat Coke.

Ell told Roger about the burning sensation she'd felt when her finger slipped momentarily through the port.

He said, "I put a mouse through a port like you suggested. He flopped around for a bit, then seemed pretty excited for another minute or two. He seems fine now though."

Ell grimaced, "Well if your whole body felt like it was on fire the way my finger did, I can imagine you'd be pretty excited alright."

Roger said, "What am I gonna do with the mouse now? I didn't think of that when I bought him at the pet store."

Ell frowned, "I think you need to get whatever we need to keep him around for the rest of his life. We need to make sure that going through a port doesn't make you sick or shorten your life span. Call him 'John Glenn.' He'll be famous as the first port traveler. How long do mice live anyway?"

Roger said, "I don't know. I guess I'd better get back to the pet store for a cage and food etc."

Allan said, "Mice live an average of 18 months."

"I think you really ought to get twenty mice. Put 10 mice through a port and keep the other 10 as controls. Then we can compare average life spans between the two groups. That way we can have some idea whether they all stay healthy. Someday we may want to put a human through a port and we'll want some idea whether it's OK."

Roger said, "Eighteen months is a long time to wait. I'll find some shorter lived animals to put through the ports too." He paused, then said, "My AI says worker bees live about 4 weeks. I'll see if I can get some freshly hatched workers from a beekeeper and put half of them through a port. Hmmm, I'll have to figure out what to feed bees..."

Roger wandered off. Sheila came back in with a bag full of fresh, hot burritos. She started shoving them through the port to the delighted astronauts.

Slager said, "Ms. Donsaii..."

Ell said, "Please call me 'Ell.'"

Slager said, "Well, you should call me 'Dave' then."

"Ouch! That makes me uncomfortable. I've been taught to respect my elders."

"Now you're making me feel old. That's not respectful! Anyway, I wanted to express our gratitude again for what you've done."

"Oh, we were just so excited to be able to help. We'd been working on these ports for quite a while and when we suddenly realized they might be able to help you guys in a time of crisis it really gave us something to work towards. I hope you don't mind the team taking the day off yesterday? They'd been working really long hours and some of them were even sleeping here on cots trying to get this whole thing to work before you ran out of air."

"Oh, my goodness no. I've worked to a few deadlines in my time. You'd completely stabilized our situation here by Saturday afternoon."

"Well, we want to make sure we've done everything we can to make you safe and to make things better for you guys. We do appreciate, even more now, the risks you've been taking in our name out there on the Station. So, are you fully bunkered up with water and oxygen in case something should happen to our ability to supply you?"

"I think we're full up, my AI'll check... but what in the world could happen to you?"

"Well, I don't know, but personally I've been kidnapped a few times and we were the victims of some industrial espionage a while back. Maybe, a fire? Who knows, but if something should happen to us we don't want you guys to immediately be back in desperate straits."

"Thanks for your concern. My AI tells me that our gauges are reading full for all of our water and oxygen storage systems now. We're a little iffy on food, but the flat packages of preserved food that NASA normally sends up here won't fit through a two-inch port."

Ell said, "Sheila got you some stuff at the store. Let me pull back the soda nozzle and hose." Ell tugged on the hose. "Can you push from your side? Be careful not to stick your finger through the port, it hurts."

Slager said, "Let me brace myself so I can push."

Ell put her hand on the port so she could pull harder. Suddenly with a snap the hose came loose from the nozzle and flew back at her. Fluid started spraying everywhere. Ell realized that actually something had cut the hose. She turned the spray down into a wastebasket and reached over to the main line, turning off the valve there. Sheila turned off the water at the sink and Ell cut power to the pump for the syrups.

Slager was saying, "What happened? Something cut the hose right across. Is there a sharp edge in the port?"

Ell wiped off her end of the hose. It was sheared cleanly across. "Um, I think I wiggled one of the wires supplying the field to the port down here. That shut off the port. Glad I didn't do that when my finger was in the port! Did it make a mess up there?" she asked, looking at the water and syrup dripping off all the surfaces in front of her.

"No, just a few drops here and there."

Ell leaned down and looked into the port, seeing Slager's eye looking back at her on the other side. "I guess wiggling the wire only cut it off momentarily and it's back on again. We'll send some food through now and clean up our mess in a minute." Ell gestured Sheila to the port but admonished, "Don't touch the wires."

~~~

Slager was astonished to see a banana wiggle through the 5 cm port, followed by ten more one at a time. Then packets of beef jerky held together with rubber bands, followed by bundles of sweet peas, little baggies full of blueberries, blackberries, cherries, strawberries and several salamis and pepperonis.

Ell said, "We're getting some dried fruit and more preserved meats that come in narrow diameters. We

really don't know much about supplying you guys
though, so we're thinking you should make some
requests. Also you could talk to NASA about sending us
some of the 'space food' they've worked out for the
station. Well, that's if they can package it to less than a
five centimeter diameter anyway. Then we could send
you a back-up supply that you could store in case you
were cut off again for some reason."

"Oh, but we'd a lot rather eat the fresh food you're
sending us!"

"We thought you would, and we've contracted with
Jose to bring his taco truck every day. He'll make you
whatever you want, as long as it can be rolled up in
tortillas. If you give us grocery lists of food you want—
and it'll fit through the port, we'll send that up too. I'm
just talking about a backup plan of preserved food from
NASA in case the ports fail or something happens to
us."

"I appreciate your concern, but we surely hope
nothing happens to you guys! I've been thinking about
how the ports change everything to do with space
science. For starters we'll be able to send up materials
for research experiments and send the results back
down. Also, with an endless supply of fuel we could fire
up the thrusters and move the Station to a higher or
otherwise different orbit. Is five centimeters or two
inches the limit on the size of port you can make?"

"Well, no. But a port's energy requirements go up as
the square of its diameter. These five-centimeter ports
require about 8,000 watts to keep them open and quite
a bit more power just to transfer stuff through them
because of the relative velocity of the Station. Also
about five watts of power have to be supplied up on
your end to energize the field of the port components

that're up there. Right now we're doing that with a fuel cell that's got its own pair of tiny ports supplying oxygen and hydrogen to it. That fuel cell and its own tiny ports are a big part of the size of the port devices you have up there. However, a ten centimeter or four-inch port would require about 30,000 watts, plus the velocity change watts, and need ten watts supplied at your end. We'll have to build power conditioners and electronics to supply that much power in the correct format to energize the port on our end. And we'll need to make a much bigger fuel cell to supply your end. We're working on it, but it'll take us a while."

"Hmm, we could supply 10 watts up here. We have plenty of energy from our solar cells."

"Maybe? It has to be very smooth DC power, which I expect the solar cells *could* supply though fuel cells do provide a nice steady source. The biggest problem is that the port has to be constantly supplied with a little bit of power to stabilize it, even when it isn't open and transferring materials. The fuel cell does that, even when the port's in transit, so it's easier for us to make the fuel cell and send it up. But, we're working on it. Then we could send you canned food!"

"Oh boy! We're looking forward to that!" Slager said in a facetious tone. Then he conceded, "Canned food would be a great back up."

"Well, we're also working on how to send your replacement nozzle for the CRV up there so you'd have a way to get back home if you had to."

"You can't put that through a port! It must be about a half-meter in narrowest dimension."

"Well, no. We've ordered larger rocket nozzles and are trying to work out methods for launching our own larger rockets. Hopefully ones that'd be big enough to carry the CRV nozzle up there to you."

"Oh! That'd be great!" Slager got an unhappy look, "Have you talked to NASA about it? I think ILX currently has an exclusive contract on deliveries to the Station."

Ell winced, "We're currently finding NASA a little hard to talk to. We're never sure who to talk to and they seem to think of me as 'just a kid.' Every time we call them we get the run around. But we're building the rocket anyway, so we could just drop the nozzle off on our way to somewhere else, free of charge. It shouldn't impinge on the ILX contract if we don't charge for the service. We would need to ask NASA to let us have the nozzle to take up there though. I guess I'll *have* to find someone there to talk to when we've gotten to that point."

"How are you financing all this if you won't even have a contract for delivery?!"

"Oh. Well, we're pretty well funded at present. Besides sending stuff to orbit isn't all that expensive when you're doing it with ports. You're probably thinking about how expensive it is to launch a regular rocket?"

Slager was silent a moment, then mused, "Oh yeah, if you aren't having to launch your fuel, it's probably a lot less expensive isn't it..."

Chapter Two

Clarkson knocked on his boss's door. "Mr. Dennison?"

"Yeah, what've you got for me?"

Clarkson pointedly unjacked his AI so that Dennison would know that the conversation shouldn't go on the record.

Dennison unjacked his own, then raised his eyebrows.

"The Space Station rescue seems to be really hush hush at NASA. No one really seems to know what happened. However, there's a rumor that a private company sent up a rocket using some new kind of technology."

"What!!! Who?!!"

"No one seems to know. Our guy heard someone say 'D5R' but he's not sure if they were talking about the company that did the rescue. A net search for 'D5R' turns up a camera model, a Sony branded AI, a research company in North Carolina, an art community, etc. etc. No space launch or rocket companies." He shrugged.

"Push our guy at NASA. We need info. He'd better earn his keep."

"Yes sir. We're working on it."

***

Rocket!

It was 7:30 when Ell stepped out the door of D5R on her way home. She thought to herself that she desperately needed a social life so she'd have something to do besides D5R. She and Roger went out sometimes. "Dinner and a movie" dates mostly, though they were pleasant enough. Sometimes she thought Roger wanted more, but he could hardly invite her and her entourage of security people to move into his apartment. She didn't feel right about asking someone who worked for her—even though their friendship pre-dated his employment—to move in with her at the farm. Gordon from her astronomy class had gone home for the summer. She didn't even have a good girlfriend to hang out with!

Amy and she did things together sometimes, but Amy wasn't as fixated as she used to be on her boss's social life. Amy'd been spending a lot of time with Randy from Ell's security detail. Usually when Ell and Amy went out to do something it was with Amy's kids Mike and Janey. They'd been down to Jordan Lake for a day and up to Asheville for a weekend trip. Those trips had been great fun, but still, there was a hole of some kind in her life...

If anyone acted too friendly to her as "Ell" she started worrying that they knew about her money. Even though she felt like she'd been fairly successful playing up the "investors" for D5R and playing down her royalties from PGR Comm, she'd suspect that they'd figured it out. Roger probably suspected somewhat, but she trusted him because he'd been her friend even back when she was broke and disguised as fat Ellen with the big nose.

She didn't like going out as "Ell" because people

recognized her and acted weird. She often thought about going out on the town as "Belle" and had even gotten some silicone padding and bigger pants in order to make herself a little less attractive if she did. Not as fat as Ellen's pants had been, but just something to decrease a little of the unwanted attention she so frequently received. But she hadn't done it yet. She couldn't bring herself go out to a bar like Top of the Hill by herself, she'd feel too weird and desperate.

She'd been thinking about taking more than one class when the fall semester started up. Maybe she'd meet more people her age on campus?

Suddenly she heard a car door open in the row in front of her. Memories of her kidnapping in Morehead City flashed. She began crashing into the zone! How had she let herself get so distracted walking across an empty parking lot! A big guy stood up out of the car...

"Phil!" she shouted in delight. "What're you doing here?! Why didn't you call before you came? How'd you even know where I'd be?"

He grinned. All six-foot three-inches of Norse God good looks smiled and held his arms open wide. She rushed into them, throwing her arms around his muscular back and squeezing.

Phil said quietly, "I wanted to surprise you like you did me back last Thanksgiving. Your Mom told me you were working here so I thought I'd surprise you when you got off." He leaned back and raised his eyebrows, "I had no idea they'd be making you work this late or I'd have thought better of this harebrained plan!"

"Oh no! How long have you been waiting?!"

"Since 4:30, when reasonable people get off work. What do they have you doing in there anyway?"

"Some research. I could've come out anytime if

you'd just called me!"

He shrugged, "Then it wouldn't have been a surprise, would it?"

Ell hugged him hard again, then let go and leaned back. "How'd you get past the gate guard?"

"Your Mom. She called someone named 'Sheila' who put me on the 'list.'"

"Hmmm," Ell lowered an eyebrow, "I'm going to have to talk to Sheila I guess. Let me take you out to dinner?"

"Nope."

Ell frowned up at him.

Phil said, "I'm about to have a real paycheck. I'm taking *you* out to dinner!"

She quirked an eyebrow, "But I've already had a paycheck for a while. Shouldn't you wait to start paying for stuff until you actually have some money in the bank?"

"Well… Now that you mention it…" he turned to his car. "Your chariot awaits, Madam." He opened the door.

Ell delightedly got in. While Phil walked around to his door she had Allan tell her car to follow them and let her security team know what was happening.

Once he was in he asked, "Do you have a recommendation for Italian?"

"Tarantinis. It's a great little place. Been around for quite a while."

"Tarantinis it is." he said, telling his car's AI to take them there.

Ell said, "So are you on your break between the Academy and astronaut training?"

"Yep," he grinned, "I report to the Johnson center in July. Meantime I'm enjoying a well-deserved rest."

"Cool!" She leaned back in her seat, "Never thought I'd get to go out to dinner with Buzz Lightyear."

~~~

At the restaurant Phil asked, "What kind of research do they have you doing at this D5R?"

She shrugged, "It's mostly to do with my physics theory on quantum entanglement. So of course I really like it. I stay late a lot of nights..." She sighed, "'cause my social life sucks. Or anyway it did until tonight when you came along!" She patted him on the arm.

Phil said, "Say, I heard that these new PGR Com chips that are overthrowing the world of telecommunications are based on your theory?"

Ell shrugged and nodded.

"Are they the same kind of chips that you made for the military to replace satellite communications during the Taiwan thing?"

"Pretty much, yeah."

"Wow! They're really great!" he said. "Look at this!" he pulled off his AI headband and pointed to the back of it. "No wire! My actual AI's sitting at home on my desk and I don't have to carry around a beltpack anymore. All I had to do was plug a PGR chip into the head band and another one into the AI!"

Nonplussed to be having something that seemed so "old hat" to Ell described as the latest thing by Phil, it brought the realization home to her that most people were just *beginning* to see the potential of the PGR chips. To Phil she said, "Pretty cool!"

He narrowed his eyes at her, "Wait a minute. Let me see the back of your headband."

Blushing a little, Ell turned her head.

"No wire! You already knew about this! And you're

just nodding and going along with me, the country bumpkin, so I won't feel bad!"

Ell ducked her head, "Sorry?"

He gave her a high five, "Hey no problem. I should've known you'd be way ahead of the curve on something you'd invented. Say, do you get any royalties on this?"

"Yeah, I do get some." Ell hoped he wouldn't ask how much.

"Woohoo!' He raised his glass to clink against hers. "I know an inventor!"

Ell felt a tap on her shoulder and turned to see a woman in her thirties there.

"Ms. Donsaii?"

Ell nodded.

"My daughter does gymnastics. She just idolizes you. Would you be willing to sign an autograph for her?"

Ell saw a wide eyed girl of about 11 sitting at the neighboring table staring at her. She smiled, "I'd be happy to, Ma'am." She got up and walked the few steps to that table then knelt and put her arm around the girl. "How about a picture?"

"Oh, thank you!"

~~~

Their dinner arrived and Ell and Phil fell to eating. Ell asked, "So how long's your astronaut training?"

He rolled his eyes, "The basic training alone is a couple of years. Once you finish basic you *hope* to get assigned to a mission and then have to train for that particular mission for a while. All this before there's any chance you can go up."

"So you aren't going to be coming back to Earth and your legions of 'googly eyed girls' for quite a while yet?" Ell grinned at him.

"I thought you promised to *be* my googly eyed girl?"

"You bet! You let me know when you get a long weekend and I'll come admire you in Houston."

"Really? That'd be cool." Phil felt a surge of delight at the thought that she'd be willing to do that. He leaned forward, "I'm really hoping things might loosen up in the astronaut business."

Ell frowned and tilted her head, "How come?"

"Well I'm sure you heard about the trouble the Space Station was in?"

Ell nodded and bit her lip.

"I was down in Houston for a briefing and orientation last week and everyone was excited about some new kind of technology that was used during the rescue of the Station. It's all really top secret right now, but the rumor is that it might make it easier to get into space." Phil leaned back and raised his eyebrows.

Ell released her lip from between her teeth and said, "That'd be really cool huh?"

"Yeah! Maybe I'll get to go up sooner?" He frowned, "Of course, astronauts wouldn't be so rare then and I'd have to share my legion of googly-eyed girls with all those other spacemen."

Ell traced a circle on the back of his hand, "What about girl astronauts? Do they get googly-eyed boys that chase them around?"

Phil's eyes widened, "Oh no, no, no! Boys are completely intimidated by intrepid girl astronauts."

Ell laughed, "I guess I shouldn't apply then."

~~~

After their dinner Phil took her to downtown Chapel Hill and had his car drop them off at UNC's Old Well. The evening was pleasant and he sat beside her on the bench in front of the landmark. After a moment he turned to her and said, "I thought we should return to the scene of my crime so I could apologize once again for the way I acted that day we first met."

Ell grinned at him, "Hey I forgave you for that years ago… I think… long before you forgave yourself."

"Well that'd certainly be true, since I still haven't forgiven myself."

She looked at him out of the corner of her eye. "I was hoping you'd brought me back here to have another try at getting that kiss?"

He grinned, "Well, I'd be a liar if I said that hadn't crossed my mind."

She reached up and cupped the back of his neck, pulling him down to her…

***

Clarkson knocked on Dennison's door again. Once inside he held out his AI's jack to remind Dennison to unjack his. "One of our guys at NASA says he's pretty sure the rocket was actually launched by the North Carolina company, 'D5Research.' He's the only one of our people at NASA who's got any clue. Doesn't seem possible because this D5R doesn't have any contracts to launch from Canaveral or any of the other launch facilities, but that's what he claims. Rumor has it that they have some new tech that lets them launch small rockets into orbit! The theory is that they're small enough that they don't show up on space-watch types of radar. Maybe they use balloons to send them up to a high altitude then launch them from their… or something?" Clarkson shrugged.

Dennison looked like he had indigestion, "Get Phelps after them. Hire some of their people, buy the tech, buy the company, whatever. Just make sure we wind up in control. Whoever they are, they're not going to cut ILX out of its own business! Tell our people at NASA to do what they can to stonewall them for now."

***

Ell looked around at her D5R group. "OK, who wants to go first?"

Braun put a hand up and said, "We've placed rush orders with GE for the construction of D3 type rocket motors with surrounding water shrouds. They've got experience working with the alloys we want for our nozzles though one of their engineers has repeatedly told me that the cooling shroud around the nozzle is a dumb idea. He's patiently explained how I should run the propellant through the nozzle walls to cool them instead. I get the impression he thinks he's working with a complete idiot, but I've just told him he has to build it my way."

Ell grinned at him, "Seems like I remember someone talking to me that way when he first came to work here."

Braun sheepishly mumbled, "Yeah, that guy *was* an idiot."

"What about a fuselage?"

"I gave it a lot of thought and we're going to order a used Lear Jet, assuming the budget's up to it. We'll remove the engines and install rockets. The nose has radar built in, a cockpit for our eventual astronauts, though we'll need to brace the chairs, and a comm

Rocket!

section that already meets FAA standards."

Ell frowned, "Will it hold up to the vacuum of space?"

"Hah! Caught you thinking old school! If it leaks, we just pump more air into it through a port."

It was Ell's turn to look sheepish.

Braun shrugged, "But it should be *pretty* airtight, Lear jets are pressurized to fly at high altitude and so they have to be fairly airtight. Of course, they do leak some at altitude but they just pump in more air, the same way we will in space. I'm planning to do some leak testing and tighten it up before we send it up. But, if you think about it, we actually *want* it to leak, at least some. Replacing losses with fresh air simplifies our problems. That way we won't have to scrub out the carbon dioxide and put in new oxygen etc."

"What about heating during liftoff and reentry?"

"We just *fly* it up to altitude so it doesn't heat so much going through the dense air down low. We retro it back down rather than aerobraking so it doesn't heat so much on the way down."

"Sounds good, are there any other problems?"

"Oh yeah! There'll be hell to pay getting the FAA to let us launch and land a rocket on a regular airfield. They're gonna take forever to decide it's safe! Have you had any luck getting NASA to let us launch and recover from Canaveral?"

Ell frowned again. "No. We've hired a lawyer with some experience in this kind of stuff, though, of course, no one's really ever done what we're trying to do. He's getting the run around too. He thinks ILX has connections in NASA that are throwing up roadblocks to stifle the competition. NASA's *supposed* to let private companies launch from their facilities, though there's usually a lot of red tape. In our case though, we can't even seem to get the red tape started. We're looking into whether we could buy an island in the Caribbean? Or maybe launch from a boat at sea? Would that be possible?"

Braun looked aghast, "A boat? Like an aircraft carrier?"

"No, like a big boat. Vertical takeoff from a launching cradle on the boat. Land the same way, or in the water and crane it out."

"Whoa! I'll have to think about those options. A boat certainly wouldn't work with my Lear Jet concept though."

Ell looked around the group. Fred lifted a hand briefly and said, "Brian and I've pretty much automated a port constructor. My entangler feeds in the entangled buckyballs as the discs rotate under the jet. Brian set up the machine so it can rotate ports of five mm and one, two, five, 7.5, ten and twenty centimeters under the jet. We'll have to retool to make bigger ports than that, but energizing big ports is gonna be a bigger problem than making them."

Vivian said, "You can say that again! I've drawn up a design for the electronics to energize a ten centimeter port and ordered parts but it'll be drawing more than 30 kilowatts. We're having to ask Duke Energy to bring in a heavier power line. We could run quite a few ten centimeter ports with the power lines the building already has, but," she chuckled, "we might start dropping circuit breakers if people used too much other equipment at the same time."

Ell turned to Ben, "How about you, Ben? What are you working on?"

He shrugged, "We don't really have need of my

micromanipulation skills. I thought for a while about just quitting here and finding another job." He made a wry face. "But I didn't want to miss out on all the excitement... So. I've started working with a couple of the new guys in the machine shop on 'macromanipulators.' Essentially we're making small rockets we can fly up to space, open up an aerodynamic shroud, then extend arms we can manipulate stuff with." He reached under the table and pulled up a rocket he set on top of it. "Meet Armstrong." He looked up to his HUD and gave a command. The tubular body of the rocket hinged open, exposing a lot of mechanical looking insides. An arm extended out of it, reached down, grasped a nut that lay on the table, lifted it and placed it into a chamber that'd opened near the top. Nothing happened for a moment, Ben gave another command, repeated it, then said, "Dammit! The specimen drops onto a 50mm port inside the rocket and was supposed to fall through that port and into the specimen jar over there," he pointed to a five-gallon glass jug with a port apparatus on top of it. "We've obviously got a little work to do yet, but the idea is that it could fly to the moon like the real 'Neil Armstrong' then use its 'strong arms' to retrieve specimens, or do some other kind of work. I'm a little worried about whether everything is going to work in space temperatures and vacuum, but as you can see, we haven't even gotten everything to work here on Earth yet."

Ell had been staring at it. It had fins like model rockets do, or like you'd see on pictures of spaceships in old magazines. With a puzzled frown she said, "Are the fins decorative?"

"Oh! No. It has port nozzles at the bottom and top of

the fins. Obviously it can use its main rocket to travel long distances. But what about when you just need to move it a couple of feet? Watch this!" Ben gave a command and with a hiss the rocket scooted across the table top. "You just open the nozzles at the bottom of all three fins and it skids across surfaces like a hover craft! If you want it to hold still while you use the arms, you blow gas out of the nozzles on *top* of the fins to pin it down to the surface and stabilize it."

"Cool! When're you going to launch?"

"Maybe this afternoon?" He shrugged. "Maybe next week, depending on Murphy... As soon as we work out the rest of the bugs. Then I'm sure we'll have to fix some bugs that occur up there in space before we'll be ready to actually send it on a mission. I thought for its first mission we'd send it to Tranquility Base, where Neil Armstrong first stepped out onto the moon?"

"Oh! That'd be... amazing!"

Ell looked around the group. They looked amused by her childlike enthusiasm. "Any other updates or issues?"

Sheila said, "I've arranged for Aerogas to deliver some really huge LOX and RP-1 tanks to our tank farm out back tomorrow. The tanks'll have sensors to let Aerogas know how full they are and Aerogas'll start making daily trips to top them off if needed. Also Vivian says we need insurance against a power outage long enough to ruin all the ports we've built already. You know, if the fields stabilizing the entanglements went down long enough for all the buckyballs to come undone. I've ordered a high-end generator to go out back."

Ell said, "I thought we already had a back-up generator?"

"We do, but it hadn't been tested for a while and when we did, it didn't work. It's been repaired now, but the new one tests itself once a week and runs off our natural gas line, presumably indefinitely. The old one'll back up the new one."

Ell said, "Great work, appreciate your thoroughness."

Brian lifted a finger, "I've just about finished making a connector that can hook up to the airlock on the Space Station. Sheila hasn't been able to get us permission from NASA to test it against the dummy lock down at Canaveral though, so we don't know for sure if it will work. We might have the same problem that the Chinese had with their connector." He grimaced, "You'd think after we saved their bacon, the people at NASA would be falling all over themselves to help us help them. Instead they're acting like a bunch of assholes and treating us like we haven't got a clue, just because we're new at this."

Vivian shrugged, "No one likes being shown up."

Ell looked around at her team. "Don't forget that, in an effort to temporarily keep the world from knowing we're the ones who saved the station, we're also keeping almost everyone at NASA from knowing about it. So, most of them don't *know* we 'saved their bacon,' and have no reason to treat us as anything but an upstart." Ell frowned, "However, from some of the friction I've seen, I'm getting the sinking feeling that ILX sees us as an adversary and they're doing whatever they can to make our lives harder. They have a history of trying, and generally succeeding, in breaking their competition."

She sighed, "Our patent attorney says we should expect them to start making attempts to infringe our patent soon. He figures that if ILX can figure out how to make ports, they'll just try to build them commercially. He thinks they'll just tell us to go ahead and sue them for infringement. They'll be happy to fight it out in court, expecting that we won't have the juice to stop them there. To figure out how to build their own ports, he thinks their most likely strategy would be to hire some of you guys away from D5R rather than trying to figure out how ports might work by reading the original paper themselves."

Ell sighed, "I think he's right because the electrical fields for the ports are really weird, to say nothing of the issues with placing entangled molecules around the periphery.

"Anyway, D5R's decided to preemptively ask you to come to them, through me, if ILX makes you such an offer. Let us make a counteroffer. I'd also like to remind you that you stand to make a pretty penny on your share of our port technology if you stay and we win any patent battle with ILX. Your contract specifies that you must maintain confidentiality about what you've learned here about ports if you want to keep your D5R shares." Ell raised her eyebrows at them.

Fred snorted, "ILX already made me an offer. I told them to take a hike." He snorted, "Although, it didn't hurt that D5R was already paying me a bigger salary than they offered."

Ell shrugged, "They may just keep coming back with better offers, but you can rest assured that D5R intends to better any offer they make."

***

Rocket!

Emma was staring at her screen, trying to absorb a paper that had implications for her research when her AI announced a call from Ell. "Put her on! Hey, Ell! How're you doing?"

Ell sounded depressed, "I'm in bad need of a social life. Do you ever go out on the town?"

"Occasionally. Mostly I'm too busy and too broke."

"Well, I've got a job now. I could finance us going out on the town?"

"Sure! I'd go out a lot more if I had a *sponsor*!"

"Alright! Saturday night?"

"Sure, what about Roger? Or your hunky wrestler in the Air Force?"

"Well, Roger and I are good friends and we go out sometimes. But I'm kinda his boss, so even though I'd like to do more with him, it feels too weird pushing our relationship. Phil's in Houston for astronaut training."

"Woohoo, you're dating an astronaut?"

"Correction, I *occasionally* see a guy who's in *training* to be an astronaut."

"Okaay. I guess I can see why you'd need a night out." They spoke a few minutes more, making arrangements.

***

Ell was working on a tiny rocket when Ben came up and said, "Hey, we're about to launch Armstrong. You want to come watch?"

"Yeah!" She picked up the tiny rocket and said, "This little guy is ready to launch too, I'll shoot him off right after Armstrong."

As they walked out to the parking lot launch pad Ben

Laurence E Dahners

looked at the little rocket Ell had in her hand. It was only about three quarters of an inch in diameter and eight inches long. "What's that one for?" he asked, thinking it couldn't really carry much except its guidance package and the port apparatus for its engine.

"This guy?" she said holding it up, "He's to test one of the predictions the math makes about the ports. The math predicts that ports will un-entangle above a certain speed relative to one another." She shrugged, "That obviously has tremendous bearing on whether we could use ports to send something to another star, so I want to test it."

Ben's eyebrows went up. "Wow, *you're* thinking a long way ahead."

She frowned at him, "Isn't that what you're paying me to do?" She grinned and winked.

He said, "Well that speed must be pretty high or we wouldn't be able to send our rockets up into orbit right?"

"Yeah, I'm estimating it's high enough to reasonably travel around the solar system, but not to another star. But, that's just what the math predicts, we've got to test to see if it's really true."

A few minutes later Allan checked for overhead traffic, then they counted down together and watched Ben's rocket streak into the sky. Ben and his team went back inside to watch the take from Armstrong's cameras on the big screens inside. Ell went over to the launching rack and clipped "Percent-c," as she'd named the little rocket, onto the test rail. She had Allan test all of its thrusters and then it shot into the sky as well, accelerating at a steady 5 gravities once it got to a high enough altitude that it wouldn't overheat.

Ell went back inside and found Ben and his little

team cussing and looking disgusted. The doors on Armstrong had failed to open in space and they had it coming back down for some more work. Ell said, "You've checked to be sure our airspace is clear before you bring it back, right?"

Ben grinned sheepishly, "I'd forgotten, but that high performance AI you sicced on me reminded us. We're holding altitude at 40,000 feet for a couple minutes before we come the rest of the way back down."

Ell was momentarily grateful she'd upgraded all her science team's AIs to PGR connected near supercomputers and had Allan put the launching guidelines onto them. She said, "Great! I'm coming out to watch us *land* our first rocket."

As Ell stood outside with the others watching for their first glimpse of Armstrong coming down, Allan said, "You have a call from a Manfred Phelps of ILX."

Deciding that she could both talk and watch the landing Ell said, "Put him on."

"Ms. Donsaii of D5 Research?" a deep voice said.

"Yes?"

"Hello, I'm Manfred Phelps and I represent ILX, the space launch company."

"Yes?"

"I've been authorized to offer your investors up to fifty million dollars for the exclusive rights to the new rocket technology D5R's been using." His tone implied that Ell should be stunned by the amount of money he was offering.

"Oh! I'm sorry Mr. Phelps, that tech isn't for sale at present. At some point in the future we do expect to license it, but not for quite a while yet."

Unperturbed, Phelps said, "Alternatively we're

prepared to offer 250 million dollars to purchase the company outright."

"Um, D5R isn't for sale either Mr. Phelps."

"Ms. Donsaii," Phelps said in a patient tone one might use to lecture a child, "please let me talk to whomever's *actually* in charge there."

Having no doubt that Phelps' AI had provided Phelps with her vital statistics and he didn't want to be speaking to a nineteen-year-old, Ell said, "*I'm* D5R's CEO, Mr. Phelps."

"Ms. Donsaii," he said, with the air of someone whose patience was wearing thin, "I haven't been able to find your articles of incorporation on the web as yet, but surely even you realize that, once we do, we can simply make this offer to your Board and they'll override you?"

Ell saw a bright light appear above as Armstrong began decelerating hard approaching a landing. With an internal grin that she hoped she kept out of her voice she said, "Oh, I don't think that'll happen, Mr. Phelps."

"Ms. Donsaii, I assure you that investors are surprisingly fickle when they see a chance to obtain a large return on their investment. Especially," he said ominously, "when they learn that the alternative would be for their little company to compete against a corporation like ILX, one that has billions of dollars in capital."

Ell watched Armstrong smoothly decelerate to a halt just above the pavement and then its main engine popped off. It settled the last inch or so, apparently lowered on jets of gas from the thrusters in the fins as well as oxygen alone from the main thruster nozzle. The watching crew applauded. The noise of the landing and applause made it difficult to hear so Ell stepped back inside and closed the door. "Sorry about the noise Mr. Phelps," she said politely. "Back to what you were saying, I'm confident that our investors won't be fickle. Also, since the technology D5R is using is based on completely new theoretical physics, the patents should stand up well to assaults by well-heeled lawyers."

"Ms. Donsaii! A patent search doesn't even turn up any new rocketry patents!"

"Well that'd be true. You can rest assured; however, that patent protection's been applied for. It *is* so recent that the application hasn't been made public as yet."

"You don't even have a patent?! It's entirely possible that a patent might not even be granted! All the more reason your investors may jump ship! I'd strongly urge you reconsider before ILX reduces this offer."

"Sorry Mr. Phelps, but we really don't have anything to worry about, either regarding the uniqueness of the intellectual property nor the confidence of our investors."

"Ms. Donsaii you're going to regret this decision!" Phelps said ominously, breaking the connection.

Ben had just walked up as Ell finished speaking. "Confidence of our investors?" he asked. "Is there a problem?"

Ell said, "No, but ILX is trying to bully us into selling the rights to the ports and they think our board's gonna roll over if they offer enough money. They're actually asking to buy our 'rocket tech' and don't seem to be aware of, or at least understand, the presence or function of ports." She grinned at him, "And, I'm not helping them figure it out."

As they walked into the research area Allan spoke in Ell's ear, "The ports supplying Percent-c have lost entanglement and closed."

"Oh! That seemed early, what speed did it get up to?"

"It accelerated at 5 gravities for 51 minutes which should have produced a velocity of 0.0510% of the speed of light though there is no direct way to confirm that velocity."

"I know that's pretty close to what we calculated, but what did the theory predict exactly?"

"0.0531% of the speed of light."

"Close enough! I'm sure our measurement error calculating the velocity from the acceleration and the time of flight isn't all that accurate."

Ben had been watching her curiously. "Do I take from that that your little rocket performed as expected?"

Ell raised her eyebrows, "Closer than I thought we'd be." She frowned, "But it definitely isn't gonna go fast enough for interstellar travel." She glanced back at him, "I've gotta go spend some time in my office."

Ben admiringly watched Ell walk away, musing over his mixed feelings about her. On the one hand she seemed so young and naïve and pretty that his instinct was to dismiss her or ask her for a date. On the other hand, talking about physics and ignoring her looks and age left no doubt that she was a frigging *genius*. Hearing her security team talk about her hand to hand combat skills gave her an eerily frightening aura. He shook his head and turned back to Armstrong.

~~~

Ell sat in her office staring at the ceiling. She'd quickly disposed of the administrative work that always stacked up, approving some Physics grants at NCSU and expenditures by her teams at D5R.

Rocket!

Now she was worrying about the possibility she'd thought of while talking to Ben. What if she was making horrific weapons available to the general public? Somehow, hearing Allan say "speed of light" this time made her think about the fact that the little rocket was traveling so fast it had a huge amount of kinetic energy. It was actually still well under the speed of light, so relativistic energy wasn't a big issue. However, calculation showed that, weighing one kilogram and traveling at 0.05% of the speed of light it had a kinetic energy of 11,000 megajoules. That was the same energy as blowing up 2.7 tons of TNT. It surprised her to calculate that 1 ton or 260 gallons of a mixture of kerosene and liquid oxygen had the same energy. She'd always had the impression that TNT had more, not less energy than kerosene, though kerosene relied on a separate oxidizer whereas TNT contained it oxidizer within itself. It really shouldn't be surprising since the little rocket had consumed nearly 400 gallons of RP-1/LOX getting up to that speed.

When Ell first started worrying about the issue she'd been concerned that a terrorist or even a teenager could build a little rocket like her Percent-c and send it out into space to circle back and impact somewhere on earth. However, Percent-c at 0.05% speed of light or 150 kilometers per second was only going about twice as fast as the fastest meteorites. Meteorites that started out weighing a kilogram or less almost always broke up passing through the atmosphere of Earth.

However, Ell had built a special circuit for Percent-c that was needed to stabilize the ports up to 0.05% of the speed of light. The regular ports they'd been building should un-entangle at much lower speeds. She had Allan run the calculation and it predicted loss of entanglement for standard ports at about 22 kilometers per second for the regular ports. That speed was nearly double Earth's escape velocity and a 1,000-kilogram spacecraft traveling that speed would be carrying 250 gigajoules energy or the equivalent of blowing up 60 tons of TNT. That sounded bad, but even a 1,000-kilogram spacecraft would mostly burn up as it came through the atmosphere at that speed. Also your hypothetical terrorist would have to burn about 38 tons or 10,000 gallons of kerosene/LOX to get it up to speed. It'd be probably significantly easier for a hypothetical terrorist to just move TNT into position with a truck than send a port rocket out into space and back.

Unless they were going to terrorize another country.

After thinking a while longer Ell resolved to build a Percent-c #2 with standard ports to confirm the 22 kilometers per second figure. Until she knew for sure she went out and found Ben, "Hey, what accelerations are you using with Armstrong?"

"Five gravities."

"OK, I'd suggest you accelerate no longer than…" she looked up in concentration, "seven minutes to make sure you don't disentangle your ports and lose control of him. You want to stay under 20 kilometers per second. At least until I check a few more things."

His eyebrows rose, "Okay, will do."

Ell decided to keep the circuit that stabilized ports to higher speeds her own personal secret. She hoped no one else would stumble across the stabilization circuit. After all it had come to her late one night in what she thought of as a lucky flash of insight.

Chapter Three

Manfred Phelps and John Clarkson arrived at Dennison's office in ILX together. Clarkson knocked and they entered.

Dennison, looked up and took in the look on their faces. He demanded, "Don't give me bad news unless you've got a solution!"

Phelps and Clarkson glanced at each other. Neither said anything.

Dennison sighed, "OK, just tell me what's happened now. As usual, I'll have to come up with a solution myself."

Clarkson motioned to Phelps who said, "I've contacted this D5R. It's being run by a nineteen-year-old girl! I've talked to some of their people, offering them jobs. They've shut me down without telling me anything about what's going on there…"

Dennison frowned as he interrupted, "How much did you offer them?"

"Twice what we'd normally pay someone with that kind of education and experience."

Dennison rolled his eyes.

Phelps continued, "I tried to talk to this girl, Donsaii that's in charge, about buying the rights to their technology. It's a little hard to know what to offer since we don't even know what the tech is; just that it let them send some kind of rocket to the Station. So I offered fifty million, sight unseen, figuring we could back out after we got a look at it, if it turned out that was too much. She didn't even blink!"

"Oh Jeez," Dennison muttered.

Phelps said, "I also offered to buy the entire company, near as I can tell a four million dollar building and 20-50 employees, for 250 million. Again, she just said 'no!' No discussion, no consideration, nothing!"

"For Christ's sake! Just go over her head to the owners."

"Tried that, haven't been able to figure out who the owners or investors are. Not even who's on the board."

"Donsaii..." Dennison frowned, "Name's familiar?"

"Yeah, you're probably remembering the gymnast with that name from the Olympics a few years back. There's also a physics paper by someone with that name that stirred the science people up. That paper is what the PGR chips that're shaking up the comm industry are based on. But, I've talked to a couple of our physicists and they don't see how that paper could be related to rocketry—in any way whatsoever. Maybe this kid that's running D5R is a relative of Donsaii the physicist? Who knows? There is jack squat about D5R on the web. They don't even have their own website; all they get is peripheral mention on a few other websites. It's like they don't care about advertising, or public opinion, or building a business. I only got put through to the kid that's running it by calling their main office and asking to talk to the CEO, not by knowing who the CEO was before I called."

Dennison leaned back in his chair and narrowed his eyes. "So hire some PIs. Have one follow that girl CEO and learn everything there is to know about her. Another one to dig up everything there is to know

Rocket!

about D5R, especially who sits on their board. Another to try to hire on as Security or Admin at D5R, or to enter the building some other way and get us some photos. Another to make friends with the people who work there and get them to tell us what's happening. Make things happen! We need to take those bastards down!" He looked off into the distance a moment and growled, "They're *not* going to beat ILX at its own game!"

***

Emma skipped down the stairs of her apartment building and out to Ell's car. She pulled open the door and dropped into the passenger seat. Her eyes flashed open wide, Ell was dressed as "Ellen" with the dark skin bronzers, the black spiky hair, the beaky nose prosthesis, *and*, Emma looked down, the silicone padded fat pants!

"What the hell are you doing in that outfit? I thought we were going out to meet guys?!"

Ell ducked her head, "Well, kinda. But people act all weird around 'Ell.' I know I'm not really famous, but too many people know who I am and treat me all different. I want them to like me for me, not because I was a gymnast."

Emma threw her head back and laughed. "I've been upstairs putting on my makeup and little black dress, trying to look as good as I could for a night out on the town and *you've* been trying to look terrible?! Most of the reason they treat you different is 'cause you look great, not 'cause you're a gymnast!"

The car was rolling toward downtown Raleigh. In a small voice Ell said, "Sorry."

"Don't sorry me! I've been worried about being the cute girl's ugly friend that the handsome guy's wingman has to hang out with. Instead I find it's the other way around! It's all good by me."

Ell and Emma walked down the stairs into a dance club. Emma eyed Ell, "Ellen lost weight, huh? Those fat pants aren't as fat as the ones you used to wear are they?"

"No, I think of these as my intermediate fat pants. The ones I used to wear as 'Ellen' are for when I *really* don't want men to notice me." She grinned, "The really fat ones make me completely invisible. I swear I could walk into a fraternity and steal them blind wearing those."

Emma giggled. "Well let's hope *someone* asks you to dance." She stopped turned to Ell, "Seriously now, before we get down into the club and it's hard to talk?"

Ell said, "Yes?"

"In my experience, if we do talk to some guys, don't tell them we do physics!"

Ell frowned, "Why not?"

"Guys get intimidated by smart women. You tell them you're a physicist and they just fade away. I usually tell them I'm a waitress. I did used to work as one."

Ell gave a dubious laugh, "Really? Men aren't that insecure are they?"

"Oh, you have no idea!"

"OK," Ell looked off into the distance a moment, "I'll say I work in the office at D5R. I don't like to lie, but I do work in the office part of the time."

They went to the bar and got a beer for Emma and a Coke for Ell, then found a standing table near the dance

Rocket!

floor to put their drinks on and looked around. Ell felt a little weird because most of the girls were wearing dresses or skirts. Tres Locos in Las Vegas had mostly been populated by people wearing jeans and Ell hadn't thought her jeans would stand out here. There were some people out on the floor doing some form of line dance, Ell grabbed Emma's wrist and dragged her out onto the floor.

Emma protested, "I don't know how to do that!"

Ell shouted over the music, "This is how you learn."

Ell was almost immediately able to follow the dance the people were doing and it only took Emma a couple of runs through the various "walls" of the dance to catch on. Once Emma was comfortable with the dance she began to notice Ell's dancing when they were turned so that Ell was in front of her. Despite the fat pants there was something graceful and fascinating about the way she moved. The extra little moves she inserted were cute too.

Eventually they walked off the floor and back to their drinks laughing. After they'd had a few sips a pleasant looking guy came over and asked Emma to dance. Emma glanced at Ell who nodded and she went out on the floor with him. Ell stood and sipped her drink through a couple dances. Emma and her friend looked like they were having fun. Ell winced internally, thinking she'd overdone her disguise. If she wanted to have a social life, she shouldn't be trying to avoid men's attention. *This get-up certainly succeeded in that.* She grimaced, wondering why in the world she'd decided to go out to meet guys dressed as Ellen.

As a song wound down she glanced at Emma and saw her shake her head at the young man she was with. Emma pointed at Ell. Ell cringed inside as it became obvious that Emma was telling him she had to come spend time with her less-attractive friend. When Emma got back to the table Ell said, "You could have stayed out there and danced some more! I'll be OK."

Emma wrinkled her nose at Ell, "It *is* your own fault for dressing that way. But Mike has a friend that he's going to get to dance with you."

Ell's brows rose, "A pity dance?!" She snorted, "I think I'd rather stand here by myself!"

Emma laughed, "Get down off your high horse girl! If you're gonna dress up like an ugly duckling you're gonna have to accept your friend's help."

Ell glared at her momentarily but then pasted on a smile as she saw Mike and his friend walking their way.

Mike stopped at their table and said "Hey Emma, Ellen. This is my buddy Arco." He waved at his obviously shy friend who stood looking at the table, holding the elbow of his straight left arm with his right hand. Arco had curly brownish hair and a mild case of acne. He was the same height as Ell's five-foot nine. Ell thought he looked like he was about to bolt back to his own table.

Attempting to produce a chipper voice over the music, Ell said, "Hi Arco."

He lifted his chin in acknowledgement, but said nothing.

Mike said, "Hey is it OK, if I go get our drinks and bring them over here?"

Emma said, "Sure!" and he turned to go.

Internally Ell rolled her eyes. Externally she turned back to Arco, "Have you known Mike long?"

He nodded. Still didn't say anything.

Ell wondered if he was only shy or actually just hated being paired up with her. Internally she shrugged, "Do you dance?"

Rocket!

He nodded.

Ell grabbed his hand and pulled him toward the floor. To her surprise, he didn't resist. Once they were out amongst the crowd she let go and he started moving to the rhythm. It was as if the music transformed him from the awkward guy who'd stood at her table into a happy disciple of the beat. He followed the rhythm effortlessly and soon was turning and moving his hips enthusiastically. Ell beamed at him. He sheepishly grinned back. She reciprocally matched the steps he was making and turned when he did.

Ell and Arco danced their way through a few songs then returned to the table and their drinks. Emma and Mike were still out on the dance floor. Ell's eyebrows rose when she saw they were swing dancing. Mike looked like he was teaching Emma the steps but Emma seemed to be a fast learner. Ell nudged Arco and pointed them out to him.

Arco *finally* said something. He leaned close and in a surprisingly deep voice said, "Mike took lessons to learn to dance like that."

Ell looked at Arco, eyebrows up again. "Do you swing dance?"

He nodded.

Ell tilted her head at the dance floor, lifting one eyebrow in question.

Arco shrugged and started out to the floor, taking Ell's right hand in his left. When they reached the floor he pulled Ell under his arm to twirl her onto the floor. In the fat pants Ell misjudged the width of her hips resulting in their having a little butt collision as she twirled under. Arco carefully led her through some more turns, then cuddles. He was a good dancer.

Ell thoroughly enjoyed it.

~~~

Eventually they stumbled out of the club and went for a 2AM breakfast at Centro, an old Mexican food place a couple of blocks from where they'd been dancing. Mike and Emma carried on a spirited conversation during the walk over but Arco said nothing. Once they had a booth at Centro, Mike said, "So what do you girls do for a living?"

Emma laughed and put a hand to her hair, fluffing it, "I'm a fashion model."

Mike's eyes widened, "Really?!"

"No silly! You have to be at least five-eight, like Ellen there." she pointed to Ell, making a little grimace of apology for almost using her real name. "I'm only five-four."

Ell said, "Yeah, *I'd* be the fashion model if only I was as thin as Emma." She rolled her eyes.

"So seriously, what *do* you do?"

Emma said, "I waitress and take some classes."

Ell said, "I work for a company out in RTP, what do you guys do?"

"We work for SAS. It's in RTP too. I'm a statistician and Arco there, he's a programmer." He grinned, "Hard to get anything done with him in the next cubicle, talking all the time!"

"Really?" Ell said, looking at Arco and trying to imagine him speaking entire sentences."

"No!" Mike laughed. "Though when you get to know him he does occasionally speak spontaneously. When you google 'introvert' his picture comes up"

Ell snuck another glance at Arco. He was blushing and staring at the table. "Well, he's a great dancer! That doesn't seem like a typical introvert trait to me."

Arco grinned shyly at Ell.

Rocket!

The conversation migrated to other topics and they eventually broke up to go home. In the car on the way home Emma said, "I *liked* Mike. What did you think of Arco?"

"He was nice. Awfully quiet though. I thought *I* was introverted until I met him."

"Hah! I'll bet that's the last time we see *'Ellen'* out in public!"

Ell shrugged and blushed, "Maybe." She felt a little embarrassed to realize how much her looks seemed to mean to her. When she was Ell, she thought being attractive was unimportant. But when she was 'Ellen,' she realized that it really *did* matter. Probably as much to her as to anyone else.

***

Ell grinned as she looked around the group. "Things are looking pretty good group. Let's update everyone's particular projects." She turned to Braun, "Rob?"

Braun looked around, "You've probably all heard D5R bought an island in the Bahamas. It had a jet capable airfield for the succession of rich people who've owned it in the past. We bought two used Lear jets. One to refit as our spacecraft and one to fly back and forth to the island. We've been testing the integrity of the one we're refitting and have patched a few leaks. We pumped the cabin up to two atmospheres pressure to be sure nothing would rip out or pop loose out in space.

"We're flying them to the island tomorrow with the rocket engines on board and ready to be installed in place of the two rear jet engines on the one that's going to be our spacecraft. Also, of course, a passel of attitude thrusters to use in space and the airlock connector that should hook us to the Space Station. We're taking a bunch of aircraft engineers and mechanics. We should be ready to lift off for test flights in space next week!"

Vivian looked aghast, "You're not sending people up in an untested craft?!"

"No." he laughed, "unmanned for the first few flights until we're sure a window isn't going to pop out in the vacuum."

She frowned, "Do you have space suits?"

He shrugged, "Not like you're thinking of probably. Nobody's made a space suit that you can actually function very well in yet. If you try to use them at full atmospheric pressure in a vacuum they're inflated so tightly you can hardly move. To use them very well at all you have to be at a lower pressure which means you have to slowly decompress to that lower pressure to keep from getting the bends. It's a huge hassle."

"What *do* you have?"

"We've got emergency bags. Essentially they're carbon fiber bags that are shaped like jumpsuits. They have a hole your head sticks out through that can be sealed with a glass bubble in case of an emergency decompression. If we have such an emergency, we'll inflate them full of good old North Carolina air through a port. That port'll stay open the entire time we're in space as assurance against getting into a pocket of stale air inside the spacecraft. You will always have some fresh air blowing out right by your face. So in case of an emergency decompression all you have to do is shut the bubble over your head and seal the sleeves. You won't really be able to manipulate your environment very well in it though because it'll be blown up pretty hard."

Vivian rolled her eyes, "Doesn't sound very safe."

Braun shrugged, "The plane shouldn't be affected much by decompression so it can just fly you back down to earth."

"What if it can't?!"

He shrugged, "If it can't, having your hands free probably won't help much either."

Ell turned to Marsden.

Fred said, "Vivian and I've set up an assembly line to make ports that are ready to energize. We've made hundreds of the small ones, dozens of the bigger ones and we should be ready to test a ten centimeter port today, now that we have the new higher power lines."

Ell narrowed her eyes at him.

He said, "Is something wrong?"

"Oh! No, I'm just worrying about people out there that may not be our friends. Let's stockpile most of your extra ports off site in case something happens to this facility."

Vehement exclamations rose from the group.

Ell waved her hands in a calming motion, "I'm probably just paranoid 'cause I've been kidnapped a few times, and we had those guys break in here a while back. Also, I recently had an unpleasant conversation with ILX. Then I started wondering about what'd happen if someone set this place on fire?"

Eyes widened all around the group.

Roger looked around the metal building. "It doesn't look like it'd burn."

"It might if you ran in some of the chemicals first."

He swallowed, "I guess it would."

"Also," Ell said. "Viv, let's dip the electronic modules for the ports in 'Dexin.'"

Dexin was a relatively new epoxy used to cover proprietary electronics because it was almost impossible to remove without destroying the imbedded circuits. It had metal shavings in it to conduct heat and frustrate x-rays.

They looked at her wide eyed.

Ell grinned at them, "I'm *sure* I just worry too much. Ben, what's happening with 'Armstrong'?"

He grinned widely, "He's working great!"

She winked at him, "And where would Armstrong be at present?"

He waggled his eyebrows, "Orbiting the moon! Due to land at Tranquility Base in…" he looked at his watch, "forty-five minutes or so… if you guys'd like to watch?"

Cheers erupted from the group.

Ell smiled at their enthusiasm. When it calmed she said, "And this afternoon at 3 we're knocking off early for our biweekly social hour. It'll also be a sendoff for Rob and the crew he's taking to the Bahamas!"

"Where are we going?" someone in the back said.

"I was thinking about another picnic at my little farm but, it being August, it's pretty hot. Fred's volunteered his racquetball club. There we can hang out in air conditioned comfort. He says those of us who don't play racquetball can play wallyball in one of the courts."

John said, "What's wallyball?"

"Volleyball in a racquetball court. You're allowed to play balls off the walls."

***

Clarkson knocked on Dennison's door. He entered at a growled, "What?"

Rocket!

He unplugged his AI and waited until Dennison had unplugged his. "Donsaii. gymnast, physicist, CEO of D5R. All the same person!"

"You're kidding!"

Clarkson shook his head.

"Who's funding the place?"

Clarkson shrugged, "No one seems to know. The PIs can't find the articles of incorporation or figure out who's on the board either."

Dennison rolled his eyes, "Am I the only one that ever gets anything done around here? We've got enough trouble with the Vulcan 5 without this pipsqueak company pulling the rug out from under us! Good God almighty! Get out there and make things happen!"

Clarkson pressed his lips together against a retort about who'd pushed them to leap to the Vulcan 5 motor based on test stand firings without waiting for it to establish a track record on actual launches. Instead he turned and left Dennison's office without saying anything.

Dennison jacked his AI back in, "Get me Sonny."

***

The D5R crew gathered excitedly in the big room to watch the moon landing together on the big screens. The rocket was descending so the center screen showed starry-black space and the four peripheral screens showed the moon at their bottom edges. Brian said, "You're bringing it down far enough away that you won't scrub out the astronauts' foot prints aren't you?"

Ben's eyes widened, "Oh! I didn't think of that!" He

Laurence E Dahners

grinned at Brian's indrawn breath, "What do you think I am, some kind of Philistine? Of *course* we're coming down far enough away to protect the foot prints!"

The inner parts of the screens slowly filled with more and more of the moon. Then someone drew a breath as the Apollo 11 Lunar Module Descent Stage came into view in the top screen.

A few minutes later Armstrong'd settled into place on the lunar surface. Roger asked, "Where's the flag they planted? Did someone get here before us and steal it?"

Brian said, "No it was blown over by the blast of their takeoff. Buzz Aldrin saw it happen. It wasn't in very firm soil and was pretty close to the module. I think I see it lying down off to the side there."

They all stared in wonderment. In a tone of reverence Fred asked, "Should we take back a souvenir?"

"Nah, it's historic, leave everything there. We're going to take some photos from all sides. Then we'll grab some moon rocks and send them home."

"OK, but check this out." Ben said with a bounce of his eyebrows. On the screen Armstrong's arm came into view holding a stake with a small plaque at the top. The arm brought the sign up close enough that it could be read in the camera. "Here landed the second visitor to this desolate place. 'Armstrong' a robotic mission from D5R. It *also* 'came in peace for all mankind.'"

A few minutes later Armstrong had planted the stake and then lifted an inch or so off the surface with its little thrusters. It skidded slowly around the periphery of Tranquility Base, getting views from all angles for the cameras. A great deal of excited talk and pointing to the various items left on the surface went

194 | P a g e

Rocket!

on. Finally, it skidded off across the surface looking for some interesting looking moon rocks to send back. The arm to gather them with as well as the port they would be sent through were both fairly small. Therefore, they had to settle for pebbles that would fit, rather than some of the more interesting rocks they saw that would've been too big. The arm's hand picked up a pebble, moved toward Armstrong's camera and disappeared from the camera's view. A moment later, with a clink, the rock fell into the five-gallon jar sitting on the table. It bounced a couple of times as cheers went up around the room.

Roger went over to the jar and tried to lift the port apparatus off the top of it. Ben frowned, "Roger, what're you doing?"

"I want to look at our first moon rock."

"The port on top of that jar's connected to the moon, dummy. You can't pull the lid off because the jar's full of vacuum. If it wasn't for the vacuum, we could just let the specimens fall on the table."

Roger colored, "Oops! That *was* dumb."

Everyone shared a little laugh at his expense. Though a number of the others had forgotten the vacuum themselves, no one volunteered that information.

Armstrong continued scooting around the Moonscape picking up pebbles and sending them through the port into the jar.

Several interesting pebbles it picked up proved to be too large for the port. Ben exclaimed, "Next time Armstrong needs to take a hammer!"

"Are you going to post this video on the net?" Fred asked.

"Yeah!" A couple of the team said excitedly.

Feeling like a wet blanket, Ell said, "Let's hold off a little while until we've done a few more of the things we want to do. I'm worried that once this goes public we'll be completely swamped with publicity and attention. We won't get much done once that happens."

The group groaned in disappointment but finally agreed it'd be better to hold off until they were ready for the notice the video would bring.

Chapter Four

Dennison unjacked his AI and slid into the booth at the rear of the IHOP. The taciturn Sonny Jones was already there. Dennison wondered momentarily, as he had in the past, if "Sonny Jones" was an alias. As usual Sonny wasn't wearing an AI so Dennison didn't need to ask him to unjack it. In the odd accent he'd cultivated for these meetings Dennison said, "We've got a problem suited to your unique skills."

Sonny lifted his chin questioningly without saying anything.

"There's a facility called D5R in the Research Triangle Park in North Carolina that's supposedly launching rockets to orbit with some new kind of technology."

Sonny shrugged disinterestedly.

"They need to have a setback. We need samples of the tech."

Sonny's eyes narrowed but still said nothing.

Dennison waited a moment, then said, "How much?"

Sonny said, "Ten grand to look it over and price it."

Dennison rolled his eyes, but nodded. Sonny'd been worth his high prices on previous jobs.

***

Fred Marsden sat down next to Ell on one of the bleachers outside the main racquetball court at his club.

That court had been converted to a wallyball court for D5R and a number of the researchers were enthusiastically playing the court version of volleyball. He nudged her, "How come you're not playing?"

"Oh! I don't think I should. I used to play volleyball in High School and I'm afraid my competitive spirit might get me in trouble in a fun game like this one."

He frowned, "What do you mean."

"Well, having played volleyball competitively I'm afraid I might not 'tone it down' enough for a friendly game. Don't want to spike a ball into someone's face."

He tilted his head. "Want to try racquetball instead?"

Ell leaned back, shaking her head.

"What, are you too competitive for that sport too?"

Horrified that he seemed to have plucked the thought from her mind, Ell said the first thing that came to mind, "Oh, no! I just don't know much about it."

Marsden almost stopped chiding her because he hated playing with beginners, on the other hand he did want to put her in her place after her comment implying that she was too good for a friendly game of wallyball. "Come on. It won't hurt you to lose a game or two." He got up and started off to the club desk as if he expected her to follow.

Ell looked at his retreating back, then back at the wallyballers, then back toward Marsden who waved her on impatiently. With an imperceptible sigh she got up to follow him, resolving to lose quickly and graciously.

Marsden checked out a rental racquet and protective eyewear, handing them to Ell. He removed his AI headband to put his own goggles on.

Ell removed her AI too, feeling naked without it. Normally, she even slept in her headband. She put on the racquetball goggles and they stepped into the court next to the wallyball court.

~~~

Marsden quickly explained the rules and objectives then said, "We'll hit a few balls to warm up." He hit a nice soft shot up the middle of the court to Ell. Beginners, even fairly athletic ones, usually had a hard time placing the ball or knowing where it would be after it bounced, so he was pleasantly surprised when she returned it right back down the center of the court. Her shot was too soft and barely reached the front wall.

He scooped it up and hit it to her again. This time she hit it a little harder and it struck the front wall about where his had. They took turns hitting and he was happy to see she seemed to be able to control the ball pretty well for someone who hadn't played before.

~~~

For her part Ell was desperately wondering how she was doing. Once she had a feel for how hard to hit the ball, the game seemed surprisingly easy. She wondered how points were to be won when the ball always went where you expected it to go.

~~~

Marsden hit one up and off the ceiling. It came down struck the back wall. He expected her to whiff it like most beginners would when they encountered their first ceiling shot. In fact, she was pretty far out of position when the ball came down to hit the floor. But, with the startling quickness he'd seen her display in the Olympics, she leapt into position and hit it, exclaiming, "Wow, that wasn't where I thought it'd be!"

With amazement Marsden realized that, out of

Laurence E Dahners

position and leaping to the ball late, she had nonetheless replicated his own ceiling shot almost perfectly. "You ready to try a game?" he said, wonderingly. *How good will she be able to play? Sure she was the world's greatest gymnast, but that's a* completely *different sport isn't it?*

"Sure, go easy on me OK?"

Fred demonstrated a serve for her, suggesting she attempt to land the ball close to the corners. He motioned to her to serve first.

Determined not to overplay, Ell thought about what she'd learned so far hitting the ball around. It seemed surprisingly easy to control the ball's position and she was sure it could be hit a lot harder than Fred'd been hitting it so far, so she suspected that he was going easy on her as a beginner. Therefore, she should probably be hitting it even softer than he'd been hitting it and probably shouldn't put it too close to the corner on the serve.

She bounced the ball then served it softly, aiming to land it about eight inches from the corner. She winced, it was going to miss her aim point and land about four inches from the corner instead.

Fred watched her bounce the ball too high and hit it softly, typical beginner's moves, but realized that it was going to land tight in the corner. He leapt over and hit it before it landed, a little harder than he wanted against a beginner, sending it up along the side wall. She gracefully stepped over to it—as if she never had any doubt where to go to meet it—and again hit it softly, this time to his backhand corner.

Fred strode to the left back corner, caught the ball after it landed, about eight inches from the wall, and lofted a ceiling shot from there.

Rocket!

As he stepped out of the back left corner, Ell stepped unhurriedly into that corner as if she already knew the corner was exactly where his shot'd end up. When it did, she carefully hit it to the other corner, this time about twelve inches out.

Fred strode over to that corner, astonished that a beginner was keeping a rally going beyond one or two hits. This time he stroked the ball down the right wall, pretty hard and low. Still without seeming to hurry, Ell appeared at the right wall to plonk the ball back to the left corner, again about twelve inches out! He had to put in some significant effort to get back to the left corner and stroke a backhand down the left wall. This time he hit it much harder.

Ell was thinking that the game was actually pretty fun. The ball was moving fairly fast now, and it was fun to figure out where it was going to be and move to that spot in time to return it. She returned it to the right corner.

Fred was amazed. She'd just returned a hard, low shot, with her *backhand* and placed it about 10 inches from the right corner. The way she was hitting it from one corner to the other reminded him of watching an instructor challenging a pupil. Was she *toying* with him?! He hustled to the right back corner and slammed a drive up the right side, only a few inches off the floor and rocketing off the sidewall about half way up the court. It was the kind of shot he'd used to win the club championship shortly after moving to the area. To his astonishment, Ell was there, racquet stretched out to return the shot. He could swear that at the last moment she slowed her reach for the ball and let it go by. Later he'd review video he got his AI to pull from the court's cameras and continue to have the eerie feeling that she'd intentionally missed the shot.

~~~

For her part, as she excitedly stretched to return the shot Ell realized Fred had hit it really hard and might be freaked out if she returned it. She turned to see his eyes narrowed on her.

"You've never played before?!"

"Nope, but it *is* kinda fun chasing that ball down. I got in a lucky series of returns in, didn't I?" She smiled disarmingly.

The rest of the game Ell continued to hit the ball at the same velocity, but place it at least two feet from the corner. She continued to chase the balls down because chasing them was fun, but if Fred had hit it hard, she hit hers into the floor or lofted it to his forehand to lose the point. When she realized he was going to win 15-0, she returned a couple of his shots so they hit the front wall an inch or so off the floor. That way she picked up a couple of "lucky" points. The final score was 15-2.

"Wow! You're really good." Ell said.

"Wow! You're really fast! I hope you don't keep playing or you'll be beating me in no time."

Ell widened her eyes and gave him an innocent look, "Oh no, that'd *never* happen." After they left the court they went back to watch the wallyballers.

After a bit Roger came and sat next to Ell. In a low voice he said, "I watched a little of your game with Fred."

Ell said, "Yeah, it's a fun game!"

"Why'd you let him win?"

She thought about denying it, but he'd been there for her foosball faux pas when she'd demonstrated what she could really do when she played full on.

Rocket!

"Don't want too much attention Roger. You'll help me keep my little secret?"

He snorted. "What, that you can kick *anyone's* ass, at *any* sport?"

"I can not!"

Roger rolled his eyes, "Did you know he's the club champion?"

Ell's eyes widened. "Damn! No... I didn't," she whispered in a disappointed tone.

***

Sonny climbed slowly down from the tree overlooking the parking lot of the D5R facility. *I'm getting too old for this shit,* he thought as he stretched his sore muscles.

~~~

Back in his motel room, he used a one-time website established only for that purpose to send an encrypted message to Dennison. It said, "125." Since he worked in increments of a thousand dollars, Dennison would know he meant $125,000.

~~~

An hour later, he checked the single use offshore account he'd set up for this project and it had the 125 grand in it. He transferred the money to his own account then stretched. *No time like the present*, he thought. *Get this done and I can retire.*

~~~

Sonny cursed in the darkness as he humped his heavy backpack back through the woods to D5R. The night-vision attachment on his AI showed him general details, but it was so dark this moonless night that its cameras didn't have enough light to work with. He kept tripping over roots and underbrush the cameras didn't show.

Once he'd reached the back wall of the building he opened the backpack and got out a tarp. He pulled off a sticky strip and stuck one edge of the tarp to the wall. He crawled under and draped the rest of it over himself. He pulled out the business end of his torch and sparked it up by feel, *Ah, finally, I can see!* He began a horizontal cut about two feet up and cut until he hit a metal stud. Then he cut the other way to the next stud and down on both sides. He lifted the sixteen by twenty-four-inch metal segment out and thumped on the inner wall. Sheet rock. He reached into his backpack and pulled out his Sawzall, twitching the trigger to activate the little light. A few minutes later he'd cut out the sheetrock. He pulled his stocking mask down and crawled into the building, letting the tarp drop down behind him.

He was in some kind of machine shop. *Nothing in here looks proprietary,* he thought. He moved into the huge next room. He wandered around using a dim light and his night vision attachment, looking for something that looked like it might be important tech. Big stainless tables, fancy research machines, various electronics fabrication equipment but nothing that looked like rocket technology.

He found a pile of small disks that were wired to what looked like epoxy bound electronic packages. They were all plugged into a power source. They didn't look like things that'd been purchased, but they didn't look like rocket technology either. He shrugged and slipped two of them into one of the pockets of his cargo pants.

Ah, a model rocket! It was sitting on one of the benches. About 3 inches in diameter and about 3 feet long, with big fins on the back like the rockets in the old sci-fi pulp stories. When he picked it up he nearly dropped it. He'd been expecting an empty shell of lightweight plastic but it was made of metal and felt substantial.

Sonny didn't see anything else and trying to break into encrypted AIs wasn't his strong suit. He headed for hole he'd made in the wall, rocket in hand. Hopefully there'd be a hose on one of the chemical tanks out back that he could drag in here and use to start a fire. That should provide the setback that Dennison asked for.

***

Allan said, "You have another intruder at D5R. This one came in through a wall."

Ell leaped out of bed, pulled on jeans and ran for her car. "Tell Steve and the ready team. Ask them to meet me there."

***

Sonny climbed out the hole and left the rocket under his tarp. He walked over to the tank farm.

After a few minutes he paused with his hands on his hips in frustration. All these big tanks full of chemicals and no hoses! What were they doing, coming out here to get the stuff in buckets? He turned in place, finally seeing a coiled hose over in a corner. He sighed and got it. Fortunately, it did attach to the fitting on an enormous tank of kerosene.

He dragged the other end of the hose into the building through the hole he'd cut and dropped it in the middle of the big room with all the research gear.

Sonny turned the corner back into the machine shop and was startled to find a girl standing there, obviously having just crawled in through the hole he'd made. She was a skinny kid, though kinda tall. Damn! He didn't like hurting people, but maybe he could just tie her up? She wouldn't be able to see anything in the dark.

He wondered if she was waiting for her eyes to adjust to the dark. That wasn't going to happen because it was *really* dark in here. He could barely see her even with his low light goggles. He reached into his bag and pulled out the duct tape then stepped toward her. Her hand moved and he heard a "pop" sound. *Taser!* He thought as his muscles spasmed and he fell to the floor. The girl actually stepped forward and caught him on the way down, keeping him from hitting his face! For a moment he was grateful, then he remembered she was the one that shot him. Before his muscles began to respond again, she'd professionally pulled his hands back and plastic tied them behind him. Then she bound his ankles. *Then* she turned on the light.

He realized she must have been using some kind of night vision too.

She squatted down next to him and he realized she was wearing jeans and a camisole! *The girl looks like a Victoria's Secret model!* She pulled out the Taser dart. Then she pulled off his stocking mask and his AI headband. She looked at the back of it and popped out the PGR chip to disconnect him from his actual AI. Then she pulled off her own AI headband and plugged his chip into a second slot on her headband. She grabbed him by the armpits and lifted him into a sitting position, leaning his back against one of the big machines. He was surprised how strong she was. She gazed at him a moment, looked up at her HUD and said, "So, Sonny Alston, who sent you?"

A spike of fear shot through him, how did she figure out who I was so fast?

Sonny couldn't know Ell's supercomputer AI'd be able to search enormous databases for his face almost instantaneously.

He shrugged.

She was looking up at her HUD. She said musingly, "I see you've been in the joint a couple of times. Breaking and entering seems to be a specialty of yours? But you went up the river for beating up some guys in a bar." She quirked the corners of her lips down. "Hmmm, you aren't a very nice person are you? You went up another time for using a weapon in a robbery? Hmmm." She turned to pick up his back pack, then glanced at him before she unzipped the front flap, "Hope you didn't bring a weapon on this little jaunt cause my AI tells me you go up the river again if you're found carrying a weapon... Aw, Sonny, look at this." She pulled open the flap to show him the gun beneath it. "It's starting to look pretty bad for you. Breaking and entering, theft of that rocket you took outside, a felon carrying a weapon." She shook her head back and forth. "And the hose you dragged in here makes it like you were planning to commit arson. You want to tell me who sent you?"

He narrowed his eyes. "Are you the police? You haven't read me my rights."

"Nope." She said cheerfully. "So I'm not bound by all

those rules that restrain the police."

"You can't make me a deal then either."

"Sure I can…" she paused. "I…" she paused again pointing to her chest, "can just let you go without pressing charges." She quirked an eyebrow at him.

"Why would I trust you?"

"Well, you'd just have to look into my honest eyes and see if you could. Course, the alternative is to go up the river for sure, isn't it?"

Sonny glared at her for a minute. "General Electric."

"What's GE got to do with this?"

"They hired me."

"Now, now, now, GE didn't hire you, some*body* hired you. Maybe they work at GE, maybe they work somewhere else? Who's that somebody?"

Sonny felt like he had pretty good control of his muscles again. It wouldn't do him much good while he was bound hand and foot. However, if he could take her out of the equation a moment, he knew he could get his hands around in front of himself. *In a machine shop there's bound to be plenty of tools that'll cut these damned cable ties*.

He moaned a little. He just needed to get her close enough. Sonny'd been in hundreds of fights. His fists might be restrained, but he knew from personal experience what a good head butt to the face could do. His own crooked nose was the result of a head butt he'd gotten in a fight. He'd been dazed and confused for minutes after it happened. How could he get her close enough? He tried another piteous moan. She grinned at him. "Sonny, you can stop the moaning. I know you haven't been hurt all that badly." Then her eyes narrowed as they focused on his leg. She leaned toward him to him to pat at the lump in his pocket where he'd put the discs with their attached electronics. Sonny lunged up, *hard*, aiming his forehead at her nose. She'd gotten so close he couldn't possibly miss!

To his astonishment, though he would have sworn it was impossible, she easily moved her face out of the way. Instead of his crushing her nose, she casually slapped *him* in the nose. His nose exploded with pain and tears poured out of his eyes.

How in all the Hells did she do that?!

She leaned back, "Sonny, Sonny, Sonny. That wasn't nice. I have to tell you, the encryption on your AI wasn't very good. My AI's finished extracting its memory, including the secret recording you made of your conversation with Mr. Dennison of ILX. I guess I'd just as well call the police." She stood up and stepped away, just as a couple of beefy security types trotted in the door, all out of breath. "Hey guys," she said cheerfully to them, "keep an eye on Mr. Alston here for me, would you?" She left as the security guys narrowed their eyes at him.

One of them squatted down to check his restraints...

***

Ell watched with the group on the big screens in the main research room. The exterior of their modified Lear jet was visible on one. Another showed the virtual remote cockpit. The plane would be flown by AI just like almost all modern jet flights, but they still had one of their pilots standing by at a console to take over in case of any unusual problems that might be outside the AI's parameters. The set up was much like the UAV control stations Ell'd been using a year ago. On one screen you could see the throttles advancing on the virtual station, on another they could see flames and steam blasting out of the engine fairings at the back of the Learjet itself. The rocket engines had been mounted inside the fairings after the jet engines had been removed. They could have removed the fairings and just mounted the much smaller rocket nozzles but they suspected there might be times when they wanted it to *look* like a standard jet, so they'd left the fairings in place. Other than the bump on the middle of the back of the plane where the airlock adaptor had been mounted, it *looked* much the same as it had before it'd been upgraded for space. The attitude thrusters were almost unnoticeable in. Allan said in her ear, "All thrusters except the main engines have been tested to full thrust without problems."

"What's wrong with the main engines?"

"The wheel brakes and chocks aren't strong enough to hold the plane still against the main engines at full power."

"Oh… yeah." Ell chuckled at herself.

A few minutes later they watched on the screen as the little plane shot down the runway and into the sky, quickly fading to a dot. They turned to watch the view out the front windows of the plane, but it was a boring sky blue. Eventually, they all went back to their own projects until someone called out that the view out the front windows of the jet was gradually fading to black.

Ell said, "Allan, how high are we?"

"Fifty-three miles."

"How's the cabin pressure doing?"

"At the equivalent of 8,000 feet, like a commercial airline, Dr. Braun has it set to start valving air into the cabin at that pressure."

"Are we having any trouble maintaining pressure?"

"No. Dr. Braun's installed a large excess of 5cm ports. They have high pressure blowers on them but, without a hull breach, he's just letting standard atmospheric pressure air from the D5R facility leak in through a few of them without using the blowers. This facility's altitude is only 456 feet, so the pressure here's a lot higher than the 8,000 foot setting in the cabin. It'd require a major cabin breach to cause decompression the blowers couldn't handle."

"How'd the main engines perform?"

"102% of expected thrust."

"Please contact Braun for me."

Ell heard Braun's voice, "Hello?"

"Rob, congratulations! It looks like a complete success from here. Are there any problems we're not seeing?"

"No! It's amazing, first launch with everything going right! That's *never* supposed to happen!"

"Bring it back down and we'll get you some supplies to send up to the Station."

"You don't want to go on up to the station this trip?"

"I'd rather go when we can send them some supplies."

"What's wrong with the supplies we've got on board?"

"You've got supplies on board this trip?!"

"Sure, my daddy said you should never plan for failure. We loaded it with fresh and canned food, bottled juices and a bunch of stuff we found on a wish list one of the astronauts put on the net a couple of years ago."

"You sneaky devil! Way to go! Station here we come.

How long'll it take to get there?"

"It won't be for about three hours. We're going up slow so there'll be plenty of time to determine whether we have any vacuum induced failures. We want to know about anything like that *long* before we arrive and find out a failure's resulted in poor control."

"Good thinking. I'm going to contact NASA and see if we can get the replacement rocket nozzle for the CRV to send up on your next mission."

"OK, I'll let you guys know about 20 minutes before we arrive at the Station."

~~~

Ell walked back to her office and sat in her chair thinking for a bit. Then she said, "Allan, let me see an organizational chart for ILX." It popped up on her screen and she studied it. David Dennison was listed as CEO as she'd already known. "Let's see if we can contact Norman James." James was listed as Chief Technology Officer.

Allan said, "Mr. James' AI says he's unavailable."

"Leave him a message that I called and let's see if he calls back."

Ell had Allan try several others near the top of the organizational chart, receiving the same "unavailable" response until she got to a John Clarkson who was listed as a "special assistant" to Dennison. "Mr. Clarkson?"

"Yes." The voice sounded suspicious.

"Can we have a full audio-video chat?"

"OK."

The screen in Ell's office blinked to life showing a taciturn man staring at her with a look of intense interest. "Do you know who I am sir?"

"You're that gymnast from the last Olympics."

Ell nodded. "Is that the only reason you know my name?"

"What is this, some kind of twenty questions?"

"No sir, it just seems surprising that you'd take time out of your busy day to respond to a call from a gymnast?" His eyes flashed. Ell wasn't sure whether in anger or perhaps in trepidation?

"Yeah, I know you work for D5R too."

Ell frowned at him, "And why would you be interested in D5R?"

"D5R's one of our competitors, it's my *business* to know."

"Really? What makes you think we're a competitor for ILX?" Ell saw the surprise in his eyes. They darted around momentarily.

He swallowed, then said, "It's our *business* to know."

"But there isn't any *public* information about our company suggesting that we'd be competitors for ILX."

His eyes flashed, "It's our *business* to know."

Ell frowned, "Have you been investigating us by illegal means?"

"I don't have to listen to this." The video image snapped off.

Allan said, "He's disconnected."

Ell rubbed her chin, "Let's try an audio video connection with Manfred Phelps next."

"Ms. Donsaii? I hope you're reconsidering our offer to purchase your technology." said the deep voice Ell remembered. Phelps had thin dark hair and a beard. He overfilled his chair suggesting he was as large and burly as his voice suggested.

"No sir. I'm just wondering what made you think we had new rocket technology like you wanted to buy."

"Are you trying to say that you don't?"

"No sir. But it was supposed to be a secret. How'd you find out about it?"

"Oh come on kiddo. You used it to rescue the Space Station. Surely you don't think that's a secret?"

"Well in fact I do. Otherwise we'd have reporters all over us here."

He leaned into the camera. "Ms. Donsaii, you're playing with the big boys now. I'd strongly advise you to take our offer before you get *squashed* in the gears of a machine much bigger than you can imagine."

"No thanks." This time Ell cut the connection.

Allan said "You have a call from Norman James, ILX's Chief Technology Officer."

"Put him on, audio video if you can. Mr. James?"

"Yes, Ms. Donsaii?" A video image snapped open showing a slender and intense looking dark man. His eyes tracked over to a spot just below Ell. Presumably the screen below the camera she was seeing him on. "To what do I owe this honor?"

"Honor, sir?"

"Well, *I* consider it an honor to receive a call from someone I fully expect to win the Nobel Prize in physics sometime soon. How may I help you?"

Ell squeaked delightedly. "Really? I don't think so. I just got lucky with that paper." She grinned, "Most people only know me for my gymnastics. I'm always excited to meet someone who's heard of my scientific endeavors."

"Well rest assured, I admire you for both, but my admiration of your scientific endeavors is much greater, probably because of my own bias." He grimaced, "I truly hate to cut this short but I've made some people wait in my outer office while I speak to you. What can I do for you?"

"Well I work for a small company, maybe you've heard of it? D5R?"

James looked mildly embarrassed. "I'm afraid not. What does it do?"

"Research. Manfred Phelps's trying to buy some of our technology."

James eyes widened. "Really!?" His tone was somewhere between surprised and dangerous.

"Yes sir. I'm sorry to have interrupted you. I'll let you get to your meeting, I'm sure we'll be talking more in the near future."

James nodded, a furrow between his eyes. He said, "OK, sure. Talk to you later."

The connection snapped off and Ell leaned back musingly, rubbing her lower lip. The Chief Technology Officer doesn't know anything about a major tech purchase? What *was* going on at ILX? At least it didn't seem like James would have been involved in the hiring of Sonny Alston.

Chapter Five

NASA Director James Epaulding was walking down the hall to a meeting with some ILX reps about the Vulcan 5. He'd been wondering how the new rockets that Donsaii'd developed should bear on these meetings. Several times yesterday he'd considered calling her company to find out how they were coming with their new technology. Interrupting these thoughts, his AI said, "You have a call from Ell Donsaii?"

"Put her on! Ms. Donsaii, what's new at D5R?" a picture of her snapped up on his HUD, but since he wasn't near a screen with a camera she wouldn't be able to see him.

"Hello sir. We've significantly improved our technology."

He grinned, "Yeah! I've seen video of your larger ports delivering fresh fruit to the astronauts. They're really pumped! How much longer do we need to keep this a secret?"

"Not much longer sir. I'll append a little video that you might want to use when it comes time to make an announcement. But what I want to ask about now is whether we can pick up the replacement nozzle for the CRV and deliver it to the station? We have a vehicle big enough to take it up there now."

"Really, that's great! When will you launch?"

"Well, we launched a flight to take supplies to the

station this morning."

"Really? I hadn't heard." He frowned, "Usually the guys make me aware of all the launches from Canaveral."

"We couldn't get permission to launch from Canaveral sir. We've launched from the Bahamas."

"What! Why couldn't you get permission?"

"I'm not sure. I even hired a lawyer with experience obtaining launch permits, but he tells me he's been completely stonewalled."

"Well there is a lot of red tape."

"He couldn't even get the red tape started sir. Perhaps if they'd known who we were? But we've wanted to keep that on the down low."

"Really?" Epaulding said in a speculative tone. "Well, I'll find out where that replacement nozzle is and get back to you." After the connection closed he went on into the ILX meeting still thinking furiously. He'd sat down when he remembered the video that Donsaii'd sent and told his AI to put it up on his HUD.

He watched in amazement as he saw a desolate landscape slowly filling his screens from the bottom. An object came into view. *My God is that... is that one of the lunar landers?! They've sent a mission to the moon? Already?* He suddenly found it hard to concentrate on this meeting about things that now seemed inconsequential. Suddenly he realized that a bunch of amateurs were about to try to dock with the Space Station! *What am I doing in this meeting?* He stood and said, "Sorry, I've just become aware of an urgent event with the Station. I'll have to go; my deputies will handle the rest of this meeting."

To shocked expressions, he strode from the room.

***

Dave Slager's AI said, "You have an urgent call from Houston."

"Yes?"

"Commander Slager, we've picked up a large object moving toward the Station."

His heart skipped a beat, "How big?"

"Largest dimension is about 18 meters sir."

"My God, that's half as big as the old shuttles." *Much bigger than the current supply capsules,* he thought to himself. "Where'd it come from?"

"We only recently picked it up and think it was launched a few hours ago from somewhere in the eastern Atlantic sir."

"Just launched? From Canaveral?"

"Nothing's been launched from Canaveral sir."

"Well, is it going to hit us?!"

"We don't know. It is decelerating at present and may be going to match orbits with you. However, sir, we would suggest you stand by to maneuver the ISS in case it does look like it could impact. We'll try to give you warning, but you might check your radar and start looking out your windows."

"OK, thanks." A shiver went over him and he started calling out to the rest of the astronauts.

Slager's AI said, "Ell Donsaii would like to speak to you."

Nervously wondering whether he should take the time, he said, "Put her on... Ell?"

"Yes sir."

"Sorry to have to rush you, but a large object's closing on the Station and I need to deal with it."

"Oh! I'm so sorry sir. That'd be *our* object. We've

launched you a resupply mission. I should've let you know a couple of hours ago, but we were waiting to make sure it was going to make it all the way up to your orbit."

"Hah! I should have known it'd be you!" to his AI he said, "Let Houston and the other station personnel know what's happening." Then back to Ell, "Are you sending up our CRV nozzle?"

"No sir. In case we're successful with this mission I've just asked Director Epaulding if we can pick it up for our next flight."

"Hmmm, how are we going to transship materials?"

"Well we've built an airlock adapter according to the engineering specs that were available. We couldn't get NASA to let us test it against their dummy lock so we aren't completely sure it will work. But we thought we could try it. Worst case, it leaks some atmosphere out of the lock and the air has to be replaced. Best case, you get some supplies."

"You're kidding. NASA wouldn't let you test against their copy of the lock?!"

"Well to be fair, remember we've asked their brass to keep our involvement with you a secret, so the people who have the lock had no idea who we were."

Slager rolled his eyes. "I still don't know why they wouldn't let you test. It isn't like it would hurt the... Woops, wait one, I have another urgent call from Houston."

"Commander Slager, this is Director Anthony Willis at the Johnson Space Center. Your AI just informed us the object approaching the Station is expected?! Expected by whom?!"

"Sorry, the people who sent up our previous rescue mission are sending up another mission. They just forgot to tell you folks."

"Who?!! Who *is* this secret group?"

"Sorry sir, I'm not at liberty to say at present."

"Commander, you cannot keep me out of this loop any longer! This caused a major panic here. My people and I have a right to know what's going on!"

"Just a minute, I've got a call from Epaulding..."

After a moment they were joined in a four-way connection. Epaulding said, "Dave, I assume you're aware that D5R is sending you a shipment?"

"Yes, but," he cleared his throat, "someone forgot to warn us until after Houston had started to panic."

Director Willis was astonished to hear the voice of a young girl, "We're so, so sorry. This is the first time we've launched anything big and we just didn't even think about how it would look on your radar. It won't happen again. I *will* need to know whom to notify though."

Willis said, "Who *are* you?!"

Ell said, "Uhhh..."

Epaulding said, "Sorry Tony. We've promised some people to keep this secret a little while longer. Right Miss?"

"Uh, yes sir. Maybe another week?" Ell almost squeaked.

"OK, one more week." Epaulding said, "Tony, I promise you'll be the first to know, and it'll be before the public announcement. OK?"

"I don't like it Jim. I think Houston has a need to know *now*."

Ell broke in. "Director Epaulding, it'd be OK with us to let Director Willis in on the secret, if he'll promise it goes no further?"

Epaulding barked a laugh, "Well Tony? Can you keep

Rocket!

a secret?"

"I don't think it's right..."

"Tony," Epaulding interrupted, "it's you alone, or it's no one in Houston. What'll it be?"

"OK." Willis muttered reluctantly.

"OK," Epaulding said, sounding like he was rubbing his hands together, "Let's get full video on this conversation."

~~~

Willis blinked as his screen popped on and showed Epaulding in the upper left, Slager in the upper right, a familiar looking reddish blond girl in the lower left and a glowing dot in the lower right.

Epaulding said, "Tony, meet Ell Donsaii."

The girl gave an embarrassed little wave. "Sorry Director Willis."

"The gymnast?"

"Yes sir." She said quietly.

"And just what in Hell do you have to do with this whole mess?!"

Epaulding interrupted, "Tony, calm down. Her company's the one sending up the mission. We'll explain it better later. First though, how close are we to matching orbits?

Willis realized that the dot had grown in the lower right part of his screen. It looked like a little cross now. A gust of material jetted out of the lumpy end of the cross.

The girl said, "Just a few more minutes."

In the background Willis heard them talking about how to transship materials but his eyes were focused in horrified fascination on the screen as the cruciform structure grew into what, for all the world, looked like a

Lear jet! "Is that an *airplane*?" he asked querulously...

***

Dennison said, "What?!"

"They want the rocket nozzle for the CRV back sir."

"Why?! We'd just have to get it back from them again when we're ready for the next launch."

"Uh, they said they wanted to send it up sooner."

"*Who* do they think's going to take it up there? We've got the contract to supply the Station! Get me Epaulding on the line!"

There was a faint click in Dennison's earpiece, then, "Hello Dave."

"Hi Jim. Someone on your team is asking us to send the CRV nozzle back over to NASA? What's this all about?"

"Yeah, we have another way to get it up there and so for the safety of the astronauts, we'd like to get it up there now rather than waiting until your next launch is ready."

"We'll be ready in six weeks!"

"But we can get it delivered tomorrow."

"Jim," Dennison said dangerously, "You *know* ILX has the contract to supply the station."

"Don't get frosty with me Dave, or do I have to remind you just what a fine job you've been doing of supplying the station this past year?"

"Sure, we've had a few bobbles but..."

"Dave! Those few bobbles nearly cost the lives of eleven astronauts!"

"We've fixed our problem and we have the contract!"

Rocket!

"And are you going to honor your contract now that your high efficiency Vulcan 5 motor is out of the picture?"

"Well, we might have to renegotiate…"

"If, you try to renegotiate, I'm afraid you're going to find yourself out of a contract. However, for right now, our other supplier will deliver the nozzle gratis, so it falls outside the contract between NASA and ILX. Please tell your folks to turn *our* nozzle back over to us."

"Who the Hell's this other supplier?"

"I'm not at liberty to say."

"Is it that damned D5R?"

Epaulding's eyes narrowed, "Who gave you that name?"

"It is, isn't it?! You haven't heard the last of this!"

To Epaulding's surprise Dennison broke the connection.

***

Ell looked around at her team. "So, 'Amelia,' as Rob has named our first launch vehicle," Ell waved at Braun, visible on the screen though he was actually on the island in the Bahamas, "successfully landed after delivery of a big load of supplies to the Station. Kudos to Brian; the airlock adaptor worked perfectly! We did have an issue with a couple of the aileron motors freezing up. Their regular lubricant hadn't been completely replaced with vacuum tolerant molybdenum disulfide and their bearings froze. The AI was able to compensate with the attitude thrusters in the wings though. So! A little 'hooah' for the team that put up a nearly perfect first space mission!" Ell pumped her fist and led a lusty cheer.

"Next—we have *one* more week, then I've agreed to let NASA tell the world what we've been doing. After which," she rolled her eyes, "we'll be besieged by reporters. So—I'd like to land small rockets on Mars and on an asteroid so we have some footage to show 'em when the time comes. And, of course," she rubbed her hands together, "I've got to get up into space myself. You guys have any other ideas or suggestions? Can we do all that or do we need to pare back?

The room stared at her in shock for a moment. Then Fred said, "*You* can't go! If something happened and you died out there it'd be an immeasurable loss!"

Ell frowned, "I can so go! It's my life, to do with what I wish. Besides, if someone else died out there, riding my idea, it'd destroy my life anyway! We'll send Amelia up a bunch more times to be sure she's safe before anyone goes up."

The people in the room glanced wide-eyed at one another. Then Ben said, "Armstrong has a couple of brothers ready to go. We've named them Buzz and Collins so that we have the first three letters of the alphabet *and* the full crew of the first moon mission. They have bigger specimen containers and their collection arms have little electromagnetic jackhammers on them to chip off specimens. For the Mars mission we want to send back some of the polar ice. John already picked a near earth approach asteroid, 2021 MG12, that's expected to pass close to earth next year. If a specimen looked promising, it might be worth trying to divert it into earth orbit for mining.

Rob said, "Amelia's ready to go up for another trial run as soon as the other Lear Jet returns with replacement motors for the ailerons. Should be sometime tonight, so we should be able to launch again in the morning.

As the meeting broke up Ell touched Fred on the arm, "Hey Fred, I do appreciate what you were saying about me there. But really, I'm just someone who's been extraordinarily lucky with a few guesses in physics. I'm *not* irreplaceable."

Fred stared at her for a moment, then in a husky voice said, "I think the human race needs someone as lucky as you then."

To her surprise Ell realized his eyes were glistening. "Hey, Fred..."

He put a hand on her shoulder as his throat labored for a moment. Finally, he said, "Working with you has been an honor and a, a, privilege. I hope to brag about it to my grandchildren someday."

Ell found a frog in her own throat, "Thank you for... for what you're saying. I don't believe I deserve it, but I truly do appreciate the sentiment."

***

"Buzz" had been launched on its journey to asteroid 2021 MG12 and "Collins" had been launched to Mars. Ell had installed her modified circuits on the ports for Collins to allow it to reach 150km/sec. Since Mars wasn't very far from Earth at present Collins could make the trip in six days. Allan was flying Collins so others wouldn't be aware of the speed it was achieving, at least until someone tried to replicate the feat someday. She hoped no one would think to calculate how long it *should* take Collins to reach Mars. It'd be landing sometime around their one-week deadline for going public.

Ell and Roger were on their way to look at Roger's mice and bee colony when Allan said, "You've got a call from the President."

Roger was surprised to see Ell stop and come to attention. "Yes sir," she said.

President Teller said, "Ms. Donsaii, I've been approached to help broker another deal like I did between PGR Comm and the existing telecomm industries. I've been informed, and my advisers agree, that your new port technology threatens to produce huge upheavals in the space and satellite launch industries like PGR did in telecomm?"

"Yes sir. Probably some other industries as well."

"Really?"

"Yes sir. This tech should result in significant changes in the delivery of liquid or gaseous commodities currently transported by pipeline and ship. The obvious ones are oil, natural gas and fresh water from areas of abundance to areas of scarcity. The Navy should want this technology for submarine supply, perhaps for surface ships. The Air Force could keep planes in the air indefinitely. In fact, probably all aircraft should be supplied with fuel by port so they don't have to inefficiently lift all their fuel into the air. I could go on?"

President Teller felt his own eyes goggling. He cleared his throat, "Uh, OK. But back to the purpose of this call. David Dennison, CEO of ILX tells me that he's attempted unsuccessfully to negotiate with you for a license?"

Ell restrained herself from snarling. She'd been talking to the police about how to go about charging someone like Dennison. She said "One of Mr. Dennison's minions, a Mr. Manfred Phelps did call about purchasing the technology, yes sir."

Teller thought that the term "minion" sounded a little prejudicial, but decided to push on. "I was hoping you might be willing to join myself and Mr. Dennison here in Washington sometime in the next few days so that I could attempt to broker a renegotiation?"

After a pause, she said, "I'd be happy to negotiate and to have you mediate. However, NASA has given us a six-day deadline to go public and I am very heavily committed to achieving certain goals prior to that deadline. My AI tells me that the best time to fly up to D.C.... would be late tomorrow afternoon?"

"One moment... Yes, that'd be fine."

"May I make a couple of conditions?"

"Such as?"

"I would like to have all or at least a majority of the ILX board present as well?"

"Okaay..." Teller said, wondering why the CEO wouldn't be enough. He shrugged, thinking, *She has the whip hand. Dennison'll just have to lean on his board to be there.*

"And I feel it'd only be fair to invite some of ILX's competitors to such a meeting as well?"

Oh ho! Teller chortled to himself, *Dennison's gonna be pissed! But he's going to have to give and take if he wants to get his hands on this tech.* Teller nodded, "That seems acceptable in the light of an effort to prevent upheavals in the industry. Would three thirty be acceptable?"

"Yes sir."

"I'll expect you here at the White House then. Directions for getting through security will be sent to your AI. I'm also going to ask Chip Horton and some of my economic advisers to video conference with you about these other upheavals you spoke of?"

"Yes sir. Perhaps Defense Secretary Amundsen also? But could those conferences wait until the next week; after we've gone public?"

"Sure. I'll see you tomorrow." The President disconnected, then stared at the ceiling a moment before asking his AI to set up a video conference with Horton and Amundsen.

Ell said, "Allan, please make a reservation for me and the on duty security team for a flight to D.C. tomorrow that'll arrive by at 2:30 at the latest."

Allan said "OK."

Roger said, "Why aren't you using your Lear Jet?!"

Ell stopped in her tracks. She'd completely forgotten the Lear Jet! She grinned at Roger, "You mean the company's Lear Jet?"

Roger snorted.

Allan said, "You'll have to fly out of RDU at 11:30 in the morning to make D.C. in time."

Ell cringed, she wanted to be here at D5R to watch Amelia's flights with the team tomorrow! "Allan, is the Lear Jet busy tomorrow?" She chewed her lip.

"No." Allan said, "But we'd need to fly it back from the Bahamas this evening to allow for crew rest."

"OK," she rolled her eyes, feeling terribly frivolous. "Do that and we'll take it to D.C. tomorrow."

~~~

The mice and bees all *seemed* healthy. Roger expressed concern that he wasn't all that great at taking care of such animals. He worried that some of them might die from incompetent care rather than the effects of going through a port.

Ell suggested that he call the pet store and see if

they had anyone he could outsource the animal care to.

Walking back Ell heard Allan say, "You have a call from NASA Director Epaulding."

"Put him on. Yes Dr. Epaulding?"

"Hello Ms. Donsaii. I'm calling about the public announcement of D5R's role in the rescue of the Space station."

"Yes sir?"

"That video clip you sent me. Was that... was that doctored video? Or did someone really take it at the first Lunar landing site?"

"Oh! That wasn't a manned landing sir. We just filmed it with one of our small remotely controlled rockets."

Just filmed by a small rocket! he thought to himself, *My God, she says it like anyone could have done it.* "Uh, so... so far you've sent a mission to the Space Station and, and to the *Moon*?"

"Yes sir."

"Is there anything *else* we'll need to be announcing?"

"Sir, that depends on exactly when you decide to make the announcement. We'll have one of our little rockets landing on an asteroid sometime this week. And late Sunday morning we'll be landing a small rocket on Mars. We're planning to land at the South Pole to collect some ice, but could land somewhere else if your scientists would prefer it?"

Epaulding felt like someone'd just kicked him. He'd been walking to a meeting while talking to Ell, but suddenly turned into an empty room and sat down. Leaning forward he rested his elbows on his knees and his forehead on his hands. He said heavily, "Anything else?"

Laurence E Dahners

"Well, if you've got the CRV nozzle back from ILX, I was thinking we could take it up, plus perhaps any new astronauts you're wanting to send up, make the announcement from the Station, and return with any astronauts that are due to return?"

Epaulding sat, stunned, contemplating the enormity of the changes that had just arrived in his world as Director of NASA.

"Director? Are you still there?"

Epaulding shook his head. "Yes, Ms. Donsaii," he sighed, "I'm still here. How many flights has your modified Lear Jet made into space?"

"It just took off on its second one sir. Our only issue with the first one was the boiling off of a vacuum unsuitable lubricant that hadn't been adequately replaced on two of the aileron motors. But we do want to make several more unmanned flights into orbit before we trust it to fly any people. I'll be going on that first manned flight, so I'll want to be pretty confident it's going to be OK."

Epaulding closed his eyes. "Ms. Donsaii, I get the impression that you're the brain trust of D5R. Are your investors really going to approve your taking a jaunt into space?!"

"Um, yes sir. The investors are OK with it."

"OK..." he said heavily, "how about if we send a couple of experienced aviator-astronauts down to your island to inspect your air... er, spacecraft and watch some of the unmanned flights. Then we can decide whether we believe it to be safe as well? Perhaps we might be able to use some astronauts that are due for a rotation to the Station at the same time. I'll have to check."

"That'd be great sir." Ell said brightly. "Might I

request one of your inexperienced astronauts as well?"

Epaulding blinked several times, "Why?"

"Personal favor, sir. Lieutenant Phillip Zabrisk has recently begun his basic astronaut training, but he's a friend who's always wanted to go to space. I'd like to be part of his achieving his dream early."

"But, but he'd be virtually untrained!"

"Pardon sir, but so am I. Flying up in Amelia will be much like a long airplane flight. Well, except for the weightlessness of course. It would, of course, be great to have some experienced people along too."

Chapter Six

Ell and five of her security team trotted across the tarmac at the RDU airport to D5R's Lear Jet. With them, bouncing excitedly, came Mikey and Janey and their mother Amy. When Amy found out they were taking their private Lear Jet to D.C. in the summer she'd decided it was prime time for a field trip with her kids and boss.

On arrival in DC Amy and her kids headed to the Smithsonian while Ell and her team took taxis to the White House. Amy'd arranged a limo, but Steve cancelled it, feeling that it was more secure, at least as concerned kidnappings, to take a random taxi than a pre arranged limo.

At the White House there was some confusion over the arrival of guests by taxi, but after some checking of IDs, Ell was admitted and her security team assigned a place to wait.

When she arrived in the conference room the table was moderately well populated with people in suits. To her surprise, many of them were asking one another if they knew the purpose of the meeting. No one seemed to know who she was, though several narrowed their eyes as if thinking she looked familiar. However, she figured they may have been wondering what a teenager was doing at the meeting.

Eventually the President entered with David

Dennison. Their entry together concerned Ell. She wondered how much cronyism it indicated. Dennison's eyes flashed angrily around the room at his competitors.

Ell had led the rise of the roomful of people to their feet when the President entered. He looked at her and nodded, "Please be seated," he said, looking around the room. "I appreciate your willingness to attend this meeting of aerospace industry representatives upon my request. Especially, I appreciate your coming without more foreknowledge of the topic to be discussed and for agreeing to keep it confidential until next week."

The people at the table glanced at one another questioningly.

Teller said, "As you'll recall, a company called PGR Comm recently released new communication chips onto the market that immediately produced calamitous upheavals in the communication industry and in the financial markets as a whole. My administration and I were able to calm the troubled seas as it were, by bringing together the industry's major players and brokering a licensing deal that has allowed many of the involved companies to survive and prosper, rather than being overwhelmed by a competitor who had a crushing technological edge.

"What you likely do *not* realize, is that a similar sea change is about to occur in your own industry. A very small company by the name of D5Research actually launched the rescue of the International Space Station during the recent stream of problems it had encountered.

"D5R accomplished this feat after developing a revolutionary new technology that is going to upend the space launch industry just as substantively as the

PGR chips did telecomm."

Startled looks had broken out around the room, though no one appeared to be panicked yet.

Teller turned to Ell, "Ms. Donsaii here represents D5R. Would you mind giving us a brief summary of the capabilities of D5R's new technology please?"

Ell felt the eyes of the room turning to focus on her as she rose to her feet. She could almost hear their thoughts as they wondered why D5R hadn't sent someone with more seniority to a meeting at the White House. She cleared her throat, "Thank you Mr. President. D5R's developed a means to create small 'ports' or 'wormholes' through the 5th dimension from one location in our 3D universe to another. The two ends of the wormhole must both be defined by a quantum entangled device we've developed. Although it is theoretically possible to open large portals, large portals require extremely large energy inputs. Thus, so far we've only focused on small portals. These have enabled us to fuel small rockets that have been able to ascend to orbit. For those of you who haven't had time to consider the possibilities, it may not be obvious that the huge rockets we use currently are only necessary because of the need to launch fuel for the rest of the flight. With our ability to port fuel to the rocket, it doesn't have to lift the huge tanks that are currently necessary, so a rocket less than a foot long can actually make orbit. More recently we've been able to fuel a craft large enough to transport eleven people to orbit in this fashion. In addition, since our first small rocket arrived there, we've been able to supply the International Space Station with oxygen, water and food through such ports..." Ell paused as the room exploded in exclamations, expletives, and vehement denials of the possibility that this could be true. With some amusement she heard the words, "pipe dream."

Even Dennison, who'd known that D5R had *some* kind of technology that he wanted for his company, couldn't believe what he'd just heard.

After a minute of vehement protest by individuals who just couldn't believe such things were possible, President Teller banged a small gavel. Once the room fell silent he said, "You may shout your disbelief as long as you wish after this meeting is completed. I'm here to tell you that what Ms. Donsaii has just told you is verifiable fact. I'm also here to determine whether we can negotiate a settlement that might allow your companies to survive and thrive, rather than wither and die in the face of such a competitive edge."

Teller turned back to Ell, "ILX tells me that you have not been receptive to offers from them, yet you implied when you and I spoke that you would be willing to consider licensing your technology. Can you explain?"

"Yes sir. The following's an audio recording of my first contact with ILX.

~~~

Phelps - "Hello, I'm Manfred Phelps and I represent ILX."

Donsaii - "Yes?"

Phelps - "I've been authorized to offer your investors fifty million dollars for the exclusive rights to this new rocket technology D5R has been using." Everyone in the room could hear Phelps' implicit assumption that Ell should be stunned by the amount he'd offered.

Donsaii - "Oh! I'm sorry Mr. Phelps, that tech isn't for sale at present. At some point in the future we do expect to license it, but not for quite a while yet."

Phelps - Unperturbed, "Alternatively we're prepared to offer 250 million dollars to purchase the company outright."

Donsaii - "Um, D5R isn't for sale either Mr. Phelps."

Phelps - "Ms. Donsaii," Phelps patiently lecturing now, "please let me talk to whomever's actually in charge there."

Donsaii - Quietly, "I'm D5R's CEO, Mr. Phelps."

Phelps - "Ms. Donsaii," with the air of someone whose patience was wearing thin, "I haven't been able to find your articles of incorporation on the web as yet, but surely even you realize that once we do, we can simply make this offer to your Board and they'll override you?"

Donsaii - "Oh, I don't think that'll happen, Mr. Phelps."

Phelps - "Ms. Donsaii, I assure you that investors are surprisingly fickle when they see a chance to obtain a very large return on their investment. Especially," he said ominously, "when they learn that the alternative would be for their little company to compete against a corporation like ILX, one that has billions of dollars in capital."

Donsaii - (Crowd noise in background) "Back to what you were saying, I'm confident that our investors won't be fickle. Also, since the technology D5R is using is based on completely new theoretical physics, the patents should stand up well to any assaults by well-heeled lawyers."

Phelps - "Ms. Donsaii! A patent search doesn't even turn up any new rocketry patents!"

Donsaii - "Well that would be true. You can rest assured; however, that patent protection has been applied for. It's just so recent that the application hasn't been made public as yet."

Phelps - "You don't even have a patent?! It's entirely possible that a patent might not even be granted! All the more reason your investors may jump ship! I'd strongly urge you reconsider before ILX reduces the offer."

Donsaii - "Sorry Mr. Phelps, but we really don't have anything to worry about, either regarding the uniqueness of the intellectual property nor the confidence of our investors."

Phelps -"Ms. Donsaii you are going to regret this decision!" Phelps said ominously, then broke the connection.

~~~

Ell's eyes swept the room. "I would not characterize *that* conversation as a 'negotiation.' I would characterize it as more in the nature of a browbeating. There was no question posed regarding what we might be *willing* to license for, or *when* we would be ready to license. There was simply an extremely undervalued offer which was rejected with no further offers forthcoming."

"Undervalued!" Dennison exclaimed. "250 *million* dollars!"

"Yes undervalued, Mr. Dennison. That offer to purchase D5R wasn't a lot more than ILX charges for an orbital flight."

Dennison took a deep breath, but before he could say anything, Ell held up a hand, looked to Teller and said, "I believe I have the floor?"

The President nodded.

Ell resumed, "The next contact D5R had from ILX came in through the back wall of our building." Video popped up on screens all around the room showing someone lifting a tarp up to reveal a hole cut in the back of a building.

A spike of fear shot through Dennison. He hadn't heard from Sonny since he deposited the hundred and twenty-five thousand in an account for him. But Sonny wasn't very communicative under any circumstances. Dennison'd only been worrying because he hadn't heard anything about the expected setback, nor received his information about D5R's tech yet.

~~~

The camera, obviously on someone's AI headband, ducked down to enter the building, then rose up in what appeared to be a machine shop. The lighting was odd, though some recognized it as typical for what's seen through self-lighted infrared night vision goggles. A man wearing gloves and a stocking mask turned the corner into the machine shop and appeared startled to find someone there. He paused a moment, then reached into his bag and pulled out a roll of duct tape. He stepped toward the camera, reaching out, obviously intent on restraining the person with the camera. A "pop" sound could be heard and the man's muscles spasmed. He fell to the floor, though whoever shot him also caught him and slowed his descent to keep him from hitting his head. Before his muscles began to respond again his hands had been professionally pulled back and plastic ties used to restrain them behind him. Then his ankles. Then the lights were turned on.

~~~

Dennison barked, "What does a break in at your facility have to do with this tech?!"

Rocket!

Ell paused the video, raised a finger and waggled it back and forth, then the video resumed.

~~~

The man's stocking mask was pulled off and then his AI headband.

~~~

Dennison's stomach clenched. *Sonny!*

~~~

Sonny was lifted by the armpits into a sitting position, his back to one of the big machines. "So, Sonny Alston, who sent you?" It was a girl's voice. Donsaii's!

She said musingly, "I see you've been in the joint a couple of times. Breaking and entering seems to be a specialty of yours. But you went up the river for beating up some guys in a bar." There was a pause "You aren't a very nice person are you? You went up another time for using a weapon in a robbery? Hmmm." She turned to pick up his back pack, then turned back toward him momentarily before she unzipped the front flap, "Hope you didn't bring a weapon on this little jaunt 'cause my AI tells me you go up the river again if you're found carrying a weapon... Aw, Sonny, look at this." She pulled open the flap to show him the gun within. "It's starting to look pretty bad for you. Breaking and entering, theft of that rocket you've got outside, carrying a weapon as a felon." She shook her head back and forth. "And the hose you dragged in here makes it like you were planning to commit arson. You sure you don't want to tell me who sent you?"

He narrowed his eyes. "Are you the police? You haven't read me my rights."

"Nope." She said cheerfully. "So I'm not bound by all those rules that restrain the police."

"You can't make me a deal then either."

"Sure I can…" she paused. "I…" she paused again, "can just let you go without pressing charges."

"Why would I trust you?"

"Well, you'd just have to look into my honest eyes and see if you could. Of course, the alternative's to go up the river for sure, isn't it?"

The man glared at her for a minute. "General Electric."

"What's GE got to do with this?"

"They hired me."

"Now, now, now, GE didn't hire you, some*body* hired you. Maybe they work at GE, maybe they work somewhere else? Who is that somebody?"

She leaned near to him to pat at a lump in his pocket. The man lunged up to head butt her. To everyone's astonishment she easily dodged him, slapping him in the face.

She leaned back as the man's nose began to bleed, "Sonny, Sonny, Sonny. That wasn't nice. I have to tell you, the encryption on your AI wasn't very good. My AI's extracted its memory, including the secret recording you made of your conversation with Mr. Dennison from ILX. I guess I'll just go ahead and call the police." She stood up and stepped away. Her cameras now showed a couple of beefy security types trotting in the door, out of breath. "Hey guys," she said to them, "please keep an eye on Mr. Alston here for me, would you?"

~~~

Dennison lunged to his feet, so angry he was

shaking, "I can't believe you're trying to imply..."

Ell simply waggled her finger again and tapped her ear. She said, "Mr. Dennison used a fake accent in his surreptitiously recorded meeting with Mr. Alston, but even without an AI's confirmation, I believe that you'll all recognize his voice."

~~~

Dennison - "We've got a problem suited to your unique skills."

A pause where nothing is said.

Dennison - "There's a facility called D5R in the Research Triangle Park in North Carolina that's supposedly launching rockets to orbit with some new kind of technology."

Another pause where nothing is said.

Dennison - "They need to have a setback. We need samples of the tech.'"

Another pause where nothing is said.

Dennison - "How much?"

Alston - "Ten grand just to look it over and price it."

~~~

Ell said, "So, Mr. Dennison claims to have attempted to negotiate a deal. But, actually, through Manfred Phelps, made a single, ridiculously lowball, offer. Then he arranged for a common criminal to attempt to steal our technology and provide us a 'setback.' The police tell me that the night that Mr. Alston broke into our facility, Mr. Dennison transferred $125,000 to an offshore account that was closed an hour later. Mr. Alston'd already dragged a fuel hose into the building from the tank farm out back when he was apprehended. He's admitted to the police that the setback he'd planned involved running kerosene into the building through the hose and starting a fire. At the end of the kerosene hose stood a device that was set to generate sparks after a delay of one hour."

She took a deep breath. "Mr. President, D5R is *willing* to license this technology to other companies, nonexclusively, at rates that will allow those companies to do what they've already been doing, but at tremendously reduced cost. Even ILX may obtain a license, but only if Mr. Dennison, Mr. Clarkson and Mr. Phelps are relieved of their positions."

Ell looked over at the people from the ILX board. "The police are almost ready to file their charges against Mr. Dennison anyway. I doubt you want to have a felon leading your company."

The board members glanced grimly at one another.

The room was dead silent. People in the room were looking at Dennison the way you might regard something particularly disgusting you'd found on your shoe. Dennison's face was ashen, he licked his lips and said, "That video has been *doctored*. I *never* said that to anyone…"

President Teller looked like he had a very sour taste in his mouth…

***

In his ear, Phil's AI said, "You've just received instructions from the Director's office to leave this class, get your travel kit with clothing etcetera, for one week's stay and report to the main entrance."

"Leave class?!"

"Yes, the orders come from the Director's office."

Rocket!

Phil shook his head; he did *not* want to fall behind on his training. On the other hand, you didn't get assigned missions by pissing off the director. He put up his hand and when the instructor recognized him said, "Sir, I've just received orders from the Director's office to report to the main entrance."

The instructor sighed exasperatedly and said, "Well, you'd better go then hadn't you."

Phil wasn't sure whether the sigh was because he'd asked permission or because the Director's office had seen fit to remove him from the class.

~~~

When Phil got down to the main entrance he found two of the more senior astronauts waiting there. He recognized Chuck Lane who was an Air Force Academy grad about fifteen years his senior. He'd been a fighter pilot before opting for astronaut training. Phil introduced himself and they shook hands. They'd all apparently received similar instructions. Lane introduced Phil to Zeke Potter, who also turned out to be an academy grad with flying experience. None of them knew where they were going or why, but they all had their travel kits with them. Phil said, "Hope it's something good!"

Zeke shook his head sadly, "It rarely is my friend, it rarely is."

One of NASA's ubiquitous vans showed up and took them to the airfield where a Lear Jet waited. They were welcomed aboard by one of the pilots who, when questioned, said, "I'm supposed to take you to the Bahamas. It's all hush-hush, so I don't know much more than that. I'm not sure I'm supposed to tell you that much."

The three of them rode in comfort in a cabin with seating for nine. They raided a well-stocked pantry, taking a few drinks to the pilots who finally confessed that they were going to a private island in the Bahamas that had its own airfield. At that point they reached a dead end on either the knowledge of the pilots, or what they were willing to tell.

Phil leaned back and waved his Coke expansively. "The Bahamas! Can't be all bad."

Zeke morosely shook his head. "Such naiveté."

~~~

At sunset they landed on a small island and were shown to rooms in a large whitewashed mansion by a staff of very polite native Bahamians. They were offered a dinner of locally caught snapper and eagerly agreed. Another jet landed while they drank High Rock Lager on a huge patio and waited for their food. It looked like another Lear Jet, but its engines had a bizarrely high pitch.

Silence settled and the sound of the surf below the porch took over. Phil tried again, "A beer, the Bahamas, someone cooking fish. Can't be all bad." He looked at Zeke out of the corner of his eye.

Zeke looked pleasantly relaxed. Nonetheless, he morosely said, "Just wait for the other shoe to drop."

Chuck snorted. "Give it up Zabrisk. Potter here has a deep suspicion of things that go well and feels that the only antidote is moaning about how bad the future's gonna be. He'd be complaining if you hung him with a carbon fiber rope."

Phil leaned back in his chair and put his arms behind his head, "Well, *I'm* happy."

Zeke moaned piteously.

Rocket!

~~~

A waiter brought out their fish and was followed by a slender man with a crew cut carrying a plate for himself. He said, "Hey, you guys must be the astronauts. I'm Robert Braun." He pointed to a man following behind him, "This is Gene Mort, my assistant. And those guys," He pointed to a group of four behind Gene, "are our aircraft mechanics, Joe, Manny, Meg, and Dennis."

The mechanics waved and sat at another table, Braun sat with the astronauts and leaned forward, "Do you guys know what you're doing here yet?"

The three slowly shook their heads.

Braun grinned and rubbed his hands together, "We're going to fly up to the ISS Saturday!"

"What?" Chuck exclaimed.

Zeke moaned, but said nothing.

Phil's hair stood on end. Did Braun work for the company that'd rescued the Space Station?!

While they ate, Braun gleefully told them that he did indeed work for the company that'd rescued the Station. However, he explained that they'd done it with a small, AI piloted, rocket.

To their wide-eyed consternation, he explained what ports were and how they allowed a small rocket to fly all the way to orbit. "But we haven't flown a manned flight yet." Braun said, "You guys are here to help us figure out if we're ready to do so."

Apparently, in the morning they were to inspect a new spacecraft and evaluate it during an unmanned flight to orbit. They were to use their aeronautical and space experience to determine whether they felt it was safe enough for a manned flight.

Phil said, "Why am I here? I just started training."

Braun stared at him. "Really?"

Phil nodded.

"Sorry," he shrugged. "*I* have no idea. My understanding was that we were getting experienced pilot-astronauts."

~~~

After a sleepless night, the astronauts were horrified to find that the craft being sent into orbit was a modified Lear Jet! Chuck and Zeke began listing all the reasons why that was a terrible idea and would never work. Braun met each objection with a well-reasoned explanation. Chuck rapped the wing, "Without ceramic tiles it'll burn up on re-entry!"

Braun looked at him in exasperation. "Have you been *listening*? It's already re-entered four times! With essentially unlimited fuel, we simply retrorocket until it gets down to where it's just beginning to engage the atmosphere. Then we point the nose up so that the rocket's thrust maintains that altitude while continuing to reduce speed until it's moving slowly enough to tolerate the airspeed. *Then* we lower the nose and let it fly into the atmosphere!"

Zeke grunted, "The tires are going to fail in vacuum."

"Once again! It's been to space and landed *four* times. The tires have spun fiber *and* are vacuum tolerant. *But*, we also use ports to lower the pressure in them after take off and re-inflate them before landing. We're still planning to change them before the manned flight though."

Eventually convinced that it might be possible, *if* all the "port" stuff actually worked, the astronauts inspected the modified Lear Jet. They had the mechanics open and close panels and answer questions. While they were doing that the other Lear Jet took off and turned back towards the States.

Late morning, they launched Amelia again, watching her turn west and climb at an astonishing rate that had Zeke shaking his head. Then they trooped back inside to watch the screens at the control station as the sky went from blue to black and the curve of the Earth became apparent. When Amelia reached an altitude of 200 miles, the instruments showed the cabin was still pressurized. In fact, it maintained the pressure of an 8,000-foot altitude using only about 10% of the ports that had been installed to pressurize the cabin and compensate for leaks. It did it without the port blowers being activated. All the equipment on board apparently still functioned. Zeke sat down at the duplicate controls and undertook some maneuvers—rolls, accelerations, end over end flips and decelerations. Then he morosely got up and let Chuck fly it some. Eventually, they had the AI turn it for home and trooped in for a late lunch.

Phil took a nap to make up for his lost sleep the night before. When he got up he saw Zeke out going over Amelia with the mechanics again. Phil went for a swim.

When he got back up to the airfield, many of the panels were still off Amelia. Zeke had his head up inside the underbody of the plane. From behind him Chuck said, "Zeke may piss and moan, but there isn't anyone that's more careful or more thorough. If he says it's safe to fly—it'll be safe to fly."

That evening as they sat down to dinner, Braun said, "So what do you think guys? Is it safe for us to take it up tomorrow?"

Chuck and Phil both looked to Zeke who sat frowning at his paella. Finally, he shrugged, "I guess so."

Braun exploded, "You guess! Did you find anything wrong, or not?!"

Chuck laid a hand on Braun's arm, "Dr. Braun, 'I guess,' is as good as you will ever get from the chronically gloomy Major Potter." He patted Braun's wrist, "Take what you can get."

"Well then, are we ready to take her up for a manned flight tomorrow morning?"

Zeke shook his head, "Chuck and I'll take it up alone the first time."

Braun said, "I built it, I've got to go."

Zeke rolled his eyes.

Chuck said, "It's just crazy to risk a lot of people on the first manned flight. It's also poor planning to take passengers on a test flight. If something goes wrong, Zeke and I shouldn't be worrying about our passengers, we should be handling the bird." He looked back and forth at the others. "How about this. What you really want is to get up to the ISS tomorrow night, right?"

Braun shrugged, then nodded.

"OK, in the morning we take it up to 65 miles, 'the edge of space.' We do it in an oxygen atmosphere and pre-breathe O2 before we go so that if there *is* a decompression we won't get the bends. If something happens, we can get down quickly and we'll be prepared for it. We come back and land, if everything went smoothly, we go up in the afternoon with you guys."

Braun said, "I should go too. In an emergency bag if you want, but I know Amelia's systems better than anyone, if you're in trouble, you'll *need* me."

"What you know, you can tell us over the comm. You've never been in free fall have you?"

Braun shook his head.

Rocket!

"Seriously, *if* we have trouble, you'll likely be contributing to it by flailing around in the weightless environment."

~~~

As they finished eating, they discussed safety precautions they could take during the manned flight.

~~~

Zeke and Chuck slept in the plane that night so they could be in a pure oxygen environment to prepare for an emergency decompression. A couple of hours later, when they landed in Amelia, even Zeke admitted that everything had gone perfectly. Well, he didn't say "perfectly," he said, "OK," but everything had gone exactly as planned.

~~~

The two astronauts and all four mechanics spent a couple of hours going over the modified Lear Jet again. Phil followed Chuck around, trying to learn, but actually so excited he could hardly pay attention. The thought, *I'm going up in space!* kept ricocheting through his mind.

They loaded the rocket nozzle for the Station's Crew Return Vehicle and some more supplies and strapped them securely into place. Finally, they all got in and put on their emergency suits. Braun watched while Phil practiced reaching back to grab the slightly dome shaped transparent cover for the suit and sealing it.

The mechanics were still working on something so Phil heard the other Lear Jet land. Braun leaned up into the cockpit to tell the two astronauts it'd be a little longer. Apparently, a few more supplies had been delivered for the Space Station along with another passenger.

Zeke practically exploded, "This is *not* a joyride!"

Braun spoke quietly, but Phil heard snatches, "...our CEO... deserves a ride..."

Phil rolled his eyes, picturing some pompous businessman with no clue about space, horning in on what Phil thought of as "his trip."

Phil's nerves jittered and he wondered if he should go back to the head and empty his bladder one more time. Then he heard the chatter of the mechanics and the door of the jet was being closed back behind him. Braun went back, apparently to help the CEO into his emergency suit and Phil wondered if *he* should offer to help. After all, the guy was probably clueless and would need baby sitting for every little thing.

Phil wasn't contributing much otherwise; at the least he could baby-sit. Before he actually unbuckled he heard them coming up the aisle so he settled back and tried again to relax. Someone leaned down next to him. He had started to turn when he heard Ell's voice! "Hi Phil," it whispered in his ear.

He leaned back wide eyed, to see her grinning down at him. She winked, "I'm all googly eyed already..."

Rocket!

Epilogue

Dave Slager closed his eyes in satisfaction as he bit into his "fruit-urrito." Taste sensations exploded across his palate and he grinned to himself. It'd been his idea to have Jose roll peanut butter, chunks of banana, grapes, blueberries and blackberries all into a tortilla. He loved fruit-urritos and the other astronauts had begun ordering them as well. As he took a second bite, his AI said, "You have a call from Ms. Ell Donsaii."

He chewed quickly and swallowed. "Yes?"

Ell's bubbly voice came over his earphones, "Dr. Slager, sorry, Dave! We've got a CRV nozzle to deliver! We should be there in about an hour and a half."

"Really! That's great! We'll be expecting you."

After they signed off, he turned with relish back to his fruit-urrito.

~~~

Eighty-five minutes later he watched as D5R's modified Lear Jet approached on little jets from its thrusters.

Anya Stolchya manned the robotic Canadarm that grab Amelia and brought her adaptor to the airlock, though Slager suspected the precision control of the AI flying Amelia, especially using all those attitude thrusters, could have done it without the arm. Once they had a good seal and had pressurized the airlock,

Slager opened the lock door and asked Ell to open Amelia's side of the airlock. As it had before, air gusted from the sea level pressure in the Station's lock into Amelia where the pressure was set to be the same as 8,000 feet. The pressure held. Slager said, "OK, Ell go ahead and close the door and we'll put someone in the lock to start the unloading."

He heard her grunt, then say, "Wait 'til we put some stuff in the lock for you."

A box slowly sailed into the lock, followed by another one. Startled, Slager realized *this* mission was manned!

One by one, the boxes kept coming until the lock was moderately full. Then a slender, reddish blond girl squirmed into the lock amongst the boxes and said, "OK, close the lock and bring up the pressure."

A couple of minutes later a few boxes sailed into the Station followed by Donsaii still yawning to crack her ears from the air pressure changes. Slager reached out to catch her, expecting her to flail around like most people did when they first tried to do things in zero gravity. He was astonished to see her sail to a stanchion and grab on without difficulty, then she launched herself to Slager and grabbed him for a big hug. "Hi, Dr. Slager! Great to finally meet you in person!" she said, grinning from ear to ear.

"Wow!" Slager said, astonished to realize the girl was *just* as pretty as she looked on screen. "You're handling yourself really well for someone experiencing free fall for the first time."

"Hah!" She laughed, "Am not! I spent 20 minutes barfing when we first went weightless." She grinned and raised an eyebrow, "Sure am glad I brought my toothbrush! But I feel fine now, probably because my stomach and *ninety percent of my intestines* are emm-teeeee!" Suddenly, she looked over his shoulder and launched herself off of him saying, "Mr. Taussan! Dr. Stolchya!" Slager turned to see her hugging both of them at the same time. They looked somewhat taken aback, but pleased nonetheless. "We can take you back home if you guys want! I know you've been here longer than your missions specified." By the time Slager had cycled the locks to let in more cargo and a couple more people Ell'd enthusiastically met and hugged everyone in the ISS.

Then she opened a Styrofoam container and started passing out small bottles of wine and lemonade with nipples on their tops. "Let's have a toast!" she exclaimed, holding a lemonade out at arms length. "To a new era in space travel."

"Hear, hear."

***

Kristen Donsaii's AI spoke in her ear. "Breaking news on CNN references Ell Donsaii."

A spike of fear shot through her and Kristen turned to look at her mother, sitting beside her on the pew at First United Methodist Church. Her mother was turning anxiously to look at her as well. Doubtless, she'd gotten the same information from her own AI. She looked the other way and saw Miles looking concerned as well. They all stood and worked their way out of the pew and from there down the aisle and out of the church.

Looking up at her HUD Kristen said, "Play it for me."

The familiar face of one of the CNN anchors filled the screen, saying. "Breaking news. After weeks of intense speculation, NASA today announced that the last minute supplies that saved the lives of the dying astronauts on the International Space Station were delivered by a little known North Carolina company called 'D5Research.' This company has virtually no presence on the web, so we can't tell you very much about them other than what NASA's told us. Apparently, D5R's CEO is none other than Ell Donsaii, whom many of you will remember to be the girl who shocked the world with her gymnastic performances a few years ago. NASA Director James Epaulding is about to commence a joint press conference on the new technology that allowed the rescue to be undertaken."

Gram sighed and seated herself on a bench, "Why couldn't the girl have told us this was gonna happen?!"

Kristen and Miles sat beside Gram, "Probably didn't think it was enough of a big deal to mention." Kristen said, exasperatedly.

Kristen looked back up at her HUD. Her AI, recognizing that she was focused back on her HUD, resumed the video. The screen split in two with a somber man in a suit on one side and Kristen's grinning daughter Ell on the other. A little subtitle identified each of them. The man was NASA director Epaulding. He launched into a long winded speech, thanking D5R and its investors and researchers for applying themselves, their resources and their new technology unstintingly to the rescue of the multinational crew of the International Space Station. "The world is in your debt." he said.

As the church service ended people started filtering out of the building. Instead of heading to their cars as usual, most of them stopped to look up at their own HUDs.

Rocket!

Epaulding continued, "The second purpose of this press conference is to make the world aware of the technology which made this possible. This technology is based on a new math devised by Ms. Ell Donsaii, the young lady you see in the other half of your screen." For a moment the video zoomed in on Ell. Kristen thought there was something odd about her?

Epaulding continued, "As you can tell by the way Ms. Donsaii's hair is floating around, she's currently aboard the International Space Station herself and therefore weightless. She and some of her D5R team flew up there last night in D5R's second manned mission." Ell waved and tossed an obviously weightless apple slowly across the screen. "To continue, this math explains many of the bizarre quantum phenomena that have long puzzled scientists. Apparently, there are ties between entangled particles through bridges crossing a fifth dimension. This connection is responsible for the phenomena that Einstein referred to as 'spooky action at a distance.' Ms. Donsaii's paper which explained this new math led to the technology behind the PGR chips some of you are already using in your communications devices and AIs. D5R was founded to explore other possibilities resulting from this fifth dimension. I won't try to explain the technical details, but their discoveries have allowed them to build small rockets capable of flying to the Space Station to deliver supplies. Such rockets also have other, even more astonishing, capabilities."

The screen blanked, then showed a black upper half and a grey lower half. "Here you see video from a two-foot-long rocket called "Armstrong." This video was taken when Armstrong landed last week at "Tranquility Base" on the moon. Tranquility Base is the location where Armstrong's namesake Neil Armstrong became the first man to step onto the moon in 1969." The descent stage of Apollo 11 came into view. The picture panned around the site and she said, "Unfortunately, you can see that Buzz Aldrin was correct when he said he thought that our flag blew over when they took off."

The screen blanked, then cleared to show a number of pebbles on a black background. "Here you see a number of moon rocks that Armstrong returned from the moon. These are the first moon rocks returned to Earth since the 1970s."

The screen blanked again, then opened to show a lumpy mass in the middle. "This next video shows Near Earth approaching asteroid, 2021 MG12, during the approach of "Buzz," another small rocket from D5R. The video jumped closer, then closer, then showed what were apparently the tail fins of the rocket gradually reach and touch down on it. Again the screen blanked and then showed some different lumps on a black background. Preliminary analysis of specimens returned from this asteroid confirm that it's metallic with high levels of platinum and tantalum in addition to the usual iron and nickel. Those metals would make the space mining of this asteroid a rewarding endeavor."

The screen showed Epaulding's face again. "Finally, if you'll watch with me a moment, another small rocket named Collins is currently landing at the Martian South Pole."

After the landing had screened, the broadcast returned to the CNN anchor. He blinked a couple of times, then said, "Ladies and gentlemen, our world has just been irrevocably changed..."

The End

Rocket!

Hope you liked the book!

Try the next in the series, Comet! (an Ell Donsaii story #5)

To find other books by the author try Laury.Dahners.com/stories.html

Author's Afterword

This is a comment on the "science" in this science fiction novel. I've always been partial to science fiction that poses a "what if" question. Not everything in the story has to be scientifically possible, but you suspend your disbelief regarding one or two things that aren't thought to be possible. Then you ask, what if something (such as faster than light travel) were possible, how might that change our world? Each of the Ell Donsaii stories asks at least one such question.

"Rocket!" asks, what if wormholes were possible, connecting one location in our space-time continuum to another? This isn't a new idea in science fiction. Many, many novels have explored this possibility, but almost all have considered the question of "what if we could travel instantaneously from one location to another." Instead "Rocket" asks, "what if we could only make little wormholes, not ones big enough to step through to a new location. Would they still have an impact?"

In short, yes they would. "Rocket" explores some of the impact such small wormholes could have and the next story will continue that exploration.

Some of you may have been interested in the energy that needs to be injected when porting things up to orbit. This is to avoid the possibility that a port could become a "perpetual motion machine." If you could port water from the bottom of a hill to the top without any energy cost, then you could let it run through a hydroelectric turbine on the way back down and generate electricity for free!

One reader has expressed concern that a port that got loose in the vacuum of space could eventually suck all the air away from our planet and become a "planet killer." Such a port would have to be beyond an Earth orbiting distance and speed or air that passed though it would eventually fall back to Earth. But, if you did have a port that far out, by my best calculations it would take more than 10,000,000,000 years for all of Earth's atmosphere (a HUGE volume) to leak out through a five cm (two inch) port.

Acknowledgements

I would like to acknowledge the editing and advice of Gail Gilman, Elene Trull and Nora Dahners, each of whom significantly improved this story.

19862434R00144

Made in the USA
Middletown, DE
07 December 2018